WHEN I OPENED MY EYES

The Dwovian Encounter

K.P. Trout

PAGE PUBLISHING, INC.
New York, NY

First originally published by Page Publishing, Inc. 2017

ISBN 978-1-64082-010-4 (Paperback)
ISBN 978-1-64082-011-1 (Digital)

Printed in the United States of America

CHAPTER

1

A short, thin gray arm and a hand with six long fingers pulled a glowing red crystalline wand from a pocket in a robe. He looked human enough. A human face—nose, mouth, and eyes. He looked like an innocent three-foot-tall toddler, except he had no ears and had a completely bald head. He waved the glowing crystalline wand silently over the stomach of a pregnant woman sleeping in her bed.

Her husband was sound asleep next to her as oblivious as she was to the happenings. The woman lay perfectly flat on her back with her arms at her sides. She looked comfortable enough, although unnatural, as though she had been posed in this position. Her sheet and blanket levitated in the air about two feet above her. This was certainly unnatural by human standards, but clearly there was something otherworldly taking place here. The alien with the young toddler features had a blank stare on his face as he stared at the wand and then back at a small device he held in his other hand. His face looked a bit like a young Opie Taylor from the old *Andy Griffith Show*. In fact, there could be no finer nickname for this creature.

In just a few minutes time, the sheet floated gently back down over the sleeping couple, and the crystalline wand was put back in the robe of little Opie. A brief flash of blue light filled the room and he was gone—silently vanishing from the bedroom in this suburban home and instantly appearing in a large shiny metallic structure elsewhere.

Chepp opened his eyes. Light poured through the gaps between the curtains. He squinted and quickly closed them again before taking a deep breath. His body felt wonderful—completely relaxed and his lungs seemed to effortlessly pull in the air and exhale. He opened his eyes again. "What day is it?" he thought to himself. "It's Monday," came morning guy's answer to night guy. He wished he could sleep longer, so he lifted himself up on his elbows just enough to roll his head and look at the alarm clock beside his bed. Plopping himself back down on the pillow top mattress, he let out a noise that is best described as half sigh and half grunt. The alarm clock was due to go off in five minutes. "Isn't that always the way?" he thought. "Why do I wake up so often with the alarm only minutes away from going off?"

Chepp pondered that question for only a second before rolling over and pulling the covers up around his body. The question seemed far less important than the extra few minutes of shut-eye he could get if he went back to sleep right now. But that was not to be. Clearly it was not his morning for the extra cat nap before rising, because his cell phone began playing the Beatles song "Help," startling him fully awake now. His ringtone was appropriate for a college professor who had graduate students. After all, they always seemed to need his help. But at this hour of the morning, it wasn't going to be a student. No college student called at—"What is it now, 6:15 a.m.?" he thought. The dimwitted students usually called late the night before a test, and the good students called at more appropriate times. His eyes caught the caller ID before sliding his finger across the smooth screen of his cell phone.

"Good morning! You've reached Joe's taxidermy for loved pets. This is Joe. How can I help you?"

"Huh?" Pause. "Oh. Very funny, Cheppie." Chepp laughed. "I didn't figure you'd be awake enough to start with something like that," came a young woman's voice.

"Well, I guess I must be, 'cause I did. What up, Leslie girl?" Chepp answered, trying to sound like the hip professor students said he was.

"I need to meet with you sometime today regarding my latest research. I've found something I can't quite explain, and I need your physics expertise."

"So you need me, do you?" coyly replied Chepp. "I thought you were over me."

"Stop messing around," Leslie replied with the familial crankiness only an ex-lover could manage. "I really need to talk with you about this."

"All right. All right. Just pulling your chain. How about we meet for lunch? I have a class at one thirty, so noonish would work for me."

"Perfect," said Leslie. "How about I meet you at Hank's? If you get there before me, get us a booth and order me one of those raspberry teas. I might be a few minutes late. One of my grad students is meeting me at eleven thirty for a few minutes."

"Got it. See you then."

"Bye."

"Yep." Chepp hung up.

That was weird, he thought to himself. Since he and Leslie broke up about five months ago, she had been politely social with him, but it was the first time in a long time that he felt Leslie was truly interested in him and his opinions. In fact, they hadn't even spoken to each other for about a month. This quick phone chat brought back memories of their early morning banter when they were living together.

Leslie McCabe was a beautiful middle-aged woman. Blonde. In excellent physical shape and intelligent. At times Chepp thought too much about her attractive body and gorgeous eyes, but it was her intelligence and personality that really turned him on. It was the rare person who conducted experiments in neurobiology but also understood as much about physics as she did. It was remarkable that she held two terminal degrees in the natural sciences—PhDs in both biology and chemistry.

Well, at any rate, this lunch was an opportunity to help Leslie and that was all that mattered. If it led to anything else down the road, he would not mind, but continuing to be the gentleman he had always been to Leslie was paramount. Chepp prided himself on being a decent man, even if he did like to goof around a good bit. He really just wanted to enjoy life and settle down now. He was pushing middle age himself at thirty-nine. He laughed out loud at the thought. Pushing? He was there.

Chepp got out of bed, used the bathroom, and moved into the kitchen. He made himself a cup of coffee with the Keurig and fed his cat, Pumpkin. He began thinking about Leslie's research. Last he knew she was working on finding the genetic foundation for sleep. What is coded in the DNA of all creatures on earth that causes them to sleep, and why has natural selection insisted on it? Animals are more vulnerable to predators when asleep because they are unaware of approaching dangers. Chepp cursed as he missed the cat bowl and dropped a bit of the wet cat food onto the kitchen floor. Could the benefits of sleep on a person's health really be a genetic improvement over a person who slept less? It was a nagging question that Leslie had been studying for years. There was contradictory experimental evidence on both sides of the topic. Studying this question was a passion for her. It drove her.

In fact, it was really the thing that led to their breakup. Unlike most other couples, it was not infidelity or a lack of compatibility that was their demise. It was Leslie's research. Chepp could not handle all the wires and electrodes she insisted on hooking up to him nearly every night. It was crazy. As beautiful and wonderful as Leslie was, her obsession with her research was maddening to him. When Chepp would attempt to get a reprieve from the regular experimentation on his head, Leslie would go into a monologue of disgust. He still remembered her arguments. "Chepp, I'm looking for any clues I can find to the origin of sleep. Studying someone very close to me provides me with my best data because I can couple it with all my observations of you. I can't observe myself as well as you, or I'd hook myself up. Maybe you just don't feel my research is that important." And of course, their conversation would spiral out of control from that point.

After so many cycles of this, Chepp had insisted he be released from his "subject 5" status at what he derisively called the Leslie McCabe Sleep Study Asylum. Yep, sometimes after sex, he would listen to her talking into her dictation software describing him as subject 5 in her research. He felt so cheap, and he felt crazy to be held in this kind of relationship. So Leslie finally obliged him and released Chepp from her research and also from his boyfriend status at the same time.

It really was very sad. When they were together, it was the happiest each of them had been in their lives. But this one issue was the Waterloo in their relationship—a decisive defeat for both of them in their battle to find true life and happiness. Chepp and Leslie both knew in their hearts that each of them had lost ground in life when they split.

Chepp finished his coffee and ate a quick bowl of raisin bran before heading back to the bathroom to shower.

A series of soft whistles and chirps and tweets and clicks filled the room. It was a complicated sound—a bit like a collection of teakettles with broken whistles boiling on a stove combined with a chorus of summer eve crickets chirping with the added clicking of zippers hitting the metal drum inside a spinning clothes dryer. But this low racket wasn't random noise; it was a conversation between five other aliens who looked like Opie—cute humanlike toddlers with no ears, bald head, gray skin, and six long thin fingers on each hand. (One of the fingers did perform something like a human thumb, so one could call it five fingers and a thumb.) The frequencies and distinct sounds easily penetrated the small pencil width opening in the skull of the aliens. They communicated in a language not unlike whales and dolphins did underwater—nonsensical noises to human ears but quite meaningful to them.

One of the aliens, the one wearing a white robe, walked straight toward Opie after he had materialized. "Did you collect all your data?" said the leader of the aliens in a matter-of-fact but stern voice.

Opie responded, "Yes. The data from all fifty of my fertilized humans has been collected today."

"But did you make any progress on the data?" he sarcastically thought to himself. Opie followed his leader, whom he had nicknamed Hero for the role he was playing in his planet's history. Hero was his superior officer after all and the one chosen to save his species. But that didn't mean he had to like that fact—or him. Opie secretly despised Hero for many things, not the least of which was how he decided to run this important research mission.

They had been on the planet running this project for five thousand Earth years, and Hero, despite his stern leadership and brief displays of brilliance, was only part way to a solution to the Dwovian problem. Considering the average Dwovian lifespan is only fifty thousand Earth years, this project was trying Opie's patience.

Opie looked around at the blank steely metallic walls of the spacecraft's laboratory. They reminded him of the desperate place his race found themselves. It fit with his mood today and his disdain for Hero. If it weren't for the immediate joy of seeing the bright orange light flooding the compartment and feeling the familiar and calming hum of the ship's reactor when Opie materialized, he may have responded to Hero with an insubordinate tone. And insubordination was not tolerated where Opie came from. He shivered at the thought of it all.

Opie and his colleagues are from the planet Dwovy, a small terrestrial planet orbiting the star Earth people know as BE Ceti. BE Ceti (also known as 9 Ceti) is about sixty-six light-years from Earth and is a yellow-orange main sequence dwarf star about the same size and brightness as Sol, the Earth's sun. However, BE Ceti is only about six hundred million years old as compared to the Earths sun, which is much older—about four and a half billion years old. Opie found it ironic that they should have to come to such an old planet to solve his race's problem. It was a bit like moving into a Model T to work on solving a NASCAR problem.

But the Dwovians' home planet and solar system are actually quite similar to Earth's, which made this mission far more comfortable than Opie had preconceived.

While most star systems in the Milky Way are binary star systems, having two stars orbiting each other, both Dwovy and Earth are in single-star systems, which means sunsets look fairly similar with only one ball of fire heading toward the horizon. Furthermore, liquid water exists on the surface of Dwovy, although not as much as on Earth. Dwovian water is not salty like Earth's oceans. Rather, the water on Dwovy has more iron in it than Earth and has a translucent rusty tint. Opie preferred his water this way and often scraped rust off Earth junk to stir into a glass of water. The recently acquired rust from an old Schwinn bicycle made his last cup of earth water taste so much better. The air is only 10 percent oxygen on Dwovy, with the other 90 percent a nearly equal mixture of argon and nitrogen mixture. Compared to the 18 percent oxygen on Earth, that made for easy breathing. Dwovy orbits farther from Ceti than Earth does from the sun, thus the Dwovian year is about four and a half Earth years long.

But the thing that Opie missed most about home, other than his wife, Nori, was the change in seasons. Seasons are more variable on Dwovy than on the Earth because they are not caused by a tilt in the rotational axis of the planet, like Earth's seasons are. Rather, Dwovian seasons result from random fluctuations in the brightness of the star BE Ceti. It is a variable star. So sometimes winter lasted only 10 percent of a year on Dwovy, and sometimes it lasted multiple Dwovian years before ending. Nobody really ever knew. The best scientific minds on Dwovy had yet to be able to predict the variability in BE Ceti's brightness. "Ha! And Earth people are frustrated with their meteorologists," thought Opie. "They have no clue." But the Earth seasons with their regular predictability would be quite boring for any Dwovian who found himself stuck on Earth for any length of time.

However, when you are a being that lives fifty thousand Earth years, you learn ways to keep from becoming bored. Dwovians are very intelligent and patient beings who have many mind games to keep them entertained—more so than humans who often twiddle thumbs, whistle, or find something to read when they at bored. In fact, even though he is growing a bit frustrated with the project, Opie has handled being away from his wife for five thousand Earth years without an emotional meltdown. It is beyond human comprehension how a loving couple could survive that kind of separation. But of course, the fact that Dwovians have such dramatic physical differences compared to humans, such as incredibly long lifespans and no need for sleep, and the fact that there would be emotional differences were not surprising. Still, Opie was struggling with the morality of this mission. "Damn this project and damn Hero!"

CHAPTER
2

Anna awoke finding herself more tired and a little less nauseated than usual. But still, shortly after becoming vertical, she found herself in her usual posture, kneeling before the porcelain bowl and puking her guts out—or at least trying. Dry heaves was a better description. But this was nothing abnormal for a four-month-pregnant woman. At least that was what the doctor and her friends told her.

After getting up, washing up, and rinsing her mouth out with mouthwash, she headed for the kitchen. She saw the small plastic tab and crumbs lying on the counter next to the toaster. Neil had put the loaf of bread back in the refrigerator without attaching the little tab to hold the bag shut—as usual. It was one of her pet peeves with him. But all in all, she couldn't complain. She frequently reminded herself how incredibly blessed she felt to have him for a husband. Yes, he was a pretty boring guy by most standards, but with his looks and stable career and money earnings, she knew she was lucky compared to many people. He was always supportive, too. His latest support in her desire to be a stay-at-home mom was incredible. With her not working, Neil had already agreed to give up his membership at the golf club and to skip paying for season tickets to Pittsburgh Pirate games. Considering what a huge sports fan he was, she felt very loved by those decisions. They spoke to his commitment to her in a tangible way.

It seemed hard to believe they had been married for ten years already. Time had flown. Especially the last five as they had been trying for a child. These years were tough on their marriage as they searched for answers to the difficulty they were having in conceiving. Still, the whole process did drive them back to church, and the spiritual growth they had experienced as a couple through their Bible study class was an unexpected but much-needed development in their lives. And it was incredibly thrilling to be this far along and to know that in just five short months, they would have a baby in their home. And their own baby—their own flesh and blood. "Thank you, Lord" was a phrase that resonated in Anna's heart all day long lately as the reality continued to sink in.

Anna made some toast and tea for herself and began to get her list for the day together. She loved toast with cinnamon and sugar and hot tea for breakfast. It was about the only thing her queasy stomach could handle in the morning. The kettle was just about to whistle when her phone rang. She jumped and her heart skipped a beat. She wasn't used to morning phone calls, and it startled her. "Hello." Nothing. "Hello?" Still nothing. She hung up. It was about the tenth time this week she got a call from an unknown number and nobody was there. Or maybe somebody was there and they just weren't answering. Or maybe they could hear her and she couldn't hear them. She didn't really care at this point. All she knew was these calls were annoying and creepy. She felt as if she were being watched.

⁓

"That will be fine, Ms. DeMarco," said Chepp, answering one of his students. "Just be sure to include our course number and your lab section when you email the report to me."

"Oh, I will, Dr. Duplay. Thank you." The student exited the classroom. Chepp grabbed his notes and netbook and threw them into his briefcase. He would have to hurry to meet Leslie on time. That was one of the annoying things about being a professor. Your schedule could unexpectedly change by five or ten minutes at any point in your day due to students who swore they need just "one minute" of your time.

He danced his way down the steps of the old stately lab building and headed for the parking lot. He breathed in the smell of the old building as he descended the stairs. There was something about the smell of the building—a sweet chemical odor probably from the aging of the old dark institutional linoleum used in the floors or the varnished, ornate hardwood trim throughout the building. Then again, it could be the old milk glass light fixtures in the dimly lit hallways and stairwells or their old wiring. It was a building from the 1930s, so who knew what it was. But the smell always brought back happy memories of Chepp's college years spent across the country at Keystone Tech, where his mind was opened to all kinds of new ideas. Some his favorite memories were of sitting in large lecture halls his sophomore year and being amazed as he learned about Einstein's relativity and the birth of quantum physics. He moved quickly to his car and pulled out.

On his way driving to Hank's, Chepp saw a Porsche Boxster and began daydreaming about owning and driving a black one with the top down. Southern California was the perfect location to own a sports car, but college professors weren't paid as well as most high school teachers these days. Even physicists who were as successful as Chepp and worked at major universities barely made six figures. And with the taxes and living expenses in California that didn't go far.

He pulled up at Hank's, found a parking space, and jogged to the door. Upon entering and looking around, he was relieved to see that he had still beaten Leslie to their favorite lunch spot.

"Hey! Chepp! Good to see you, my scientist friend!"

"What's up, Hank? How's business today?"

"Can't complain. Things are fair to middling. You want a table or booth?" asked Hank, the older but stylish ponytailed owner of the college town's best bar and grill.

"How about a table for two under an umbrella out on the patio?" suggested Chepp.

"Right this way, buddy. And Angela will be your server today." Hank led Chepp to an intimate table at the back of the patio area, away from others, as he held up two fingers for Angela. A large red umbrella shaded the cute rod iron table covered with a matching red-and-white checked tablecloth. A vase of beautiful fresh cut flowers were in the center of each table on the patio. The fresh, mild air and sunny blue skies completed the perfection of the setting.

Angela was quickly behind with two ice waters and menus. "We'll both have raspberry iced teas to start, please," said Chepp.

No sooner had he ordered the drinks than he noticed Leslie coming in the front door confidently heading right for him. She looked beautiful, thought Chepp. She wore a cute yellow and orange sundress that hit her midthigh. Her toned tan legs looked like those of a woman a decade younger.

"Wow! You look wonderful," Chepp told her. "Looks like you've lost some weight since the last time I saw you, or is it just the way that dress looks on you? You look terrific."

"Actually, yes, I have lost some. Thanks for noticing, Chepp. Nobody else has much noticed, but I'm down about ten pounds. I haven't been sleeping or eating much lately," answered Leslie.

"Well, you wouldn't know it to look at you. You look very healthy to me."

"Thanks, Chepp. It's amazing how well tea bags on the eyes and makeup work to cover up puffy dark circles under your eyes. Did you order me a raspberry iced tea?"

"Yep! Here they come now." Angela set two ice-cold dripping glasses of fresh iced tea in front of them each and went over the lunch specials. They both quickly decided on the chicken Caesar salad.

Hank's Caesar salad specials were to die for and very filling. They came with fresh bread too, one of Chepp's favorites. He and Leslie used to buy loaves of Hank's fresh baked bread to take home. He didn't sell them to just anyone, but for Chepp and Leslie he made an exception. The fact that Leslie had used her biology knowledge to help Hank acquire a superior grade of bread yeast may have greased the wheels on that decision. In fact, Leslie's yeast helped put Hank's on the map, and if the truth were to be known, he should be paying Leslie monthly in a profit sharing deal.

"So how have you been, Chepp?" Leslie asked.

"I'm doing well. My career is still going well. I was in Denver a couple of months ago at a conference. Found some time to ski. I still suck at it."

Leslie giggled. "Yeah, the sight of you trying to ski is not your best choice of physical activity if you're trying to impress someone.

But on the other hand, your baseball skills in college were pretty awesome. I love those old VHS tapes of you playing in the college World Series. You were pretty sexy."

Chepp blushed a little, and his heart beat a little harder. "Really? Well, I'll have to keep that in mind. But my guess is I'll be most impressive to you if I can help you with your research. What's going on?" Chepp asked.

"Oh, Chepp, it's awful. I've discovered something incredible. If I'm right—which I'm very confident I am—then this is very big . . . and very disturbing at the same time. It's almost too hard to believe. I can still hardly believe it myself. I really need help nailing this down before I can talk publicly about it."

Chepp looked at her concerned. He rarely saw Leslie this distressed. In fact, he had never seen this. Leslie was always confident and under control. "What is it, Leslie? What's this all about? I'm guessing it relates to your sleep research?"

"Yes," answered Leslie, "I've found what I was looking for. I found the genes responsible for sleep."

"That's incredible, Leslie! That sounds like great news!" answered Chepp with a smile and excitement. Even having heard Leslie's concerned words a minute ago, Chepp reacted instinctively as a scientist. He knew this discovery was groundbreaking.

"Yes. It is and it isn't. Along with discovering those genes, I discovered something else, Chepp," responded Leslie in a more hushed voice now.

"Like what?" Chepp asked, cluing in on Leslie's tone and speaking more quietly.

"We're not supposed to sleep, Chepp."

"Uhhh . . . Did you mean to say that you and I aren't meant to sleep together?" said Chepp with a look of confusion and a bit of levity in his voice to lighten the weight of the moment.

"No. I mean we're not supposed to sleep! None of us! We are not supposed to sleep—at all!"

"All right. Is this some kind of joke, Leslie? There's probably a camera around here somewhere picking this all up, isn't there?"

"No, Chepp. I'm totally serious. This is not a joke. Humans are not supposed to sleep. In fact, no animal on planet Earth is supposed to sleep for that matter, so far as I can tell at this point."

"Whoa, whoa, whoa, slow down here," said Chepp. "Did you or did you not just tell me that you discovered the genes responsible for sleep? How can that be true and then you turn around and say we are not supposed to sleep?"

"That's just it, Chepp. They both *are* true. I'm telling you that somebody at some point has messed with the DNA of all humans and all these animals I've checked."

Chepp's face turned to a blank stare as Leslie continued.

"We've been redesigned on the genetic level! You and I aren't as we are meant to be! We've been altered, violated, tinkered with. We are meant to be awake all the time! Sleep is not necessary! Somebody, long ago, put us to sleep for some reason! This was done to us on purpose!"

CHAPTER

3

Opie's footwear tapped across the metal floors of the spacious spacecraft. He had recently taken a liking to the Earth shoes called Crocs. More specifically green Crocs. One of Hero's benevolent permissions was to allow his Dwovian team to enjoy certain aspects of the unique culture on planet Earth while they were here. Opie appreciated that. He had always been one for embracing life, and he found the cultures on Earth fascinating. Dwovy had only one culture. The one agreed upon by the High Council.

Opie walked into his work cubicle, and he began entering the recently collected data into his jerblonk. A jerblonk is like a netbook, although much more advanced than any Earth computer. Dwovian computers are quantum computers and function at speeds and memories at the limits set by nature.

Because Dwovians have incredible coordination in their long fingers, they make use of a keyboard-like device in order to enter information as quickly as possible. But their keyboards angle upward and have two sides so that the hands are more ergonomically positioned while typing. The keyboard collapses down flat along with the flat screen when the jerblonk is closed. The keyboards also have far more keys than QWERTY-style Earth keyboards. But not because the Dwovian language has that many more letters. Some common letter combinations have special keys at locations to speed up data entry. This is ideally suited for the long reach of the slender Dwovian fingers. Opie was moderately proficient on a jerblonk and could enter about one thousand words or data chunks per Earth minute.

He tapped away on his keyboard at lightning speed when his colleague Grenko popped in.

"When did you return?" asked Grenko. "Have you eaten anything yet?"

"I just got back. And no, I haven't eaten yet. What have you made?" answered Opie.

"You're in luck. I made your favorite tonight. Dwovian pizza!" said Grenko with a flare in his voice and a smile.

Opie laughed out loud with a belly shake, and Grenko started laughing too. There of course was no such thing as Dwovian pizza—at least not officially. Because their food supply from Dwovy was limited when they came to Earth, about all that was left was some spices and some canned Dwovian spritfink. Spritfink was the Dwovian equivalent of dried chipped beef and literally was the pickled and dried meat from a small Dwovian animal called a shloonk. A few months back, Grenko had taken an Earth pizza, removed the cheese (Dwovians cannot digest cheese), and then lay thinly sliced pieces of spritfink on top of the sauce like pepperoni.

"Mmmm. Yeah, I do like me some Dwovian pizza." Opie chuckled. "I'll go get some in a little."

"It's funny how well we've adapted to Earth food. I have a feeling these creatures will have an everlasting impact on Dwovian culture when we return and share our experiences. Especially if we are successful in saving our species. What Dwovian family would not want to honor the Earth people by eating Dwovian pizza on occasion."

"I'm glad you get that, Grenko. They certainly do deserve to be honored after what we've put them through," said Opie.

They smiled at each other with a heartfelt and deep smile, then Grenko left to allow Opie to continue his data entry.

It's true that Opie and his colleagues would never be the same and that these Earth people had influenced them. But sometimes it amazed Opie how much he and his colleagues had influenced the development of humankind too.

On occasion, an Earthling would end up interacting with a Dwovian. In order to minimize the exposure, the person would be given hallucinatory drugs that caused most of the encounter to be remembered as a dream. Sometimes, however, the faint memories of the encounter that were still left in the person's mind—like the image of a jerblonk, for example—would lead to a human inventing something similar to what they had seen.

And every generation for five thousand years had some Earth people who became aware of the Dwovians' presence on Earth. Some were even intuitive enough to realize they were being studied. They spoke up, but there was never enough momentum in their views or evidence to overcome the push of humans with average levels of observation and curiosity. Hero had correctly predicted this characteristic of indifference and resistance in humankind. It was one of his selling points to the High Council for why this project on Earth would work and why it should move forward. And Hero was right. Opie hated that Hero was right.

And Hero was very competent in developing protocols through the years that minimized evidence that the Dwovian expedition to Earth was living among and studying humans. The drug protocol had been highly successful. But he had even orchestrated some very clever cover-ups when Opie's colleagues had made the rare gaffe. Hero's general strategy was to see that false evidence was planted and documented, which made it look like more than one type of alien and alien spacecraft had been visiting Earth. The doctored photographs and stories that could be proven wrong helped to muddy the water, creating confusion in the Earthlings' UFO and abduction communities, thus reducing their credibility. This strategy was also highly effective. The truth was, other than the failed scouting attempt of the Ridonians that ended in their crash in Roswell, New Mexico, it was just this Dwovian expedition, with their one saucer-shaped spacecraft, who had visited planet Earth. In addition to the Ridonians, the Dwovians were aware of several other intelligent races in this sector of the galaxy, but none had the technology to travel to Earth, nor did they have any interest in Earth at this time.

The improved communication and photographic ability of humans that came with the recent invention of things like iPhones had led to Hero's new policy that the spacecraft stay in its usual parking spot—a mile deep hole in the ground under an active volcano in

Guatemala. They had burned this hole in the ground upon arrival five thousand years ago. So the chance of authentic (i.e., unimagined) flying saucer sightings was now zero on planet Earth—for the first time in five thousand years.

Opie had no problem with this new "staying parked" policy. It really made no difference to him since they all lived on the spacecraft anyway, and transport on and off could be just as easily performed underground as above. And the bright artificial orange light that lit up the inside of the spacecraft and warm, thin air was a perfect representation of the natural light Dwovians received from BE Ceti. The ship felt like home, and the proper light, warm temperatures, and thin air onboard kept them healthy. Besides, they had already collected a sufficient amount of general observation data of the planet during their fly-arounds, so Hero correctly deduced that the risks outweighed any further benefits that could be gained.

Also, the mission was now in the final phase. The observation of this particular group of fertilized earth women would likely provide the solution to the Dwovian problem. If not, at the current pace, the project would take another five hundred Earth years. That would be just barely in time to return to Dwovy and implement the cure. Everyone was growing anxious. Particularly Hero, whose family name would be forever praised on Dwovy or would endure a generation of shame before Dwovy would slide into extinction.

~❧~

Chepp didn't know what to say. He knew Leslie seriously believed what she was saying, but it all sounded unbelievable.

"Leslie, please don't be mad at me for asking this. But is there any chance your lack of sleep and appetite are being caused by some illness?"

"Ooh. That's just like you, Chepp! You've always been skeptical and unsupportive of my research! Leslie blasted back, "I'm not crazy! I can show you the proof!"

"Okay. Okay. I'm sorry. I just had to ask," Chepp countered. "But I would like to see the proof. You know me, Leslie, I won't feel right about this if I don't see it."

"It's all right, Chepp. I'm sorry too. I did kind of expect that. The truth is, I know it's going to be hard to get anybody to take me seriously with a claim like this, but I've got the proof all tied up with a bow at my apartment. Once I came upon this, I started keeping my records at home—call me paranoid if you want. Can you come by this evening, say about seven thirty to look at it?" asked Leslie.

"Yes. Actually, that would work perfectly for me. I have a prescription to pick up at the Rite Aid just down the street from you. Hey, but you know, if you've got this thing all tied up with a bow, why do you need me?" Chepp queried.

"I know our DNA was tampered with about five thousand years ago. It seems to be worldwide too. But surprisingly the thing that caused the DNA to change wasn't biological or chemical. That's how I know someone or something did this to us. I know the culprit is some kind of physical phenomenon. And it's highly unlikely that it was something natural, like a nearby star exploding, because just specific genes were altered—the phenomenon was tuned somehow to particular genes. That's where I need your help, Cheppie," answered Leslie.

"Well, I'd be crazy to say no to this," stated Chepp. "If I were to walk away from this after everything you just shared, I'd never stop thinking about it anyway. This is huge, Leslie. And I'd probably call you like practically every day just to see what the latest is. So I'm definitely in."

"Then it's a date. I'll see you tonight at 7:30 p.m.," said Leslie, just as Angela was arriving with their Caesar salads.

She must have overheard, because she said, "Oooh. Are you two getting back together? Hank said you two used to be such a cute couple."

"Well, it all depends," said Leslie with a bit of a hush in her voice but a very serious look at Angela. "First, Chepp has to help me kill my husband. That's what we're discussing now. If we can pull that off, then yes, we will probably be getting back together."

"Oh . . . okay . . . well, enjoy the salads," said Angela with a nervous stutter and turning a bit pale. She set the salads down and was gone. Chepp laughed.

"You are so bad! Classic Leslie McCabe. Love it!"

"Well, that'll teach her to stop butting into people's business. Can you believe that?" said Leslie, clearly annoyed at the teen's lack of discretion.

"Hey, she's in college—probably still a teenager. What do you expect?"

"That's true," Leslie replied, "but hopefully that will help her grow up," she said matter-of-factly.

Chepp smiled and shook his head in amazement and admiration as he put his napkin on his lap and grabbed his fork. Leslie always found a way to tickle his fancy.

"Oh and here's your bread," Angela said, startling Leslie and Chepp as a basket of fresh baked bread was practically tossed on their table, and in a whirl she was gone.

"Pffft." Leslie buzzed her lips in a derisive raspberry razz sound and laughed without opening her mouth. Chepp smiled. He was becoming captivated with Leslie all over again.

CHAPTER

4

Neil arrived home from work a little later than usual—about 6:30 p.m. He put his briefcase on the entranceway table and started to loosen his tie. "God, I hate wearing a tie and suit," every day he thought to himself, but it was necessary with his job as an assistant VP at the Petemyer Pharmaceutical Company in Pittsburgh. And truth be known, the suit fit his personality and dashing good looks perfectly; he just hated the way it felt.

"Hello! I'm home. Anyone here? Anna?" He called out his announcement like this every day upon arrival at home. Due to his obsessive-compulsive personality and true pride in his consistency and steadiness, it was almost always this same exact announcement. Sometimes Neil was as close to a programmed robot as any human could get, but at other times, his emotions would burst through. He was hard to categorize. A bit of an enigma.

"In here, honey!" Anna called from the kitchen. "Dinner is almost ready. Come here. You can feel the baby moving."

Neil ran in. "Really? Let me feel!" He placed his large, strong hand on Anna's slightly rounded belly. "I can't feel it."

"Just wait. It's been moving all over the place this afternoon. Just keep feeling for a while," Anna reassured him and then quietly stood still.

After about another five seconds, Neil yelled, "I felt it! I felt our baby moving! It was just a little tapping feeling, like the flutter of a butterfly, but I felt it!"

"Yep! That's our kiddo!"

"That's so cool!" He smiled ear to ear, then *mwah*, he planted a big decisive, flamboyant kiss on Anna's cheek. "God, I love you!"

"I love you, too. Now go get washed up for dinner. I'll get us plates fixed, and we can sit out on the back porch for dinner tonight." Anna loved the back porch at this time of year. It was mid-June—a clear, dry, comfortable summer day. Now that the sun was getting lower in the sky, it was just the perfect temperature on their screened in porch.

Neil quickly washed up and changed into some Bermuda shorts and a polo shirt. He joined Anna on the back porch.

They chatted about their day and enjoyed a delicious chicken and rice dinner that Anna had made—her grandma's recipe. She had also made a Waldorf salad, not that it went great with the chicken and rice, but she was craving it earlier in the day and figured her body, and the baby, must need it. The apples, walnuts, and mayo made her mouth water as she ate it.

After dinner, as usual, Neil moved to the stately desk in his den to check the sports scores on his laptop computer. And as if following a computer algorithm, he followed that up by checking the UFO blogs. Anna knew Neil was fascinated with the possibility of life else-where in the universe, but she didn't know that he actually had his own blog site. In fact, his blog site, called NotAlone, was one of the most popular blog sites for the believing community to share UFO and alien experiences and to ask questions. He was also a member of the popular MUFON, the Mutual UFO Network. But the coup de grâce was his secret that he, at one time, had worked in a special branch of the military that actually investigated UFO sightings.

Neil loved his short time (roughly four years) working on legiti-mate UFO research. He investigated state-of-the-art drugs that lead-ers in his research team believed were related to UFO sightings. Some believed the newly discovered drugs were accidental and rare combi-nations of street drugs. These drugs led their partakers to experience a hallucination that caused them think they had been abducted by aliens. Others believed the drugs were from beyond, actually admin-istered by aliens to people who had legitimate encounters with them.

Neil fell in the latter camp. He believed that hypothesis fit the data better.

Regardless of who was right, with the military focus on the war on terror following the attacks of September 11, 2001, his department's budget dried up, and he soon found himself out of a job.

So in 2003 he left the military for civilian life, moving from New Mexico to take a job at Petemyer Pharmaceutical Company in Pittsburgh. Working in the private sector in pharmaceuticals was steady, reliable work, and the pay was good. He actually liked it more than he thought he might.

He met Anna shortly after moving to Pittsburgh, and they were married in 2005. Because Neil had just left the secret work on UFO-related drugs at that time, and because he had just met Anna and did not want to freak her out, he never told her details about those years. Early on, he just told her that he served in the military for four years after college as a way to help pay his college loans back. That part was basically true, and he had enough nonspecific pictures of himself and others in military uniforms that Anna never really pried. When she did, he just said, "It was typical military. I don't like to talk about it much." That seemed to work.

Anna respected his feelings on that, and since Neil had no PTSD, bad dreams, or other psychological problems, she didn't see the need to pry. And the longer time went, the less Neil felt the need to explain that short period of his life to Anna. Her not knowing was a status quo they both were content to live with.

⁓❧⁓

Chepp arrived at Leslie's apartment right on time. He knew she liked promptness, so he wasn't going to be late. He was actually early, so he waited in the drug store parking lot until it was time to drive down the street to Leslie's. He parked, splashed on some cologne he kept in his car, then went and knocked on her door at precisely seven thirty as she requested.

He was a bit shocked when Leslie quickly opened the door with a glass of wine in her hand, and wearing what appeared to be sleeping shorts and a nightshirt. Her hair was pulled up in a hair clip.

She looked very casual and ready to curl up in bed. For a second he thought maybe she had forgotten she had invited him over. But then she said excitedly, "Cheppie! Right on time!" This was apparently her second glass of wine. Or third.

"Hi, Leslie. You look . . . comfortable tonight," said Chepp, trying not to seem surprised and fumbling a bit for words. "These are for you." He handed her a bag of Hershey's Kisses. He knew they were her favorite.

"Oh . . . my . . . God. Kisses! I've been so busy. I don't think I've even had one in weeks . . . maybe months. They look so good. Thank you so much, Chepp. Dare I say that this was *sweet* of you." Leslie giggled at her pun. Chepp politely giggled too.

She waved her hand inviting him in and took the bag of chocolates toward the kitchen. Chepp came in and slipped his shoes off as Leslie began pouring the bag of Kisses into a crystal bowl. Then he followed Leslie to her kitchen table, which currently had papers and books laying all over it, but in an organized way.

"Here you go, sweetie."

She handed him a glass of wine, which she had obviously poured for him before he arrived.

After hearing her call him sweetie, he was sure Leslie was on her third glass of wine. He took the glass and downed a gulp. It was a dry red wine, Leslie's favorite.

"So here's the proof you requested." Leslie waved her hand over the table like Vanna White might when showing a new puzzle on *Wheel of Fortune*. "What do you want to see first?"

"Well, let's start with your area of expertise—biology. Why couldn't the change in the DNA have been caused by a virus or bacteria or some biological agent?" Chepp said. "After you explain that, then we can move onto chemical possibilities and finally wrap up with my expertise with the physical."

"You certainly *are* an expert at the physical," Leslie said with a playfully sexual connotation. Then, as if catching herself and recognizing her inebriation, she quickly followed with, "I mean you *do* have a PhD in physics."

It was a good recovery, but Chepp could tell Leslie was still interested in him like he was in her. His heard skipped a beat at the thought. Leslie looked so cute and comfortable. For a moment, he thought about getting drunk with her and carrying her off to the bedroom. But the gentleman in him would not let the thought take root. He decided it would be best if they were both sober before jumping back into an intimate physical relationship. If he had another shot at a relationship with Leslie, this time he wanted to be sure they did things properly. He would not disrespect Leslie or take her for granted again.

"Yes. Okay. Well . . . uh . . . let's just start with the biological possibilities and eliminate those one by one, shall we?" said Chepp, doing his best to suppress his male sex drive and to be the mature one at the moment. Fortunately, Leslie took his lead and started to go over her scientific masterpiece.

"Okay. Well, let me start by introducing 'my babies'—the genes that make modern humans sleep."

Leslie quickly transformed into her world-class scientist alter ego as she showed Chepp her ingenious approach using her first-of-its-kind quantum molecular sleep study data along with data available from the human genome project, to identify them. Then she compared the appropriate section of modern human DNA to a strand of DNA extracted from an early *Homo sapiens* woman who had recently been found frozen in ice on an Alaskan mountainside. Leslie emphasized the serendipitous fact that the DNA strand recovered from the frozen woman was the section containing the same series of genes, and it provided a way to compare the sleep genes of early woman to modern woman. She showed Chepp the very unusual pattern of genetic difference. Even though he was not a genetic expert, he knew enough biology to follow Leslie's arguments and he agreed the differences were striking and odd—highly unlikely to occur so specifically and rapidly through an evolutionary process.

The odds of it all reminded Chepp of his favorite childhood story, *Charlotte's Web*. What Leslie had found—the change in our DNA—would be a bit like studying a spider web hanging in a pigpen, then coming back the next day to find the same spider web had the words "some pig" spelled out in it. If that were to happen in real life, you would know something odd is going on. That's the kind of thing that happened to Leslie as she made her genetic comparison. The unheard of—the miraculous—had happened in our genetics. "Astounding" was all Chepp could think as he thought about it all.

Then Dr. Leslie McCabe spent the next six hours, almost uninterrupted, except for another glass of wine, some delivery pizza, and the occasional Kisses wrapper playfully thrown at Chepp, going through all the possibilities of what could potentially cause this genetic change, and providing sound evidence for why each was impossible. Chepp was truly impressed. Her notes were detailed and exact, and her scientific approach was spot-on.

She had a long list of plausible explanations for how the sleep genes could have been altered in such a unique and specific way. Chepp could see no possibilities at this point that Leslie missed. Her list was comprehensive and her logic irrefutable.

Using her PhD-level knowledge and the help of a few unsuspecting grad students, she had considered and thoroughly investigated all the biological and chemical possibilities. None could explain it.

And even though Leslie did not have a PhD in physics, she did have a fairly extensive understanding of it. This led her to be able to eliminate most of the physical possibilities as well, although she did want Chepp to carefully check her work over the next couple of days. She considered every physical environmental phenomenon that Chepp could think of, including electrical effects from lightning, pressure, sound, and heat effects from volcanic eruptions, meteor or comet collisions with the Earth, and on and on. She even considered the possibility of a humongous worldwide earthquake (9.9 on the Richter scale) and found that there could not be enough energy generated on the submicroscopic level from such a phenomenon to disrupt anything in the DNA.

There were four possibilities that she had not yet officially scratched off her list. These were the ones for which she needed help—they involved electromagnetic radiation. She needed someone who could help her with these. Of course, her handsome ex-boyfriend, Dr. Cheppard Duplay, was the perfect choice for the job.

Being an astrophysicist, he had experience working with radiation from space.

"Well, Dr. McCabe. This is really, truly quite impressive. I am blown away by it all," said Chepp. "We really need to get some other science experts to double-check all this, but I agree with everything you presented so far. And I doubt the radiation phenomena are going to explain it either. But I'll check them out."

As Chepp considered the unlikeliness of radiation explaining the genetic change, the reality of the lone remaining possibility began to sink in. As Sherlock Holmes would say, when all other possibilities have been eliminated, whatever remains, however unlikely, must be the truth. Chepp began to seriously entertain the idea that someone or something may have purposely altered humankind's DNA. He felt a shiver go up his back and the hairs on his arms stood up as if they were electrically charged.

"Your heavy wine drinking this evening makes a little more sense to me now. After seeing this, I personally don't know whether to suggest you pop a bottle of champagne or . . . or . . ."

"Or what?" she interrupted.

"Or . . . I don't know . . . burn all this stuff and run away I guess."

"You see what I mean! It *is* incredible, isn't it? And I think you *do* get it. I feel both excited and blessed to have come upon this important discovery, but I'm also scared to death about how people are going to react to it."

The four possibilities that Leslie McCabe had not yet crossed off on her list were (1) radiation from the sun, (2) radiation from space, (3) radiation from the earth (terrestrial radiation), and (4) purposeful manipulation by an intelligence. But she and Chepp already realized that 1, 2, and 3 were long shots.

"Wow. Yeah. This is really something, Les." They looked at each other with stymied faces for a few seconds, then after this brief pause of silence, Chepp continued, "Okay, so, it's getting late . . . like one thirty in the morning late. So how do you want me doing this? Do you want me to take these radiation calculations home to check them over the next couple of days?"

"Uhm . . . well, how about we just leave this stuff lying here, and I'll take a picture of the relevant pages tomorrow morning using my phone and message them to your phone. Will that work?"

"That sounds perfect. Now . . . please let me help you clean up before I go," said Chepp.

"Okay. There's not a lot to clean up, but you'll help me stay focused to actually get it done. I'm so distracted and also quite exhausted."

Chepp threw the paper plates, napkins, and pizza box away while Leslie put the left over pizza in a baggie and then the fridge. Then they washed the wineglasses together. The most time consumed cleaning up was picking up the little aluminum foil wrappers from the Kisses, which were scattered around the room. Then they walked to the door together. Chepp slipped into his shoes.

"Well, thanks for coming, Chepp, and for agreeing to help me with this." She looked into his face with eyes starting to tear up and her voice starting to crack.

"Sure thing, Les. And hey, it's going to be all right. You'll get through this. God made an incredible person when he made you, and you have all you need to handle this. He apparently chose you for this historical discovery, so you can count on him to guide you through this. And you have me, too. If there's anything you need, just say the word and I'll be here in a flash."

She wrapped her arms around Chepp's firm body and squeezed hard while turning her head and burying her cheek into his shoulder. Chepp hugged her back and squeezed her close with his head touching hers. Their bodies melded together perfectly, and they both simultaneously realized how great it felt to be in the other's arms again. After a long while, they finally looked into each other's eyes. With deep sincere eyes, Chepp said, "I'll check in with you tomorrow. Get a good night's sleep, Les. Gosh, it's good to see you again."

She looked back with a twinkle in her eye and a nod. "You too, Cheppie." Then he walked out the door as she slowly closed it shut.

Chepp was home asleep in his own bed within thirty minutes. And amazingly, so was Leslie. She slept soundly for the first time in weeks.

CHAPTER

5

"What's going on?" asked Neil as he suddenly awoke, rolled over in bed, and wearily opened his eyes and rubbed them. His eyes were quickly drawn to a red glowing object being held by a toddler on the other side of the bed. The small boy stood beside Anna, who lay flat on her back in bed beside Neil. Her face pointed straight up toward the ceiling, and her arms lay straight at her side. She looked comfortable but unnaturally positioned for someone asleep in bed. Her eyes were closed. Then suddenly—"Oh, nothing," Anna replied, "he's just playing with that thing of his."

"Huh? What thing?" asked Neil.

"Oh, you know, that toy of his." She calmly spoke but her eyes remained shut. Neil had originally thought she was asleep, but apparently she wasn't because she was following and participating in a conversation with him.

It was pitch black in the room except for the eerie red glowing object, and it was late at night—about 4:00 a.m. Neil looked at the glowing object again. He was feeling strange and was having trouble focusing.

It looked like a red crystalline stick, or wand. The crystal structure was apparent, with distinct ridges and bumps like one might see on cut glass. However, the structure was more random and larger than the fine cuts seen in expensive crystal goblets. It was almost as if a series of small crystalline rocks, about the size of marbles, with sharp edges like diamonds, had somehow been melted together into a stick about a foot long, with the smaller stones toward one end so the wand tapered to a point. The wand was translucent and was glowing red throughout. It was just bright enough to provide the previously mentioned eerie red glow to the room, and it provided a faint illumination to all the objects in the room.

"What are you talking about!" Neil queried with urgency and confusion in his voice. He watched as the toddler boy waved the wand over Anna's stomach. He was doing it for some reason, and it reminded Neil of something, but he couldn't think straight.

Suddenly, Neil blacked out for what seemed to him like only a second. But he heard a bang as if Anna's nightstand was bumped into by someone, and he was instantly awake again. However, his body was in a different position. He was not on his side facing Anna anymore but rather was lying on his stomach in bed, a position he rarely assumed when sleeping in the middle of the night.

He lifted himself onto his elbows and looked over at Anna. She was in the same position as he remembered—on her back—but now the covers were over her. "Wait," he thought. "Where were the covers when I saw her a few seconds ago?" He remembered that they were somehow being held up off her. And where was the little boy who had been standing beside her? And where was the glowing wand? Neil's heart began to pound. Someone was in his house! He had an intruder in his home!

"What the hell is going on!" he yelled as he reached over Anna to turn her lamp on.

"What's wrong?" asked Anna.

"Where is he?" Neil anxiously blurted out while rolling off the bed and standing up.

"I think he's back in his bed now," Anna calmly replied as she finally started opening her eyes.

"What are you talking about!" Neil raised his voice again and repeated. "What the hell is going on!"

This was unlike Neil to become so animated and upset, and finally Anna was almost fully awake. "I don't know. I was dreaming that our child was playing with me here in bed with a toy. And I guess I thought he went back to the nursery next door."

The bedroom next to Anna's and Neil's had been converted to a nursery about a year ago by friends from their church. Neil had them make over the room in one weekend as a surprise for Anna. It was symbolic and was meant to provide hope and faith that their child was on his way. Neil thought his confidence being displayed to Anna would somehow help them conceive. He was right.

"What? What kind of toy?"

"I don't know. It was some little thing that glowed. He was waving it around me."

"Was it a little boy?"

"Yes. How did you know? He seemed like he was about three years old in my dream."

"Oh my god! It wasn't a dream, Anna! Where is he? Where is he?" yelled Neil as he quickly looked around the room and under the bed. "Do you remember me talking to you in your dream?" he asked as he ran over to the nursery and turned on the light to look.

"I just remember you asking me what was going on, and I told you he was playing with a toy," Anna replied. "Neil, what's going on?"

"It wasn't a dream, Anna! It couldn't have been. We wouldn't be dreaming the same thing. And the conversation seemed very real to me, and you remember it the same as I do. No. Something weird is going on. Somebody was in our room!"

"Well, if it wasn't a dream, then where are they now?" Anna asked.

"I don't know. I guess they're gone." Neil was now fully awake and remembering the details better. He checked the clock. It was already 4:30 a.m. A half hour had passed in what seemed like a few seconds to Neil. "There was this crystalline wand, like no toy I've ever seen before, and it was glowing. And he was waving it over your stomach. And now that I think about it, he didn't have hair. What toddler of three doesn't have hair on his head? He was completely bald! And you know what else! I don't remember seeing any ears either. Whoever he was he didn't have ears!" Neil was in a full state of panic and terror at the moment. The volume of his voice had been climbing as he spoke.

"Okay. Calm down, Neil. He's gone now apparently. So it's okay. We are fine. So can we go back to bed now? I'm exhausted."

"What are you talking about? This is creepy. I can't sleep now! How could you just go back to sleep, Anna?" Neil looked at Anna with an expression of unbelief.

"I don't know. It was probably just a weird dream, honey. Weren't you asleep, too?"

"No. Well, kind of. I was awake but feeling weird. You know, I don't think that person was human. I think it was some kind of alien!" said Neil as he did his best to reason through what he had seen and experienced.

"Oh, come on, Neil. I doubt that. Now, come on back to bed," calmly encouraged Anna. She lay back down and pulled the covers up further over her.

It was dawning on Neil that Anna was convinced this was all a dream. Could she remember more than she was letting on and that somehow the shock of what she experienced was causing her mind to cope with it all through a strategy of complete denial. There was something odd about the way Anna was reacting to it all—almost as if she had been brainwashed into believing it was all a dream.

"Well, you can go back to bed if you want. I'm going to check around the house and get to the bottom of this."

"Suit yourself, honey. But I'm sure it was just a weird dream, and I'm going back to sleep." She rolled onto her side and added, "Turn off my light for me when you're done checking this room, please."

"Very, very odd" is all that Neil's mind could think as he observed Anna. The adrenaline was flowing through his body in a full "fight or flight" mode, and Anna looked as indifferent about an intruder in the home as she would if she had just found out that a housefly had snuck in.

Reluctantly, longing for a partner to help him investigate this mystery, Neil kissed her on the cheek and told her he understood. It was just a small lie. He tucked her in and flipped on the hallway light. Then he came back and turned off the lamp on Anna's nightstand. He wouldn't ever have admitted it to another human being, but he was a bit afraid of the dark at the moment.

❧

Opie stared at the screen of his jerblonk with widened eyes. Could it be? Zero percent, the line on his screen read. He began to breathe a little faster. The data he was studying was the most encouraging he had seen in the last one thousand Earth years of their efforts. Finally. This could be it. He was very excited to share this news with his colleagues, but he wanted to wait a bit longer to be sure. The baby was only three months along; what would another six months be compared with the five thousand years they had already invested into the project?

Besides, Hero was becoming suspicious of Opie's dislike for him; at least he thought so. If Opie shared this news now, and in a few months, it turned out he was wrong, Hero may suspect Opie of purposeful deception for an ulterior motive. That was the last thing Opie needed—more strain between himself and the commander, especially if this project did continue for another five hundred Earth years.

But the development of the baby girl in this particular female Earthling was right on track—healthy and normal by all known standards. Additionally, the baby was not producing the protein responsible for the Dwovians' plight—the deadly illness on Dwovy known as Plinks.

The Plinks illness had developed on Dwovy some six thousand Earth years ago after the Dwovian star, BE Ceti, had undergone an unusual variable cycle of solar eruption. The prominences during that cycle produced a unique pattern of pulses of gamma radiation that altered the DNA of all Dwovians. Immediately after that particular solar cycle, all offspring on Dwovy started being stillborn. There has not been a live birth on Dwovy for six thousand Earth years. Unfortunately there had been no Dwovian astronauts out of the solar system when BE Ceti's radiation struck, so the Plinks illness affected every living Dwovian.

Dwovian scientists moved with urgency once it was clear their race was in trouble. Within a Dwovian decade, they had narrowed it down to a protein that was now being produced in the bodies of the fetuses that hadn't been there before. The protein inhibited the proper development of the circulatory system in the babies. The walls of the arteries and veins in the baby's bodies now leaked blood, like a bucket of water would leak if it had a screen for a bottom. The babies would all die in utero while they were still peanut-sized.

The protein that developed in the babies, called foyerik-bento, turned out to be deadly to the Dwovian body. Earth scientists had not yet discovered this protein, but that was not surprising. It was present in humans in small amounts and was fairly unimportant in human physiology.

So the Dwovian scientists knew the DNA had been altered by their home star, and they knew this was causing the troublesome and deadly protein. But it was unclear what part of the genetic alteration was responsible for the production of foyerik-bento. It was an extraordinarily complex problem.

Dwovian anatomy and physiology are remarkably similar to humans. There are some one hundred thousand proteins produced in a healthy Dwovian body, but there are only twenty-something thousand genes. So the first complication is that some genes direct the production of more than one protein.

Furthermore, more than 98 percent of the Dwovian genome is noncoding, as in humans, which means it doesn't code protein production. However, this 98 percent of the DNA includes directions to turn off or turn on certain genes that produce the proteins.

So there are literally millions upon millions of genetic possibilities to consider. And the DNA of humans and Dwovians is in a state of constant mutation and alteration. Imagine a gun that shoots a single grain of sand. Finding the cure is a bit like trying to hit a specific single piece of sand in a dump truck full of sand by shooting a grain of sand while it drives by at one hundred miles per hour and not knowing what grain of sand to even aim at.

To make matters worse, Dwovian babies develop very slowly. It takes about one hundred Earth years for a Dwovian baby to go from conception to live birth. This long pregnancy time is caused by the slow Dwovian aging process. This limits the rate at which potential genetic cures could be tested.

But now Opie was staring at the data from a precious human baby girl who may cure a whole world. It was very unusual for Dwovians to cry, but Opie felt an iron-rich orange tear streak down his face. This could be it. Perhaps this last round of genetic manipulation had produced the long hoped for answer.

CHAPTER

6

The solid wooden door in the hallway of the Wexford Science Center at the California University of Sciences (CUS) had a red placard with white engraved letters that read "Cheppard E. Duplay, PhD." Just below that was a thin strip of corkboard from which hung by thumbtacks a piece of photocopied paper showing the good doctor's semester schedule. Behind that door, the physically fit, brown-haired, green-eyed man sat at his desk. It was a beautiful, antique oak office desk that he had just inherited from his grandfather, and Chepp was busy at work on his laptop answering emails. His office still had a new smell from the recent renovations in his portion of the building. He had just noticed it once again and took a couple of quick sniffs trying to figure out if it was the carpet that was causing the smell when his phone rang.

"Hello. This is Chepp Duplay," he said as he picked up the desk phone and held it to his ear.

"Hey, Cheppie! It's Leslie. I hadn't heard from you, so I thought I'd call."

"Hey! Leslie! What a coincidence. I was just getting ready to send you an email. I couldn't remember when you had class today. I think I already told you yesterday that I went through all your calculations and didn't find any errors."

"Yep, you said you checked the ones I had done—the ones I knew how to do." She quickly added.

"Right. And the others you needed help with—the radiation calculations—I finished those up late last night."

"Cool. Soooo . . . Dare I ask? What's the scoop? Was I right?"

"Are you sitting down?"

"No. But okay . . . I am now. Come on, Cheppie, don't keep me waiting. What did you find?"

"Well, according to me, the only feasible way radiation could have caused the odd change in DNA you discovered is if the sun had a highly unusual, very fast change in its solar rhythm. Technically, that could induce a large solar prominence lined up with Earth and it could cause a change in DNA."

"Oh," said Leslie, with a bit of disappointment in her voice. "So you're saying that radiation could be the cause then, huh?"

"Well, here's the thing. It would have to be a rhythmic change in the solar cycle that occurs at a very high frequency and has a very specific pattern to make such a change. And this is really not possible with a stable star like the sun. It would require a star with a variable output—a star either influenced by a neighboring star, like we see in a novae arrangement, or a star with some sort of cycling helium flash event."

"Okay. So what's the bottom line, Cheppie? Am I hearing you right? Are you saying there is no way the change in DNA I discovered could be caused by radiation?"

"That's what I'm telling you, Leslie. The sun cannot do this, and there are no other stars close enough that could have done this. Unless there is some other possible explanation that we are missing, it looks like your hypothesis that somebody tampered with our DNA is the only remaining possibility. But I'm getting a couple of very credible colleagues to double-check my radiation calculations."

"Oh my god, oh my god, oh my god!" Leslie said in a panic. "This is really happening to me, isn't it, Chepp?"

"Stay calm, Les . . . But yeah, this apparently is really happening. And yes, it's huge! But we will get you through this, so don't panic. I'm here for you, and I know you can do this."

"Oh, Chepp, thank you for saying that. I am definitely going to need help. I am so nervous lately. But since I've been spending a little bit of time with you, I have been doing better. I've even gotten some sleep the last couple of nights."

"That's good, Leslie. I'm glad I've been helpful. Whatever you need, I'm here."

"But what do you think I should do next, Chepp? I really don't know what to do from here."

"Well, if it were me, I'd get all your data and calculations checked by the best colleagues you know—like I'm doing with the radiation calculations—and then present your findings at the next big biology conference and publish your results. But chances are, something as big as this, it's going to leak before it gets published. So I'd be prepared because you're eventually going to be interviewed or asked to do a press conference. This is perhaps the most significant discovery in human history."

"Oh god. I hate the thought of interviews. I've never been good with that kind of thing."

Chepp was surprised to hear Leslie say that. She was one of the most confident people he knew.

"You'll do great, I'm sure. But it probably would be wise to prepare brief, accurate answers to the common questions you'll get. I was a writer for my college paper, *The Tech Observer*, when I was at KTC. I could help you by doing a mock interview of you to help get you up to speed."

"You're a godsend, Chepp. And I am going to take you up on that. But what are you doing for dinner tonight? You want to get together over some Chinese food and we can just take a break from this? I haven't told any of my grad students or even my girlfriends from church about any of this. I want to try to unwind a bit, but I'm afraid I might let this slip out if I hang out with anyone else."

"Yeah. I can understand that. I have to agree, I'm probably the logical choice at this point. And you know how much I love Chinese food, so yeah, I'm in."

"Can we meet at your place tonight? It might help me to be out of my apartment tonight, but I don't really feel like doing the whole restaurant thing. We can order the Chinese food to be delivered. Will that work?"

"Sure! Sounds like fun to me! I'll get home around 6:00 p.m. tonight. I have class until five, and then I need to make a quick stop at the grocery store before coming home. Actually, I can pick up the Chinese food at Fu Ling on my way home, too. So why don't you plan on getting to my place about 6:30 p.m."

"Perfect! Thanks so much, Chepp. See you then. I can hardly wait."

"Me, too, Leslie. I'm so proud of you." Chepp took a deep breath, not sure if he should have said that. He was proud of Leslie, but it sounded a little odd to him, and he was feeling self-conscious. "Okay. I'll see you tonight. Goodbye."

"Bye, Cheppie." *Click*—the phone hung up.

〰️

"Come on, Neil, just get through the day," he thought to himself. It was 2:30 p.m. on a sunny, Friday afternoon. Neil felt very tired and nauseated, but somehow he was making it through. Using his elbows to prop himself up at his desk was the key. The sun coming in through his office window helped too. His office faced westward in a modern building just south of downtown Pittsburgh. He had been up since 4:30 a.m.; the adrenaline rush and the response of his nervous system had taken its toll. His muscles were sore, his blood sugar was low, and his heart was palpitating due to the stress of the last ten hours.

Last night, after Neil had kissed Anna and turned on the hall-way light, he spent the next half hour searching the house—opening closets, looking behind doors, and all the rest of it. He found nobody. On one hand, he was relieved, but on the other hand it reinforced his belief that they had experienced an alien intruder. Who else could have entered and exited their home without leaving a trace or a sound? All their windows and doors had been locked. And what other explanation could there be for what he saw?

Neil had always imagined he would be happy and excited to meet an alien face to face. But now that it happened the way it did, Neil didn't like it. In fact, he had to keep fighting the temptation to deny what he saw. It reminded him of Anna's reaction.

"It had to be a dream," he mumbled under his breath. "No! I know what I saw. When I opened my eyes, I saw a small person—or

42

something—standing there. And there was that red glowing stick of crystal," he answered himself a little bit louder and with conviction.

He decided it was time to share his experience. If he could put it in black and white, then it would help him feel more confident in himself and what he saw. So even though he was at work right now, he logged onto his blog site, NotAlone, and wrote his account of what happened. It flowed out of his mind through his keyboard and onto the screen without hesitation. This was not a man trying to remember the foggy details of a dream; it was a person giving an eyewitness account.

No sooner had he posted his story, the responses began to come. Most of them were from the delusional, loony UFO bloggers who apparently had no job and were online nearly twenty-four hours per day. For example, one person told him the aliens enter through windows in a beam of light, so he and his wife should cover all the windows with aluminum foil to keep the aliens from coming back.

But there were other responses that were legitimately helpful. One in particular caught Neil's attention. This blogger suggested Neil take Anna for a newly developed hypnosis regression therapy being performed by a young postdoc student at Keystone Tech named Shelly Warstein. Perhaps her therapy would help Anna remember anything her mind was suppressing.

The new therapy included some new drugs related to Neil's old research. So he liked this idea. Even if the therapy didn't work out, Neil could perhaps collaborate with Dr. Warstein about the drugs. He would be interested in learning the pharmaceutical chemistry of these new drugs and seeing some of her data. Even though it had been about ten years, Neil never lost his passion for investigating drugs that affect memory, especially as they related to UFO research. And the experiences of last night had whetted his appetite for getting back into it.

Tech Station was only about three hours or so away. Maybe he and Leslie could drive up there to see this Dr. Warstein and make a weekend out of it. He had never been to Keystone Tech, but had heard stories about it from colleagues whose children attended there.

Everybody told him he should visit the creamery to get ice cream if he ever was there. Anna loved good ice cream.

Maybe it was the sleep deprivation or maybe it was just the driving desire to better understand last night, but Neil was in a mode of action, and he didn't like the thought of leaving this possibility untouched all weekend. He pulled up his internet browser and found the website for the Keystone Technology College. He searched the directory for Dr. Shelly Warstein. He searched the list that came up on his screen and began talking softly to himself. "Nothing. Wait. There she is. Dr. Michelle Warstein. Chemistry department of all places." Neil was thinking she must be in the psychology department since she was offering therapy, but perhaps the drugs were more her specialty. "She must collaborate with psychologists," he thought to himself.

The directory listed her office address, email address, and phone number. Neil boldly picked up his phone, listened for a dial tone, then dialed the number. The phone on the other end began to ring.

"Hello."

"Hello. My name is Neil Reese. May I speak with Dr. Shelly Warstein?"

"This is Shelly Warstein. How can I help you?"

"Well, I was wondering if it might be possible for me to make an appointment for my wife and me to meet with you on a weekend sometime."

"What is this regarding, Mr. Reese?" she asked.

"Well, I understand you do drug-assisted hypnotic regression therapy for folks who are trying to recall suppressed memories. Is that true?"

"I perform research in this area, but I don't have a practice of any sort. I'm a postdoc student in the chemistry department at Keystone Tech. My strength is more in the development of chemicals—drugs, if you will—to assist in such activities. My colleague, Dr. Ben Krutch, in the psychology department performs the hypnosis therapy."

"Oh. Well, that's interesting. That's what I was actually thinking. I have a master's degree in chemistry and a bachelor's degree in business, too. I used to do research in the military on drugs related to memory, and I currently work at Petemyer Pharmaceutical Company. When I saw you listed in the chemistry department, I thought maybe you dealt more with the drug end of it."

"Yes, Mr. Reese. I'm not sure what your research was, but I mostly work on new combinations of currently approved drugs— drug cocktails, if you will—that have good penetration through the conscious part of the brain. Excuse me, but how did you say you got my name?"

"Oh. I'm sorry. I didn't say. I had an acquaintance tell me about you. They were somewhat familiar with your work. And after what my wife and I experienced, they thought I might want to contact you."

"I see. And what was it that happened, Mr. Reese?"

"Well . . . uh . . . I'd rather not say at this point, Dr. Warstein."

"I understand, Mr. Reese. But I assure you, as a scientist, regardless of your experience and how embarrassing or private it might be, if there are suppressed memories involved and you want them investigated, my colleague and I will need to know the whole story. And with all due respect, I'd rather know a little about your situation now and what your interest is in me before scheduling an appointment. My time and my colleague's time are very valuable."

"I understand. Okay. Well, to stop beating around the bush, I can tell you that I believe my wife and I had an experience last night with an alien—as in extraterrestrial—and I think my wife might be suppressing some memories of the event. I might be, too. So we were interested in possibly undergoing the hypnotic regression therapy. But I am also interested in getting back into research on memory drugs like you are working with and would like the opportunity to consult with you in that as well."

Neil's heart began to beat faster and his throat started tightening. He was convinced the next sound he would hear through his phone would be the click of Dr. Warstein hanging up. But instead, it was as if he had pushed a magic easy button that morphed Dr. Warstein into a long-time friend.

"Shut the front door! You and your wife interacted with an alien? How soon can you get here?"

"Well . . . uh . . . I don't know. You mean you're not shocked by what I just told you?"

"Yeah. I'm shocked but more excited than anything. My colleague, Ben, and I are huge UFO nuts. We love all things extraterrestrial. Alien encounters are our favorite regressions to do. Seriously, when would you and your wife like to come, Mr. Reese?"

"Well, Dr. Warstein, perhaps—"

"Please, call me Shelly," she interrupted.

"Oh. Okay, Shelly. And you can call me Neil. Like I was saying, perhaps you could suggest a weekend that is good for you?"

"Well, the sooner you come, the easier it will be to extract any memories you both have. I couldn't do this weekend, but next weekend Ben and I will both be in town. Would next weekend work, Neil?"

Neil glanced at the calendar app on his phone. "Yes, next weekend will be fine. We can come into town Friday evening, and I can give you a call Saturday morning, say around 9:00 a.m., to see what timeline will work out best for you. Does that seem reasonable?"

"Yes, that's perfect, Neil. I'm excited about this."

"Me, too," said Neil. "Thanks for talking, Shelly, and I guess we'll see you next weekend."

"Sounds good. Have a safe trip."

"Thanks. We'll certainly try. Goodbye, Shelly."

"Goodbye, Neil."

Click. The line went quiet. Neil smiled and then quietly and very slowly laid his office phone down on its base. He could hardly believe how well all this had worked out.

Now he just had to convince Anna.

CHAPTER

7

Chepp got off the elevator, carrying a full paper grocery bag in his left arm while simultaneously carrying his soft leatherback briefcase in his right hand and a plastic bag containing Chinese food hanging over his right forearm. He turned left and started down the hallway toward his apartment. Leslie, who had already arrived and was waiting, spotted him. Then she did her best to run down the polished tile hallway quickly toward him. "Oh my—let me help you, Chepp." The light tan, fabric-topped, wedge-heeled sandals she was wearing made a soft echo as she ran. She immediately grabbed the bag of groceries from his left arm when she arrived.

"I guess I'm a little early," she said.

"Actually, you're right on time. I was hoping to get home about ten minutes ago," Chepp answered.

"So what do you have in here?" asked Leslie as she opened the bag top with her free hand while cocking her head to look down into the bag.

"Just some staples I was running low on—eggs, bread, and butter. But I did stop and pick us up a bottle of champagne. I think we need to toast your big discovery—even if it won't be official for a while. We need to pause tonight, relax, and celebrate, Dr. Leslie McCabe."

"Aw. That's so sweet, Chepp. That sounds like fun."

"I thought so," he said as he pulled out his keys and unlocked the apartment door. "Come on in and make yourself at home while I put the groceries away and get the champagne on ice."

"How about I get us some plates and silverware so we can eat? I'm famished. Do you still keep them in the same place?"

"Sounds good. I'm hungry too. And yes, everything in the kitchen is in the same basic places they were when you lived here. Well, except I don't have silverware anymore. I eat everything with chopsticks now to save on dishes. I hope that's okay."

Leslie's eyes opened wide and she stared at Chepp, not sure what to think. "Uh . . . you're kidding, right?"

Chepp laughed. "Yeah. I'm just messing with you. I've got silverware. I was just remembering that time at the physics graduate students' potluck dinner when you tried to use chopsticks with that piece of sushi. Remember? That was such a riot." Chepp started to giggle.

Leslie's face turned a little red, but she began smiling and giggling, too, as she remembered. "Oh my gosh. Do you remember that? We can laugh about it now, but that was so embarrassing."

Chepp was laughing harder now. "As a physicist, I still can't figure out how you got that little piece of fish to pop out of your chopsticks and fly across the room like that. I mean that thing had to be moving Mach 1."

Leslie was starting to laugh harder now, too, as the event began to replay in her mind. "I know! Then remember where it landed?" She continued laughing even harder while she spoke. "Right on the front of Dr. Cortez's wife's low-cut dress—" She was hysterically laughing now. "Right near her cleavage . . . Oh my god . . ." Leslie was now in a full-out belly laugh and Chepp was joining her.

Gasping for breath between laughs, Chepp continued the story, "The fish was moving so fast, nobody even saw it happen except for you, me, and I think my one grad student. I don't know how she didn't feel it when it hit. Remember how it just hung there . . ." Chepp was starting to get tears in his eyes now from laughing so hard.

Leslie was in a full-out deep belly laugh now and tears began to stream from her eyes. She did her best to finish the story, but it came out in a soft weak voice that could hardly be heard due to the laughing muscles in her stomach being so tight. "And then her husband finally pointed it out"—she caught two breaths—"and told her she needed to be more careful"—she breathed, then laughed, then breathed again—"eating with her chopsticks . . . oh my god . . . She had this stunned and confused look on her face when she saw it and then realized she hadn't been eating any fish." She was then quiet, intensely breathing out and laughing with her lungs empty from laughing so hard.

Leslie was now doubled over and gasping for air. She and Chepp shared in a deep belly laugh with tears streaming from their eyes. It was the kind of laughing where you can't even breathe and it started to hurt. It was a "had to be there" story, and they both were.

Finally they got it back together and the laughing calmed. "Oh my gosh. I needed that," said Leslie. "I haven't laughed that hard in a long time. It felt good." She looked at Chepp with a relaxed and healthy glow on her face.

"Well, I have the groceries put away. How about I put the champagne in the fridge for later? We can eat now and do whatever you want—maybe a movie on the TV or a board game. How's that sound?"

"Perfecto!" answered Leslie. "Exactly the kind of relaxing evening I was hoping for. And I vote for backgammon. It's been a while since I kicked your butt at that."

"You got it," agreed Chepp as he unpacked the Chinese food onto the coffee table and sat down on the couch with Leslie. "I assume it's okay with you if we sit on the couch to eat?"

"Like you even need to ask," she said with a fake roll of the eyes and a giggling smile.

They each grabbed a paper plate, napkin, and silverware. Then true to their Christian faith and their past routines as a couple, Leslie said grace and they clanked their forks together and said together aloud, "For strength to gain knowledge." They smiled at each other, then dove in.

✎

Hero stomped down the hallway in the living quarters of the flying saucer. He was not in a good mood. "Colonel Skrako! Where are you?" he began calling. "Where is my lead researcher? Present yourself!"

Opie stuck his head out the door, looked, and said, "Here I am, Commander." He stepped forward in his doorway standing in a respectful fashion as expected by Hero. Dwovian height is very consistent. All Dwovians are between 3'4" and 3'6", so when they stand in front of each other, for the most part, they were face to face.

Hero was dressed the same as everyone on the expedition. Well, except his robe was white. Everyone else wore a dark robe. Hero was distinguished as the commander only by this white robe. There were no other markings or insignias.

Well, he was also distinguished by his general sloppiness. Hero's personal hygiene and appearance were subpar compared to most Dwovians—certainly compared with the others on the expedition. And his breath was horrid.

"It has come to my attention, Skrako, that you have been deliberately hiding important progress in our research. Come clean and explain immediately, or I'll call a hearing to have you terminated for sabotage of the mission right now." Hero was speaking loudly and spittle was flying forth from his wretched mouth. The whistling and clicking noises of his Dwovian speech filled the ship and drew attention. The others came out of their living quarters to hear and observe. Opie looked around at the four other members of the expedition, wondering who might have found out his secret and how.

As if he knew what Opie was thinking, he said, "Don't bother looking at them. None of them told me anything. I've been reviewing your research personally, on a daily basis, these past few years. I've had misgivings about you lately, Skrako, and now I have evidence for why I've been feeling that way. Why did you not report this information?"

"Sir, the woman is only three to four months along. It is too early to claim success."

"Agreed. But it is not too soon to protect this woman and be sure this baby goes full term. Losing even *one* pregnancy is too much right now, Skrako! We are running out of time!"

"I know, sir. I'm sorry, sir."

"Good. I'm glad you're sorry. You can prove that on the night of your next data collection by assisting me in retrieving this woman and bringing her to this ship for the duration of her pregnancy."

"Don't you think it would be best to leave her in her natural habitat? The fear and stress of bringing her here could jeopardize the pregnancy," said Opie.

"What's jeopardizing this mission right now is *you*, Colonel Skrako, by challenging my leadership! The pregnant human will be brought here and kept here. That's an order. You and I will retrieve her next round."

"Yes, sir. Thank you, sir."

Hero turned toward the command area of the vessel and started walking away. He turned his head back and said, "Meeting at third nutrition tomorrow—everyone!"

First nutrition was the first meal of the day for Dwovians— the equivalent of breakfast on Earth. However, since Dwovians don't sleep, they eat approximately every six hours around the clock. So there are four nutrition times per day while they live on Earth, and they are simply numbered. The first nutrition is at sunrise, and the last (fourth) was roughly at midnight.

Grenko walked over to Opie and tilted his head sideways toward the door indicating that he wanted to speak in private. They went inside and the door automatically materialized behind them.

"Holy shit, Skrako! I think the commander is losing his mind." Grenko spoke in a forceful whisper with a concerned face and muscles in his forehead tense. Being that all Dwovians look like children, Grenko looked a little bit like a schoolboy who had just found out someone ate his cupcake. "He's been incredibly agitated this past week, and his idea of bringing the Earth woman here is insane as you correctly pointed out. We don't know how she may react to us, and if she were to lose the baby that carries the cure . . . We should *not* be risking that!"

"I know, Grenko. And he's been forgetting things lately, too. We left Dwovy with all the genetic manipulations already prepared. Each nano machine injection we have is coded with one unique genetic manipulation, and we only have two of each. We all know that.

We've all known that fact for five thousand Earth years. Losing even one baby is risky to our mission because of these limitations. Since we stopped our surveillance flights, it's almost as if the commander forgets we are not on Dwovy. He seems to think we can whip up another batch of nano machines at any time. But as you know, we don't have that ability on this spacecraft."

"Exactly! Exactly! So what are we going to do?" asked Grenko.

"Well, for now we are going to do as he says and pray for the best. With his temper like it is right now and his unpredictability, we dare not risk a mutiny. We have no idea what he might do, and with the potential cure nearly in our hands, that would be equally as foolish. We need to know everyone onboard is in agreement before we do anything."

"You're right," answered Grenko as he looked at the bracelet on his wrist. The small blue crystal on it began to glow, meaning the sun had just set. The Dwovians are the galaxy's experts on crystals, having discovered a vast number of crystal structures that have peculiar properties. "Well, it's almost dusk now, so it's time to get ready for tonight's rounds. But I'm going to talk with the others tomorrow during uni-time and see what their impressions are about it. Personally, I think the pressure on the commander has finally gotten to him, Skrako."

Uni-time (that's what it is called in English) is time set aside each day for Dwovians to focus on self-improvement and reflection. It is usually spent alone. It is a time of meditation, learning, and study. Traditionally this is done while it is dark outside. However, nighttime is an active work time for this mission on Earth because the Dwovians perform regular data collections from sleeping, pregnant women. So uni-time occurs during daylight hours right now, between the second and third nutrition, or noon and 6:00 p.m. Earth time.

Opie said goodbye, and Grenko turned and walked toward the door. It quickly disintegrated, and Grenko walked out. The door rematerialized as Grenko turned in the hallway to walk toward his living quarters.

Opie quickly flipped open his jerblonk and pulled up a picture of his wife. God, how he missed her. But he would have to wait until he got back to Dwovy to speak with her. Traveling at near light speed, the distance from Dwovy to Earth had length contracted and their flying saucer had reached Earth in only one year's time. However, to send a radio communication back to Dwovy would take sixty-six Earth years, so communication was not very practical. That's the strange math of relativity with its time dilation and length contraction. Opie's wife, Drinko, was the same age as Opie when he left Dwovy. But now she was sixty-six Earth years older than him. He knew she was still alive. He had been receiving regular radio updates from her since the time they left, and she was receiving his updates as well, although she would receive only one year's updates over the course of about sixty-six years. So she surely felt even less connected to Opie than he did to her. He found it hard to swallow as he thought about that. As much as he missed Drinko, he couldn't imagine how she felt.

Opie took the next Earth hour to write a love note to his beloved and sent it off into space. Then he quickly used his hygiene station and changed into a clean uniform. After hanging his dirty uniform in his closet, the door materialized over the closet opening and a soft whirring noise began. The Dwovian closet began irradiating his uniform with gamma rays to kill germs, while a strong electrostatic filter and fan drew the vaporized germs and soil particles from the uniform.

Opie grabbed his jerblonk and checked his assignment for the night. He was familiar with almost all the households to be visited. However, there was a new one tonight. As pregnancies finished up and were found to have not been the cure to the Plinks, new cases were assigned. Opie would need to reprogram the router tonight to include this new location. The router was the name of their transporter. It used the phenomenon of quantum coupling to allow people and objects to be transported from one location to another without ever having existed in between. It took tremendous amounts of energy and computer technology as well. The onboard fusion reactor provided all the energy needs for the ship, including the energy for the ion engines. The Dwovian computer technology was beyond compare. Furthermore, the Dwovians had nearly perfected the process, and there were extremely few mishaps when using the router. Dwovians commonly claimed that you were much more likely to be injured by lightning than from a router mishap.

"Another day, another try," Opie said as he flipped shut his jerblonk, tucked it under his arm, and grabbed a small bag containing his crystalline transceivers. Then he was quickly on his way out the door and heading for the router room.

CHAPTER

8

Neil and Anna had just finished dinner and sat down together on the porch. It was a beautiful summer evening, and there was a fresh smell of something sweet in the air from the neighbor's flower garden. Neil put his arm around Anna and they snuggled up beside each other on the porch swing.

"Honey, can I talk with you about something?"

"Of course, Neil. You know you can talk with me about anything."

"Well, have you ever been to Keystone Tech?" Neil asked.

"You mean the college? No. Why?"

Neil answered, "Well, I heard its beautiful this time of year. It's just the summer students on campus, so it's not very crowded. It's also the best time of year for going to their creamery for ice cream. It's supposed to be some of the best ice cream in the country."

"Okay . . . so I'm picking up on the idea that you want to go to Keystone Tech. But why do I think it's not just the ice cream making you want to go there?"

"You really are too smart sometimes. No, it's not just the ice cream. There's a chemistry professor up there I want to see." Anna had a serious look on her face as she looked into Neil's eyes. She was not sure where this was going.

"Yes. Go on," she said.

"I'd like to consult with her about the drugs she's researching, but I'd really like to do it on a weekend and have you come along."

Anna looked at Neil and with a heartfelt response immediately said, "Okay." She smiled.

"Really?" said Neil. "I thought I might get some resistance. I mean, you are pregnant and it would mean a four-hour car ride up, then back. Are you sure you don't want more time to think about it?"

"Yep. Honey, I know you. You've made up your mind that you want to do this consulting trip on a weekend for whatever reason, and you'd like me to come along. I love your bulldog persistence when you make up your mind, Neil, and I trust it. I'm your wife, so my answer is yes. I choose to stick with you."

"God, I love you!" Neil answered. He gave her a kiss and a hug. "You really are a special woman."

"When do we go?" Anna asked.

"Well, if it's good with you, next weekend. I can book us a room this evening if it's all right."

"Perfect," she answered.

"Great. And I promise you delicious ice cream, too." He smiled at her.

"I'm counting on that. That's actually the reason I agreed." She looked at him and giggled. "Just kidding." Anna snuggled close to Neil and laid her head on his right shoulder. He lowered his head down and rested the right side of his head on the top of her head, feeling her soft hair against his cheek.

Neil stared off into the distant scenery thinking and praying, 'Thank you, Lord. I am truly blessed. Thank you so much.'

⠻⠻

Chepp and Leslie had finished their dinner and enjoyed a fun movie they found on Netflix. So far, they had not discussed Leslie's research at all. Chepp picked up some of their mess—paper plates, napkins, and silverware—and headed for the kitchen.

"That was a fun movie," said Leslie. "I always enjoy Will Smith."

"Yeah. Most of his movies are pretty good. Some actors are like that. Most movies with Gene Hackman are pretty good, too."

"Yeah, I like Tommy Lee Jones, too. He and Will Smith were great in *Men in Black*," Leslie said. "Loved the way they made the whole aliens among us seem so natural and real. Hey, you know, if my research is right, then maybe that movie wasn't so farfetched. Have you ever researched alien abduction or UFOs online?"

"Of course. But I've never known what to make of it all. Some sites seem pretty far out there. Maybe we should start to look for a real UFO expert who is levelheaded and whom we can network with. Maybe we can figure out why somebody would have tinkered with our DNA if we can find some true stories." Chepp suddenly realized what they were talking about. "Wait, I'm sorry, we're not supposed to be talking shop tonight, are we."

"That's okay," Leslie answered, "I'm the one who brought it up. In fact, get your laptop. Let's search a few UFO stories online because now you have me curious. Then we can pop that champagne and watch another movie."

"You sure?"

"Yep!"

Chepp grabbed his laptop and walked back to the couch. He pushed some empty Chinese food cartons out of the way and plopped it down in the space he made. Soon they were browsing alien abduction and UFO sites on the web.

Many of the stories seemed as though they were unique and could have been hallucinations by someone dreaming or tripping on drugs. But one site caught Leslie's attention as they were browsing.

"Wait," she said, "go back to that site . . . What was it . . . NotAlone. It seems the way that site is organized is different."

"Here it is," replied Neil as he found the open page in his browser.

"Look!" jumped Leslie. She pointed to a spot on the laptop screen. "There are over a thousand people who have blogged about a visitation from aliens while they slept."

"Yeah. I see that. But don't you think those people might have been dreaming?" Chepp was playing devil's advocate as usual.

"I don't know. Let's read some of them. All I know is that I stumbled upon this whole thing by investigating sleep, so it may be connected with these stories somehow."

"As usual, I can't argue with your logic, Les."

They pulled up that story section and began reading first-hand accounts of alien encounters at night. After reading the first few, they came upon an encounter described by Neil Reese.

"Reese. Where did we just see that name?" questioned Chepp. He pressed the back button on his mouse twice and the screen was back on the site's homepage. "Here it is. Neil Reese. Wow! He's the owner and moderator of this whole blog site. When did this experience happen to him?"

Neil pressed the forward button on his mouse twice and they were back reading Neil's story. They sat quietly, leaning toward each other with their heads side by side so they could each get a good angle on the computer screen.

"Interesting!" sang out Leslie. "His wife is pregnant and this alien is waving a glowing wand over her stomach."

"Yeah. The way he writes, he doesn't sound crazy like some of the others, does he. His description of the event is intriguing."

"Go back to that homepage again, Neil. Does he have his contact information listed anywhere?"

Click, click on the mouse. "Yes. There is an email address listed," answered Chepp. "Do you want to email him?"

"I'd rather call him so I can hear what he sounds like. Isn't there a phone number for him?"

"Not on this site, but we could search him on the web and see if we can find one," suggested Chepp. He began clicking away. Leslie watched the screen as Chepp searched for Neil Reese.

⟳

Opie was standing in the command center at the command console when he finished preparing for his nightly visitations. The command console desk had a glassy smooth surface. It doubled as a computer screen with the surface of the desk acting as the screen. Information flashed across the surface. The command console even had a built-in keyboard. The entire vessel and everything in it could be controlled from this location.

Opie had the coordinates and timing of his visits worked out in detail, so he typed in the coordinates at the command console and sent the information to the router. Then he turned around and pulled his red crystalline transducer from one of the charging slots in the wall behind him. The wall was adjacent to the ship's reactor, and the slots in the wall penetrated through the shielding that contained the reactor. The crystalline transducers received and stored up energy from the reactor. High-energy particles, which were by products of the fusion reactions that generated power for the ship, were absorbed by the crystals as they hit them.

Opie put his red crystalline transducer into the customized, long, narrow pocket of his robe. Then he grabbed a small, hand-sized jerblonk, much like a smartphone, that interfaced with the crystal. This amazing device allowed the Dwovians to quickly gather and store detailed data on the humans they were tracking.

He also snatched a small box of syringes containing a narcotic drug that caused human minds to enter a dream state. For several hours after receiving the drug, their memories become foggy. Most are unable to distinguish whether their memories are of actual events or dreams. This was a very useful drug for the visitations, so each Dwovian who ventured into the field to gather data carried this emergency pack for quick sedations.

It was rare that the syringes had to be used. Each visit takes an average of only twenty Earth minutes, so most humans sleep through the visit and data collection. But on occasion, a human will wake up and wonder what is going on. At that point, the dark robe and standing very still is usually all that is necessary. Often the person will quickly fall back to sleep.

On occasion, a person will get up and use the bathroom before falling back to sleep. But again, quiet and still in a dark robe works well. Opie began thinking, "I have experienced humans walking within a gerklin [an Earth meter] of me on their way to or from the bathroom and never notice me. Human minds are weird."

The Dwovians were fascinated by this feature of the human mind. The unconscious mind of a human being was an unnatural state, of course, having been caused by genetic manipulation. The funny thing was that the part of the brain still active in the unconscious state controls most of human behavior. It's amazing what people will never notice when they are not looking for it, and their mind has been conditioned by previous experiences. They will walk right by a short gray-skinned Dwovian as if he isn't even there.

But only a few days ago Opie had to use a dose of the drug on the mate of a female subject. Coincidentally, it was the husband of the "maybe miracle mom." That was the term that popped into Opie's mind when he thought about the woman who might save his race from extinction. He was having fun with the English language in recent years. He especially enjoyed phrases with words that rhymed or even just started with the same sounds. Poetry—in fact, any type of metered or artistic language—was uncommon on Dwovy. Language was primarily used to communicate ideas and not generally seen as a mechanism for recreational or artistic outlet. But Opie was an emotional being, so he liked it. He memorized the few Dwovian poems he had been taught in school. So human language was fascinating to Opie.

It was time. Opie stepped into the router—a small, rectangular room about the size of a typical elevator and lined with crystals. The crystals covered the walls, ceiling, and floor completely. There was no surface area left bare. The crystals looked clear and translucent at first, almost like glass rocks. Suddenly they began to glow with a soft flickering blue glow. They blinked quickly and dimly at first, but the flashing became progressively brighter and slower until they remained steadily on and each crystal was brighter than a typical blue Christmas tree bulb. This whole process took only about two seconds, and it culminated with a bright flash of blue light with everything inside the router, even the air, brightly glowing a beautiful blue color. After the flash, the crystals immediately dimmed and Opie was gone. He had been routed to another space-time coordinate.

❧

"Found him!" Chepp yelled to Leslie who was standing in the kitchen. "He works at Petemyer Pharmaceutical Company in Pittsburgh."

"Cool! Hey, you ready for this?" she responded, looking at Chepp.

"Well, it seems like I should be the one doing that since it was my idea, but you have me searching for a phone number right now. So yes, let it rip, in celebration of your accomplishment."

There was a very loud pop and a cork went flying. "Woohoo! I'll bring over the glasses and bottle so we can have a proper toast."

"Yes. I definitely want to toast you," said Chepp. He was still scrolling around on his laptop. "Hey, here we go. I've got a phone number for you. Based on the number, I think it may be his cell phone."

"Wow. You really are good at hacking, aren't you? Let's toast, then we can call this guy. What's his name, Neil Reese?"

"I thought you wanted to watch another movie."

"Yeah. That too, but first I want to call this guy before it gets any later."

"Okay." Chepp lifted his hand off the computer and made a waving motion with his hand inviting Leslie to come over. "But right now, let's have that toast."

With one hand, Leslie set the bottle of champagne down on the coffee table. The bottle was cold and sweating, with a few drips of condensation running down the side. With the other hand, she set the tall, skinny champagne glasses down. Neil looked at Leslie and smiled as she sat down. He took the bottle in his right hand and poured them each a glass about two-thirds full.

They each held their glasses up and Neil began his toast.

"This is the day one man gets to toast the amazing qualities and accomplishments of a true friend, and that makes this a very special day. Dr. Leslie McCabe, the world is blessed by your presence. You share your gifts and passions with humankind, unselfishly pushing yourself to try to give back what you feel blessed to have received. Your recent discovery, made through the special persistence and scientific genius you possess, will no doubt be a landmark scientific discovery and will bless humankind and steer the scientific community for many years to come. There will be great changes coming, and I know you will courageously face them with grace, love, and beauty, properly representing all the goodness in your heart. Leslie McCabe, you look stunning tonight, even in this humble environment, because you have a beauty about you that can't be diminished by your surroundings. With true gratitude to have this opportunity right now, I toast you, Les—who you've been, who you are, and who you will be."

He pushed his glass forward to toast. With tears welling up in her eyes making them sparkle, Leslie moved her glass to softly clink against Chepp's.

"Thank you, Chepp." They drank some champagne and looked into each other's eyes. "You are so sweet. I don't know what I'd do without you. And I have a confession to make." Leslie set her glass down quickly, then stood up and began walking back and forth in a straight line as though a bit upset. "I made a huge mistake ending things with you. I have been such a fool. You have been the love of my life—all that I could ask for. And my life has felt incomplete since we went our separate ways." Her pacing stopped and she looked into his eyes. Chepp began to stand up as Leslie continued. "This last week has made it concretely clear to me that I will never stop loving you. Will you forgive me, Cheppie, for making a mess of things?"

The room was quiet for an instant that seemed to drag out as Chepp put his hands out and softly grabbed Leslie's. He turned her gently sideways to the left as he turned himself to the right to bring them face to face. He leaned forward some to get his face a little closer to hers. She did the same. Chepp smiled a peaceful smile that only a man staring at the woman he loved could smile.

"Leslie, in my heart I never left you. So maybe there's not such a mess after all." She stared into his penetrating green eyes and smiled. They were both captured in the moment, as if their whole lives were lived to bring them to this place and this time.

An instant later, their eyes were closed and their lips found each other as they had so many times before. But this was no ordinary kiss. This was a forever kiss. A kiss that sealed a truth they both had carried in their hearts for some time. They were meant for each other.

Chepp wrapped his strong arms around Leslie's thin waist, and he lifted her up and pulled her close so they're bodies were touching firmly. She wrapped her legs around Chepp's hips and locked her feet behind his back. As they continued to passionately kiss again and again, Chepp carried her toward the bedroom.

CHAPTER

9

Chepp opened his eyes. The sunlight was shining through his bed-room window, and there was the smell of freshly made coffee in the air. He could hear Leslie in the living room moving around. He smiled inside as he thought about her and the night they had just spent together.

He wiped the sleep out of his eyes, got out of bed, and hit the head. Then he made his way toward the kitchen. His cute orange-and-white cat, Pumpkin, began jogging alongside him. He knew it was breakfast time. Leslie was sitting on the couch tapping on the keyboard of Chepp's laptop.

"I didn't feed your new cat yet because I wasn't sure which food you gave him in the morning," Leslie explained. "I saw the can of soft food in the fridge, but then I saw the bag of hard food in the pantry when I looked for the coffee. I didn't want to upset your system with him."

Chepp walked over and gave Leslie a kiss on the cheek. "Good morning to you, too. Don't worry. I'll take care of my little buddy. I make him bacon and eggs each morning. Isn't that right, Pumpkin?"

Pumpkin, who was standing right next to Chepp, looked up and meowed. Chepp picked him up, and Pumpkin immediately began to purr and brought his nose close to Chepp's for a gentle sniff.

"You have got to be kidding," said Leslie in a slow deliberate manner, staring at the love fest between man and cat.

Chepp laughed. "Yes. I'm kidding. I give him soft food each morning and night, and the hard food is a treat for him on occasion."

Chepp put Pumpkin down. "The bacon and eggs are for my other kitten if she wants some."

Leslie chuckled. "Kitten, huh? Does that make you my big strong lion?" She smiled at Chepp. "Yes, I would love some bacon and eggs."

"Coming right up." Chepp poured himself a cup of coffee and then began feeding Pumpkin. "Whatcha workin' on?" inquired Chepp as he craned his neck to try to see the laptop screen.

His apartment had a nice open layout. There was no wall separating the kitchen from the living room. Only a midheight row of cabinets with a counter on top, creating a small breakfast bar, divided the spaces. So you could easily see back and forth between the living room and kitchen.

"We left the laptop on. Something"—Leslie fake-cleared her throat—"distracted us last night before we could shut it down." She smiled at Chepp with her eyes opened wide and her eyebrows raised. "So I was just pulling up that Neil guy's phone number again. I'm going to call him."

"You're going to call him when?"

"I'm going to call him right now. I figure it's 7:30 a.m. here, and he's East Coast, so it's 10:30 a.m. in Pittsburgh. That's not too early to call."

"Yeah, I guess that makes sense." Chepp pulled out a frying pan from a kitchen cabinet to make eggs, and he got some bacon going in the microwave. Leslie began dialing her phone.

"Put it on speakerphone so I can hear," said Chepp. Leslie did as suggested and the soft sound of the phone ringing on the other end could now be heard. After a couple of rings, the phone was answered.

"Hello."

"Hello. Is this Neil Reese?"

"Yes, this is Neil Reese. Who is this?"

"My name is Dr. Leslie McCabe. I'm a scientist in Southern California, and I was hoping to discuss your blog site with you."

"Uh, okay . . . uh . . . What was your name again? McCabe? How do you spell that?" Leslie responded and spelled out her name for Neil. "Are you working with a journalist or something, or is this purely for research purposes? What is the context of this discussion you want to have?"

On his end, Neil quickly opened up the browser on his computer and searched for a Dr. Leslie McCabe. Sure enough, she quickly came up as a scientist in Southern California just as she had said.

"Well, first, no, we are not working with any newspaper writers or anything like that. We are just curious scientists. Call it research, combined with personal interest."

"Okay, then, Dr. McCabe. What would you like to know? Am I on speakerphone? There seems to be a slight echo on your end. Is there anyone else in on this conversation?" Neil had been burned before by opening up to the wrong people, and he was wanted to know what he was getting into.

"Yes. My colleague, Dr. Cheppard Duplay, is also present here. Last night we stumbled upon your personal entry on the blog site, and we were hoping to talk with you about it."

"Okay. I'm still trying to work through it myself. I'm not sure if you noticed when you read it, but that encounter just took place a few days ago."

"Yeah we noticed that," called Chepp from the kitchen. He walked into the living room and stood behind the couch, looking over Leslie's shoulders at the phone. "What do you think this alien was up to? What was his interest in your wife?"

"Well, that's what freaks me out so much," said Neil. "My wife is pregnant. She's only a few months along, but my gut tells me the alien was interested in the baby. He or she was waving this red crystalline device over my wife's stomach, almost like it was taking measurements for him or something."

"Fascinating!" said Leslie. "I think you're right. That's what it sounded like to me too, based on your description."

"The problem is, I don't know if there were other things that happened because I was just waking up when I saw all this, and apparently things were already in progress when I tuned into the show, so to speak. But my wife can't remember much of anything. That's why I'm taking her to Dr. Warstein at Keystone Tech this coming weekend. She and her colleague will hopefully perform hypnotic regression therapy on us to see if we can recall anything else about the event."

"Hey! Keystone Tech is my alma mater!" Chepp excitedly added.

"Any chance we could join in and be there for the regression therapy?" surprisingly popped out of Leslie's mouth.

"Well, I guess so. Uh, I mean . . . I mean, if you really want to be there and the doctor approves. My understanding is that we will be given medication to put us into a subconscious state, so I guess your presence wouldn't be distracting to the process."

Chepp leaned over the couch and softly spoke into Leslie's ear.

"Leslie, are you sure about this? It means a long weekend. We would have to fly there on Friday late night. Remember, they are three hours ahead of us. Then we'd have to return Sunday evening. There will some serious jet lag involved."

"Neil, will this number we called you on be the best number to reach you on this next weekend? What time is the therapy?" Leslie's answer to Chepp's concern was obvious by her response.

"Yes. This is my cell phone, so you can reach me at this number regardless of where I am. We are supposed to contact Dr. Warstein on Saturday morning. I suppose we will get the time then." Neil sounded a bit surprised by all that was happening, but Chepp and Leslie seemed legit, and the truth was he was excited to have a couple of other scientists interested in what happened. He wanted some partners in this investigation and for some reason they were coming his way. "Thank you God," he thought.

"Cool!" said Leslie. "We'll get in touch with you next weekend, Neil. We look forward to seeing you then and discussing all of this further with you. My latest research might tie into all this. Of course, it might be totally unrelated, but your story has me intrigued."

"Great. I look forward to hearing more about your research at that time, Dr. McCabe," answered Neil.

"Please, call us Leslie and Chepp. We've been calling you Neil, so let's keep things on a first name basis."

"Thank you, Leslie. I look forward to meeting you both this coming weekend. See you then."

"Yep, see you then. Goodbye."

"Goodbye." *Click*. The telephone on the other end could be heard hanging up, then Leslie hung up her cell phone.

"So we are really going to Keystone Tech this coming weekend?" asked Chepp.

"Yep! He didn't sound crazy to me, and I need to learn more about this. Pack your bags, honey, we are going to Pennsylvania." Leslie smiled.

"Okeydokey, then. I guess we better look for flights and a hotel room. Should I book just one room, or do you want one of your own?"

Leslie laughed. "Based on last night, what do you think?"

Chepp smiled and looked at Leslie. "One room it is."

❧

"We go tonight, Skrako. Here's the plan." Hero addressed Opie across the command console. However, the entire abduction support team—which was everybody onboard—sat and listened for the next half hour as the commander outlined his plan and timeline. The plan involved incapacitating Neil with an injection, while Anna was lightly sedated and transported to the ship using the router.

The router was not Opie's main concern. They had transported humans numerous times in the past, and there appeared to be no danger to human minds or bodies. Human physiology and Dwovian physiology are remarkably similar considering they are from solar systems so far apart.

Opie's main concern was that Hero intended on carrying out this maneuver with only the two of them on site. Opie and Hero together could have trouble dealing with Neil, a well-developed human man, if he were to fight back. Neil was nearly twice their height, and Opie had documented the fact that Neil awoke during his last visit. In the last go around, the Dwovian drugs had barely put Neil to sleep.

Opie expressed his concern to Hero who promptly reminded Opie once again—in front of the entire crew—who was in charge. Hero had decided to make an example of Opie in an attempt to stifle the rumors going around the ship that Hero had flipped his wig.

"Is everyone clear on the plan?" The whistles and clicks of his speech were sharp as Hero spoke with intensity. A prompt and unison response came back, "Yes, sir!" Then, almost as if Hero had timed his question for extra drama, everyone's blue crystals began to glow on their bracelets simultaneously. The sun had just set.

Dwovian astronaut bracelets have ten different crystals. Each crystal is tuned to a unique environmental variable. The crystal activates and glows when the environmental variable changes abruptly. This has been particularly helpful to the Dwovians in space exploration. One crystal is orange and glows if there is a sudden change in the Dwovian's blood oxygen level, which often indicates they are about to lose consciousness. This crystal, nicknamed the lifesaver, has saved many Dwovian astronauts' lives. When it glows, there is often enough time left to make an adjustment in what is happening to keep from losing consciousness. Of course, the blue crystal is particularly helpful on Earth because it is sensitive to the radiation given off by the Earth's Sun.

"Let's get the gear together, Skrako, and don't forget we each need one hypodermic of each drug. That way we can adapt the plan and reverse roles on the fly if it becomes necessary. Grenko, you prepare some appropriate nutrition for the pregnant Earth woman. Chenko, prepare a room and medical supplies to help care for this special 'mother of the cure.'" Hero was in full control and in his glory.

This abduction was going to happen—tonight. And in spite of Opie's concerns about Hero's mission strategy this evening, he was a soldier trained to follow his commander's orders. He would die for Dwovy if necessary. He only hoped that Dwovy would not have to die because of Hero's stubbornness.

⋘⋙

It was nearly bedtime. Anna was in bed, watching television. Neil was in his underwear just about to crawl under the covers himself when he realized that he had unfinished business. He hopped up and ran to get his briefcase.

"Where are you going?" asked Anna.

"I'll be right back," called back Neil. "I have data on some of the drugs we are developing at work that I want to take to KTC this weekend." He was just in the next room over at his desk and was quickly on his way back with his briefcase. "I want to have Dr. Warstein check it out."

"Who is Dr. Warstein?" queried Anna.

"She is a chemistry postdoc student who researches drugs used in hypnotic regression therapy. I called her to see if she would be willing to look at some of the data I have been collecting at work." He paused as his conscience got the better of him. "Well, actually, that's not true. I'm sorry. I really called her to ask if she would see me for a therapy session this weekend while we are up there."

"Therapy? What do you need therapy for Neil? What's going on? What's wrong, honey?" Anna was clearly concerned.

Neil explained that it was not traditional psychotherapy but therapy to help him remember repressed memories—specifically memories of the odd event that occurred last week.

"Oh, Neil. I told you—that had to be a dream," she said. "Does she know that? Why would she want to help you recall a dream?"

"It wasn't a dream, Anna. And I'm not going to be settled until I try to get to the bottom of it. If you let me do this, and if you participate as well, I think I can prove to you it wasn't a dream," Neil looked directly into Anna's eyes with all seriousness. "If we end up remembering totally different things under hypnosis—things that definite don't go together—then that will prove it was a dream and I promise I'll let it go and accept that it was a dream. Will you do this with me?"

"Oh, I don't know . . . Come on, Neil." She looked back at him. "You said you wanted to consult on drugs." She could sense the seriousness in his eyes. "Would there be any danger to the baby?"

"No. I would never let that happen. I read up on their technique. At most, they would use a very mild sedative that is totally safe. And you won't ever really be knocked out. It's mostly a hypnotic event. The drug is even optional if you can relax enough. They just have to get your conscious mind out of the way to see if there's anything you remember." Neil stared into Anna's eyes with almost tears in his own. "Please, Anna. For me?"

The gorgeous eyes, handsome face, muscular body, and loving charm of Neil Reese had always been impossible for Anna to resist. He was so good to her and she loved him so much. "Certainly I can do this for him," she thought to herself.

"Will I still get ice cream if we do this?" Anna smirked at him and tilted her head in a playful way to lighten the mood. Neil laughed.

"Of course! We can get ice cream twice!" He smiled at her optimistically with his eyes opened wide and eyebrows raised anxiously waiting for her yes.

"Okay then. I'll do it," she said.

"Thanks, honey! I love you so much!" Neil leaned over, put his arm around Anna, and kissed her on the cheek. She turned her head toward him and they stared into each other's eyes, and she kissed him on the lips.

CHAPTER

10

The router activated and Opie began to experience the familiar shrinking feeling associated with the transport system. It didn't hurt, but it did feel a bit strange, as though your body shrunk out of existence and then quickly expanded back into existence. He often started reciting one of the few Dwovian poems in his mind as the feeling began to see if the poem picked up in the same place in his mind when he rematerialized. It always did. So other than the temporary odd feeling and the flash of blue light, the router did not otherwise disrupt or disorient the person being transported.

As he materialized, he looked over toward Hero. It was dark and hard to see, but apparently, they had both arrived safely in the bedroom of Neil and Anna Reese. It was 4:00 a.m. local time, and other than a small mechanical clock ticking in the hallway outside the bedroom, the house was quiet. Hero activated his red crystalline wand and hand held jerblonk to begin collecting data. The soft red glow revealed Neil and Anna in bed together. Both were asleep according to the data being received on Hero's jerblonk, so he used his hand to give the "good to go" sign to Opie. (Ironically, on Dwovy the "good to go sign" is made by bringing the five fingers together, spreading the thumb out wide and holding the hand up with the palm pointing toward the other person. On planet Earth, this is generally the hand signal for "stop.")

As they approached the bed, they noticed Neil's hand was lying up over Anna's hip and their legs were touching. Neil was on his back and Anna was lying on her side facing him. Usually, when they were not intertwined like this, Opie could avoid using the drugs. He would simply use the levitation device built into his handheld jerblonk to slowly lift the covers off Anna. Then he would levitate Anna and slowly turn her over and bring her back to rest on her back. The freshly charged crystal transducers, which interacted with the handheld jerblonk, had plenty of energy stored in them to perform this type of maneuver. Anna was such a sound sleeper that as long as he did this slowly and didn't wake Neil, his visit would go smoothly. But Neil slept lighter, so Opie always had to keep an eye on him.

Tonight, they would have to give injections, and simultaneously, too, so that any involuntary flinch one of them might make would not wake the other. Opie was nervous about this part of the plan because Hero was not practiced up at these visitations. Only on the rare occasion would he substitute for a team member on a visitation. Usually Hero stayed on the spacecraft, along with Grenko, while the other four team members collected data in the field. Hero had not been in the field for about fifty Earth years.

Opie and Hero pulled out their syringes. Hero had the strong sedative and Opie the mild sedative. As long as Neil was knocked out, Anna and the baby would be safer with the mild sedative. Opie and Hero should be able to handle a mildly sedated female human of Anna's size if she were to fight against them. Anna was only five feet, three inches tall and weighed scarcely more than 110 pounds.

They looked at each other and Hero gave the countdown with his fingers. Six . . . five . . . four . . . three . . . two . . . Suddenly a neighbor's dog started violently barking outside the bedroom window. Neil's body jerked and he woke up. His eyes opened and he drew in a sudden deep breath as if he had just been holding his breath. Opie quickly plunged the needle into Anna and injected her. "Inject, inject, inject!" he shouted at Hero, who was startled and froze for just a fraction of a second. Anna instinctively kicked her leg as the needle went in. Hero began to plunge the needle toward Neil, but his reflexes were too quick. He instinctively threw his left arm up and outward toward Hero and pushed him away. Hero fell backward onto the floor, still holding the syringe in his hand. None of the sedative was injected. Neil jumped out of bed and spun around like an animal that had just been bitten. He heard odd sounds of whistles, pops, rattles, and clicks coming out of the two aliens.

Anna screamed. Opie pulled out his second hypodermic with the strong sedative and ran toward Neil with an outstretched arm. He lunged for Neil, his body leaving the floor. Neil saw him coming, and with lightning speed, he spun sideways and tackled Opie ripping the syringe from his hand. The room was still glowing an eerie red glow from the crystalline wand, and as Neil turned his head, he could see that Hero was back up on his feet and heading quickly toward Anna. "Don't you touch her!" he screamed and simultaneously lunged for Hero. Neil managed to wrap his arms around his legs and easily tackled the child-sized Hero. Hero fell face-first onto the floor with a thud with Neil shortly behind him. Neil squirmed into a straddle position over Hero and rammed the syringe he had grabbed from Opie into Hero's back. Hero whistled, clicked, and spat as the sharp needle pierced deeply and Neil injecting the full load of medication.

Suddenly Neil felt a pinch and burning sensation on the back of his right calf muscle. He quickly kicked hard and met a mass that felt like a bag of sand. Opie went flying into the dresser and bottles of Anna's perfume and a small lamp crashed to the floor. Neil grabbed at the back of his right leg and pulled the syringe out. He rolled over into a sitting position and the room began to spin. He concentrated hard to try to focus his eyes. Opie was dazed from hitting the dresser. Neil dove toward him and injected what was left of the strong sedative into Opie's left thigh. Neil began to feel sick in his stomach. He pulled himself over and sat up against the dresser beside Opie. The room was spinning quickly and sounds were becoming faint. He heard Anna calling his name in slurred speech. "Neil . . . Neil . . ." Hero had somehow pulled himself up by the sheets of the bed and he had hold of Anna's foot. Suddenly there was a flash of blue light and they were gone. Neil's vision faded to black and he lost consciousness.

It was a beautiful, sunny southern California day at Hank's Bar and Grill. Chepp and Leslie were enjoying lunch at their usual table on the patio. Lovers and best friends, the happiness they felt in their hearts again was apparent by the glows on their faces.

"Hey, call me crazy, but there's a special conference in three months that focuses on genetic manipulations of human DNA. It's sponsored by the GSA—that's the Genetics Society of America— and it is being held in Phoenix. I submitted an abstract a couple of days ago to see if I could present my work. Do you think I'm out of line? Is it too soon, or does that seem appropriate to you?" asked Leslie.

"Actually, that sounds perfect, Les. I think following traditional protocol and announcing your research at a conference would be a great way to go," answered Chepp. "Just because you've discovered something earth shaking is no reason to abandon the proper process. And no, it is not too early. In fact, we need to get others onboard now. There are a lot of unanswered questions to be investigated here, and as my mother always said, many hands make light work."

"Gosh, I loved your mom, Chepp. She always had so many of those wise sayings to share. I'm so sorry the world lost her. I can't imagine how tough it must be to have both of your parents gone."

"Yeah, I miss my folks a lot. But they still live on in my mind and heart, and of course, I'll see them again someday," he confidently answered.

"Yep. We both will," she answered with encouragement and hope.

"So am I going with you to this conference or what?"

"I certainly hope so. In fact, I'm glad you brought that up. Can we talk about *us* for a few minutes?" Leslie inquired.

"Of course, Les. What's going on?" asked Chepp.

"Well, I was thinking. If it's okay with you . . . I'd like to move back in with you," announced Leslie.

Chepp stared at her with loving eyes and a smile. "I would love nothing more. It is our home, Leslie—not mine. We picked it out together. And to tell you the truth, it hasn't felt like the same place since you left."

"Cool. I wasn't sure you would be ready for that yet, but I'm glad you are. How about after we get back from this trip to Keystone Tech, we make arrangements to get me moved back in? Do you think you can get some of your grad students to help us? Would Gary and Dave be willing to help?"

"Gary is a few ticks away from crazy right now from writing his thesis. And Dave's been struggling with some equipment issues. Some physical activity and a couple of beers would be just the thing for those guys about right now. And of course, being their thesis advisor, they will probably do just about anything I ask them to do." Chepp chuckled. "Oh, to be a grad student again, huh?"

"Tell me about it. I'm glad those days are behind us. So much hard work and you had to jump through everybody's hoops. Being a grad student in the natural sciences is about as close to slave labor as you can legally come in America. And to think its universities—institutions that proclaim fairness and equality to all—who sustain the system and turn a blind eye to it. Honestly, how is paying $12,000 per year to a research assistant a fair trade for all they do for the university?" Leslie asked.

"Hey, you're preaching to the choir, sister! I agree with you totally. Maybe you will be able to use the clout that will undoubtedly come your way soon to help draw public attention to this situation. Universities need fewer administrators and more money for paying the faculty and assistants in my opinion. But we need to get the public onboard with that. As long as wealthy donors are supporting the universities and the government continues to pour out grant money, the administrators are going to keep living fat."

Suddenly Leslie's phone began to vibrate. "I don't recognize this number, but I guess I better take it. We've got a few irons in the fire right now, so I need to stay on top of things."

Chepp picked up his raspberry iced tea and drank a few swallows as Leslie answered her phone. Man that Hank knew how to make a good raspberry iced tea. And the atmosphere he created on the back patio was just about the perfect setting for a romantic lunch. Fresh flowers, tropical plants, a small circulating water feature with a small pond, natural sunshine with umbrellas to shade the tables—he had created a paradise in the middle of a city.

Chepp listened to Leslie's side of the conversation, and he took note of the serious wide-eyed look she was giving him. Something was up. He mouthed, "Who is it?" Leslie held up her index finger to indicate she would let him know in just a minute. Leslie was finishing her conversation.

"That will be fine. Tomorrow at noon at my office. I'll see you then." *Click.* She hung up her phone. Looking at Chepp, she said, "Well, you are either very smart, or you are clairvoyant. Either way, you were right."

"Right about what? What's going on?" Chepp anxiously inquired.

"That was a reporter from the *Los Angeles Times*. Some *AP* reporter put a small blurb about my upcoming presentation at the conference in Phoenix, and apparently this *Times* reporter wants to do a feature story on me and my research."

"Wait. I thought you just submitted that abstract a few days ago. You didn't even hear back yet as to whether it was accepted for presentation, have you?"

"Nope, I haven't even officially heard back from the organizers of the conference and somehow my abstract has leaked to the press. Unreal. But what can I do? Like you said, once the cat's out of the bag, they're going to want more information." Leslie seemed a bit nervous about it but not altogether shocked that it was happening.

"And so it begins. Fasten your seatbelts, ladies and gentlemen, and be sure to keep your arms and legs inside the ride at all times." Chepp quipped.

⟳

"Damn it! Something's gone wrong!" shouted Grenko to the other crew members. "The commander's vital signs are critical and his auto-return device is activating! Emergency protocol! Repeat. Emergency protocol!" Crew members began to scramble around the control area of the ship.

All Dwovian astronauts had an electronic device implanted in their neck. To a human being, it would simply look and feel like a small metal BB that a child would shoot from a toy gun. But it was actually a very technologically advanced device, one of the Dwovian engineering community's crowning achievements. The device continuously interacted with the crystal bracelet and monitored the important biological vital signs of the Dwovian astronaut. If the astronaut was seriously injured or became deathly ill in the field, the device would automatically activate the router to return the astronaut to the ship.

Grenko ran around the command console and grabbed a gurney from the wall. He activated the levitation device built into it. The gurney began to hover. He pushed it forward and then waited at the entrance to the router. The crystals in the router pulsed and suddenly with a blue flash of light, Hero and Anna were standing before Grenko—but only momentarily. As quickly as they both arrived their legs gave way and both came tumbling down to the floor of the router.

"Denko, grab a second gurney for the Earth woman! Put her in the exam room and care for her! Manko, you're with me in the intensive care room! Hurry!" Anna was barely conscious, but the adrenaline was surging through her body and she screamed. Then her eyes rolled backward and she lost consciousness. Denko lowered the levitating gurney and pulled Anna onto it. Quickly the gurney was levitating again and he was pushing it toward the exam room.

In the intensive care room, Grenko had moved the gurney to the middle of the room where an unresponsive Hero laid.

"Get the analyzer down, Manko! Quickly! Get it down!" yelled Grenko.

Manko worked at a small control station at the side of the room. A large metallic device covered with electronics and blinking crystals on top lowered down from the ceiling. It looked like a shell that would fit over top of a person, shaped like the lid of a casket. It levitated down until it rested just over top of Hero on the gurney. You could no longer see his body as the device surrounded him now. A computer at the small control station began speaking in a gentle female Dwovian voice: "Condition critical. Analyzing. Immediate concerns: no pulse, no breathing. Restarting heart and breathing."

The crystals on the top of the device began blinking at different rates. First, the orange crystal blinked faster, then it became bright and steady for a second before the green crystal blinked. The red crystal followed suit. The computer spoke again. "Heart restarted, breathing restarted, condition critical. Analyzing. Concerns: poisoning, heart damage. Injecting antidote. Analyzing."

Grenko and Manko stood at the small control station observing Hero's vitals and monitoring the computer's responses, ready to override the computer if necessary. Dwovian emergency medicine was mostly a hands-off process. The computer and crystal transducers interacted quickly and performed lifesaving procedures. However, doctoring decisions were still made on occasion to override the computer. If the doctors had insight about the patient that the computer did not know about—for example an allergy or a prior condition—they could steer the computer program a different direction. However, this was not a common occurrence.

"Analyzing. Immediate concern: no pulse. Condition critical. Restarting heart."

"Come on . . . come on!" Grenko said with stress and anxiousness in his voice. Grenko was the health officer on the mission and seeing that the commander got the proper care was his responsibility. He was an experienced doctor and had served on numerous missions in the past. He also served as the nutrition and exercise officer. Manko was the mission's physician assistant, but he was only twenty thousand Dwovian years old—a mere child for a Dwovian doctor.

"Analyzing. Condition fatal. Heart unable to restart. Lethal dose of poison injected. Damage to electrical center of heart from needle injection or similar object. Unable to restart heart. Cause of death: heart failure."

Grenko closed his eyes and then inhaled deeply and exhaled. Manko bowed his head. Hero was dead.

CHAPTER

11

Neil regained consciousness about an hour after being stuck. The summer sunlight was just beginning to trickle in through the window. He was leaning up against the dresser in an awkward position, and his head felt like it was being beat from the inside by a sledgehammer. With each heartbeat—*bam, bam, bam*—he was nauseated and took a deep breath and held it for a second. He exhaled, blowing the air out of his mouth. He hadn't felt this hungover since his fraternity days.

Suddenly his mind began to remember what happened. "Anna!" His eyes opened wide as he sat himself up straight and looked over to the bed. He felt as if a dagger was piercing through his heart when his eyes confirmed she was not there.

He looked left and was initially startled to see the small boy-sized alien still lying next to him. Neil looked in disbelief at the oddly robed creature. He had a bald head, small holes in the skull where his ears should be, gray skin, long fingers (six digits per hand), and—what in God's name!—"Is he wearing Crocs on his feet!" He could hardly believe his eyes, but yes, those were Crocs.

Opie was still unconscious, and Neil realized that this little being was his only lead for finding Anna. He began thinking and going down a list in his head. "The police, the FBI, the military, the government—whom should I call? What should I do?"

It didn't take long for him to come to his senses. The people who came to mind would be of little or no use to him. Even if he could get them to believe what happened, they would be far more interested in this alien for their own purposes than helping him find Anna. He had seen the movie *ET*, and he knew human nature well enough.

Neil stood up and fought the urge to vomit. Assuming this little creature was still alive, he knew he had to restrain it. He didn't know when he might regain consciousness, and he could not risk losing him. He knew he needed to frisk him and remove any devices that he could use against him. The thought of touching him and picking him up was not pleasant to Neil, but it had to be done. He ran his hands up and down over his body. He felt something. Neil removed a translucent crystalline wand from a long pocket in the robe. Continuing, he removed a bracelet with crystals on it from the alien's slender and bony wrist. He also found a small device that resembled a cellphone clinging to the robe by something like Velcro. He pulled that from the robe.

Based on Neil's quick frisk, he guessed the creature was male. At least he seemed anatomically similar to a small male human. "Ugh!" Neil said out loud and shivered in disgust as he thought about what he just did. He debated in his mind about going further with his search of the body, but he stopped short of a strip search and convinced himself that the quick frisk was probably enough.

Neil bent over, scooped the creature up with his arms, and threw him up over his right shoulder. Neil walked to the kitchen and propped the young-looking thing onto a kitchen chair. He rested the bald head and arms on the table so he wouldn't slide off the chair, then he ran to the garage for some rope and zip ties.

It didn't take long to find what he needed, and Neil quickly ran back to the kitchen. He pulled out a pocketknife that he kept in a kitchen drawer and cut some rope. He wrapped the rope around the creature's waist and the chair where he sat and pulled tight, securing the rope with his best knot. Then he pulled the gray arms backward behind the chair in order to zip tie them. Because the alien was so short, Neil could not get his hands to touch. So he improvised and put a zip tie around each hand and added an extra zip tie between them. The gray skin and long fingers were creepy to Neil.

His heart was pounding and the adrenaline surged through his body. Neil had never held a captive like this, and he didn't like the feeling. But it was necessary. The small alien's legs were about the size of a four-year-old's, so his legs would not bend at the knees and hang over the edge of the chair like a full-grown human. Neil pulled one leg each way so that the creatures legs were spread wide and somewhat straddled the kitchen chair. He zip-tied the creature's left ankle to the left leg of the chair and then repeated with the right side.

He also pulled off the child-sized Crocs the alien was wearing and threw them into his bedroom. He figured if the creature did get loose, it would be harder for him to make a run for it in bare feet. He didn't know anything about this alien's feet, but he figured if he preferred to wear Crocs, then maybe his feet weren't that different from ours, and therefore, it would be better to remove them.

He put the blinds in the kitchen down and then went around the house and did the same in each of the other rooms. He also grabbed his gun from the lockbox under his bed. He heard some movements in the kitchen and ran back out. He turned on the kitchen light and sat in a chair facing the alien.

The creature lifted his head groggily and began opening his eyes. The eyes looked like human eyes. They were green but a much darker green than he had ever seen on a human being. The alien looked at Neil. Then in a rattling, metallic voice that eerily reminded him of Stephen Hawking.

"Neil Reese. Please tell me—was your wife, Anna, taken?"

As Leslie walked around the corner, she saw about ten10 people standing outside her office door. A couple of them had cameras around their necks, and there was even one man holding a television camera that said "Action News" on the side of it. She took a deep breath and swallowed hard. This was not what she was expecting to deal with this morning, but she would do her best. As she approached her office, one of the reporters—the one with the news camera—ran over to her. He was wearing a light purple dress shirt, black pants, and a gray sport coat. Suddenly a bright light was shining in her face and a microphone was pulled out.

"This is Josh Branin with Action News, and I'm here with Dr. Leslie McCabe, a tenured scientist in both the biology and chemistry departments at the California University of Sciences. Dr. McCabe, I understand that you have recently made the discovery of a lifetime. My understanding is that you have evidence that humankind's DNA was altered by aliens. Can you explain?"

The microphone was thrust up to Leslie and several camera flashes began to flash away while a few soft whispers could be heard from among the small crowd. The reporter didn't even ask for an interview—apparently the media was beginning to aggressively pursue this story.

Leslie was a bit annoyed by this reporter's blunt approach, but she put on her best smile. "The results of my research will be presented for scrutiny by the scientific community in the coming months, and we will see where things go from there and what conclusions can be drawn. It is true that my hypothesis involves purposeful manipulation of DNA in animal life on planet Earth via an intelligent source."

"When you say an intelligent source, are you referring to a supreme being or intelligent alien life?" asked the reporter.

"We are attempting to investigate how the genetic manipulation was performed. Once we can determine that, we will have a better understanding as to *who* performed it. I can tell you that, based on my research so far, my hypothesis is that no known intelligent force native to planet Earth could have performed this genetic manipulation five thousand years ago when it took place. In fact, current state-of-the-art equipment and techniques barely have the power to detect it," Leslie answered confidently and smoothly.

"Then you are saying that part of your scientific hypothesis is that an outside intelligent being or beings—very possibly intelligent alien life-forms—exist and have interacted with humankind for as long as five thousand years?" The hallway grew quiet as everyone hung in the moment waiting for her answer to this question.

"Yes." Leslie gave the answer bluntly and moved quickly toward her office door. The cameras flashed and the reporters each started shouting overtop of one another attempting to ask questions. "No more questions at this time please. If you will excuse me, I have things to do. Thank you."

With that, Leslie squeezed through her office door, shut it, and locked it. She leaned her back against the doorframe. Her heart was pounding. She took a deep breath. The reporters were hanging out in her hallway, and she could tell they were not going anywhere for the foreseeable future. She could softly hear one reporter on his cell phone talking to a person. "Bob, we need to get a full team down to CUS right away to cover this story. It's going to be huge. We need to interview some other faculty and administrators and get the full scoop on this Dr. McCabe."

Leslie was feeling a little nauseated and she took another deep breath. She was not ready for all of this. Her need to escape was overwhelming. She turned on the light in her office as though she were getting to work. She left it on, then quickly walked through an interior doorway from her office to one of her research laboratories. She kept those lights off and then quickly navigated through a maze of lab tables covered with expensive equipment and a few oddly placed lab stools. She made her way about thirty feet to the other end of the lab where there was another doorway out of the lab; it was around the corner from her office door.

She prayed none of the reporters were in this other hallway. She softly opened up the door, stuck her head out, and turned it to look up and down the hallway. The lights in the hallway were still half-off, their usual overnight setting, and she saw nobody. The coast was clear at the moment. She took off her heels and quietly snuck out the door. She turned and very quietly closed it behind her. Then she ran down the hallway toward the stairwell. She could hear the reporters talking around the corner. Fortunately, it was still early in the morning for a college campus in the summertime, and she was able to get into the stairwell unnoticed.

She quickly ran down the steps, then slipped back into her heels and exited the building. She took another deep breath and blew out of her mouth with puffed cheeks as the door closed behind her.

"Good morning, Professor McCabe!" she immediately heard called out from behind her. Leslie turned around with a start to see one of her female students from her senior level neurobiology class.

"Good morning," Leslie politely replied, smiled, and waved. Then she quickly turned and walked off the opposite direction as though busy and late for an appointment. She could not afford to get caught up in a conversation right now. She needed to escape and regroup.

She pulled her cell phone out of her briefcase and pressed the speed dial button for Chepp. "Hey. It's me. Please stop what you're doing and come pick me up at Hank's as soon as you can. I need to get off campus, but I want to leave my car parked here. I'll explain when you get here."

⁓᠑

"What the . . . You speak English! Yes, Anna was taken. Where is she and what has happened to her?" Neil was clearly shocked, but also angry and anxious.

"If your wife was taken, I am quite certain she is on our spaceship at this time," answered Opie.

"You listen to me. If anything happens to Anna or our baby, I will kill you! Do you understand that English?" Neil spoke in a threatening tone, and Opie got the message loud and clear.

"Trust me when I say that your goal of keeping Anna safe is our goal as well," explained Opie.

"What does that mean? What is going on? Why is Anna so important to you and what have you been doing to us? I have a lot of questions, and you're not going anywhere until I get some answers and I get my wife back."

"I understand, Neil, and I don't blame you."

"How do you understand English? Are you speaking English or are you altering my brain somehow? Your voice sounds like it's computerized or something."

"When you spend five thousand Earth years on a planet, you have time to study and learn the languages," answered Opie.

"Are you telling me you are five thousand years old? No way. You look like a child. Actually you look just like Opie from the old *Andy Griffith Show*, except you're bald and don't have ears," Neil remarked.

"You mean Ron Howard? Yes, that is not the first time I have heard that. And no, I am not five thousand Earth years old. I am approximately twenty thousand Earth years old."

"No way, little Opie. No way any creature lives that long. You better start telling me the truth or I'm going to start using this thing we call a gun and find out what color you bleed!" Neil stood up and held the gun to Opie's head. "Now take me to Anna!"

CHAPTER

12

Anna awoke. She felt no pain, and she felt very relaxed and rested. She felt as if her body were floating on a soft cloud. However, she was disoriented. She couldn't remember what had happened, or where she was, or how she got there. In fact, she couldn't remember much of anything. But she didn't feel afraid or panicked by that. She felt strangely calm.

She looked up and saw what appeared to be an instrument panel very close above her with red, blue, green, and orange lights distributed along it. It was hard for her to focus on it because it was so close. She had no idea what the lights meant, but she thought to herself, "At least I know they're called lights."

Anna could hear soft, short whistles, squeaks, and some metallic clicking in the background. The soft metallic clicking sound reminded her of the sound the lid on her large pot made when she boiled potatoes on her stovetop. "Yes, that's right—I have a home with a stove and a kitchen," she thought to herself.

With her peripheral vision, Anna became aware that there was someone with her. She saw some blurry shadows to her side, and then the instrument panel began to rise.

A gentle-looking childlike face leaned over her face and spoke.

"It takes a while for the effects of the medicine to wear off. How are you feeling?"

The boy alien spoke in English, but the sound of his voice was metallic and raspy, as though generated by a voice synthesizer. It reminded her of that famous scientist with Lou Gehrig's disease who uses a computerized speech synthesizer. Neil loved the guy, but she couldn't remember his name. Then, like a child opening her favorite Christmas gift, she suddenly remembered Neil. She remembered her handsome and wonderful husband, Neil. The drugs still had her feeling very calm and carefree, but she began to have questions come into her mind. She tried to fight through the cobwebs in her mind to concentrate.

"Where is Neil? What am I doing here?" Anna was remembering more with each breath.

"Stay calm and wait for your mind to recover and I will answer your questions. For right now, just know that I'm here to take care of you. Are you thirsty or hungry? Is there anything you need?"

"I don't want anything except some answers. You're one of those aliens Neil said was in our house, aren't you? Bald, no ears . . . just like he said."

"My name is Denko. My colleagues and I are from the planet Dwovy, orbiting a faraway star."

"I hear you in English, but your voice sounds computerized. What have you done to me? What do you want with us?"

Anna was beginning to remember what happened. There was a struggle with a couple of these aliens in their bedroom. "Maybe Neil is here somewhere, too," she started thinking. She couldn't see out of the room she was in, but she began to cry out, "Neil! Neil! Where are you? Are you here? Neil!"

⚜

"Hop in!" Chepp yelled out of the passenger side window as he pulled up beside Leslie. Hank's was about a fifteen-minute walk from campus, and she had been walking steadily for fourteen minutes. She had just turned the corner on the sidewalk beside the beautiful outdoor patio at Hank's when Chepp pulled up.

"Thanks for coming so quickly, Cheppie," Leslie expressed to him with relief in her voice as she slid into the car and shut the car door. "Where were you anyway?"

"I came from home. I was trying to get a little bit of grading done before heading to campus. But guess what I found out?"

88

"What?" Leslie looked over at him with curiosity but also trepidation. She did not need more drama today.

"Well, I was just getting ready to head to campus—I had entered all my grades on my laptop—and I decided to jump on Facebook quickly for a few minutes."

"Yeah, so?" Leslie said in a questioning tone implying Chepp should hurry up and get on with his news.

"Somebody—I'm guessing the person you submitted your abstract to—posted it on Facebook and it's gone viral. It's had over four hundred thousand hits already and it was just posted last night."

"Good grief! No wonder there were reporters lined up at my office this morning!"

"No kidding! So that's why you called me so frantically. How many?"

"About ten to fifteen, including photographers and one television cameraman," answered Leslie.

"Wow! Well, we pretty much knew this was coming, right? We need to find a place to lay low until we can get some of those canned answers practiced. Also, we can wait to see what direction the media goes with the story."

"Sounds like a good plan, Chepp, but do you have any place in mind?"

"No, not really. It needs to be somewhere people would never suspect you would go—so good friends and relatives are out."

"Maybe we could head to Keystone Tech early instead of waiting until the weekend."

"Hey, that's a pretty good idea, Les. We would have to cancel a couple of classes, but we can put some work online for the students and catch up next week. It's early enough in the summer session that we could probably make that work," agreed Chepp.

Leslie's cell phone began ringing. She grabbed it and looked at the screen.

"Don't answer it! It could be one of the reporters," Chepp excitedly blurted out.

"Maybe, but this number is from the 412 area code and it looks familiar. I think it's that guy Neil, the alien blogger," said Leslie as she slid her finger along her phone screen to answer the call.

"Hello, this is Leslie McCabe." Chepp was driving, and Leslie did not put the call on speaker so Chepp could only hear Leslie's side of the conversation.

"Hey, Neil!" Leslie smiled and looked over at Chepp satisfied that she had guessed right. But then her facial expression grew very animated as her eyes widened.

"No way! He's right there with you! Uh-huh. Holy cow! Okay. What's this one look like—same as the other night? No kidding! Uh-huh. Okay. Just hang in there and don't do anything too crazy, Neil. My colleague Dr. Duplay and I can be there later today. We will get the first flight we can and be on our way shortly." After a brief pause, she said, "Neil, I totally understand. You don't have to apologize. I think you did exactly the right thing by calling us. Just text me your address, and we will be there ASAP. Yep. See you soon." Leslie hung up.

She turned to Chepp and said, "You are *not* going to believe this!"

Later that day, Neil sat in his chair gripping his semiautomatic handgun. He tapped the barrel against his thigh and gently bit his lip sideways as he thought. He continued to stare in disbelief at this small being he had tied up in his kitchen. Being tough with Opie was getting harder. It was now early evening, and after a whole day of interrogation, Neil found himself softening toward his prisoner. The fact that Opie looked like a popular, cute Earth boy from an iconic TV show didn't help. Thank goodness for the missing ears, gray skin, and raspy metallic voice because they helped him remember that Opie was certainly not a little boy.

"Okay. So let's review. You have Anna and my baby to keep them safe. And we can't just return to your spaceship to get her—unless we have a very good plan—because this loose cannon Hero guy—your leader—would not hesitate to kill me. And it's all because your race is dying from some strange disease caused by an odd harmonic in a solar flare from your sun. Okay. I think I've got all that. But would you please explain to me one more time what you did to the human race using the volcanoes?"

"Please keep in mind, Neil, that all of this was done in desperation. And most of it is reversible. Also, for the record, this is not how I would have carried out this mission. But I had no choice in that matter. I am a military man, as you have been, and I'm simply following orders." Opie spoke fluent and eloquent English for the most part. It was the Earth language that he and his Dwovian colleagues had learned the best due to its importance in human history, especially the last two hundred Earth years.

"I understand," said Neil. "Your whole planet united behind this master plan to save your race, and you want me to know that you are just a cog in the gears of the whole operation. I get that. But you still bear responsibility for your actions, little Opie. Now, please get on with telling me this volcano thing again." Neil was anxious to hear it one more time because it was boggling his mind. He was having a hard time believing it and accepting it. But as he stared at Opie— this short, gray, bald-headed, earless alien from another planet—it reminded him that his whole foundation of knowledge had changed drastically since yesterday.

"When we arrived five thousand Earth years ago, one of the first things we did was drill deep holes below some of your active volcanoes. We used a special laser array on our spacecraft that—" Opie was interrupted by the doorbell ringing. Neil reacted immediately.

"Shhh! Be quiet!" he whispered while jumping up and placing his hand over Opie's mouth. Then, with his other hand, he raised the gun at Opie and very quietly said, "Don't you dare move or make a sound while I check on this. If you think this gun and I are your worst nightmare, try imagining that you end up pickled in a big jar of formaldehyde in the corner of some government scientist's lab. Because if anybody else on this planet gets ahold on you, that's probably how it ends for you. So, I suggest you listen to me." Opie nodded, acknowledging that he understood.

Neil walked down the hallway toward the front door. It was getting late in the day and the hallway was dimly lit. Only the natural light coming in the very small windows above the front door was lighting it. Neil turned his head around looking back down the hallway toward the kitchen, which was well lit. He could see the end of the table where he had been sitting just a few seconds before. Fortunately, Opie was out of sight.

Neil looked through the peephole. It was a man and a woman he did not recognize. The woman was holding a small luggage bag. It suddenly dawned on him. This was Dr. McCabe and her colleague, Dr. Duplay.

Neil unlocked the door and pulled it open while he put the gun behind his back and tucked the barrel into the waistband of his jeans.

"Hello. Dr. McCabe, I am guessing?"

"Yes," Leslie answered, "and this is my husband, Chepp." Chepp looked over at Leslie with one of those odd upside-down smiles on his face. The kind of smile you do when you find something surprising but refreshing to see—like a parent seeing their teenager clean up their room without being asked.

"Oh, your husband? I thought he was just a colleague," responded Neil.

"Well, he's that, too. But he's also my husband. Not many people know it though because we eloped and we don't talk about it much. It's a long story," explained Leslie.

"Well, okay then. I look forward to hearing more about that. But for now, please come on in and set your bag down there." Neil pointed to a spot near a beautiful entryway table. "We really need to get out to the kitchen pretty quickly. I have our uninvited guest tied to a chair out there and I don't want to leave him alone for too long." Neil turned around and pulled the gun out from his waistband, raised his arm, and waved the barrel of the gun in a "Come this way" fashion for Chepp and Leslie, inviting them to follow him down the hallway.

Chepp and Leslie were a bit startled by the gun but began following Neil down the dimly lit hall. As a gentleman, Chepp was walking behind Leslie, but he put his hand on her shoulder to stop her and whispered in her ear, "I love you. Are you ready for this? Are you ready to see a real alien? Would you like me to go first?"

"No, I got this. I'm a little nervous, but I'll be fine."

As they came into the kitchen and they glanced to the left, there he was. Tied to a kitchen chair was a boy-sized alien with a cute face and bald head. Leslie walked past Opie, staring at the pale gray skin and ear holes. She sat down in a chair at the far end of the table, beside Neil who was already seated in a chair directly facing the alien. Chepp followed around the table and sat next to Leslie. They were handling it all fine but were shocked to hear Opie speak.

"Neil, I have been tied to this chair all day. I really need to use the bathroom and a drink of water would be good. I'm getting dehydrated. I also request a blanket. It is quite chilly in here for me." Opie's metallic, techno voice shocked Leslie.

"Oh my god, he speaks English! Are you sure this isn't some neighborhood kid who's had his ears and hair whacked off?" Leslie blurted out.

"I assure you, I'm no neighborhood kid," Opie responded looking at Leslie.

"Why does your voice sound computerized? Are you using a speech synthesizer of some sort?" asked Leslie.

"We do not usually speak like humans. Our native language is more similar to your Morse code than English. So our voice boxes are much simpler than yours. We have only two vocal cords and they have a high metallic content—mostly iron. My planet is rich in iron," Opie explained. "Now, Neil, may I use your facility or would you like me to relieve myself right here on your kitchen chair?"

"Okay, but I'm going to accompany you and we are not shutting the door," explained Neil as he handed the gun to Chepp. "Doctor, I'm assuming you know how to use a gun. Shoot to wound if he tries anything. But by all means, do not let him escape. Remember, they have my wife and unborn baby." Neil knelt down and began cutting the zip ties around Opie's feet and hands.

"Yep. You got it. And don't worry, I can handle a gun," said Chepp.

"This is so weird," pronounced Leslie. "How do you know English so well, Mr. Alien?"

"I've been calling him Opie because I think he looks like a bald Opie Taylor from the old *Andy Griffith Show*," Neil said as he quickly glanced at Leslie but stayed focused on untying the rope.

"Yeah! He does! I knew he looked like some little boy I knew!" she responded.

"To answer your question—it's amazing how natural a language will become for you when you've been observing it and studying it for thousands of years," Opie answered.

"Did I forget to mention that? He says he's twenty thousand Earth years old," Neil blurted out with some doubt in his voice. The last knot came loose and the rope slid away. Opie stood up.

"I am, Neil. I am twenty-thousand Earth years old. Why would I make that up?" said Opie, "Now, can you please get me to your bathroom before I burst?"

Opie hardly seemed a threat as he stood and walked with Neil toward the powder room, which was a short distance away. At noticeably less than four feet tall and wearing a small black robe, he looked like a child ready to trick or treat with a parent.

"This is unbelievable," said Chepp as he shook his head slowly back and forth with a shocked look on his face and his mouth slightly hanging open.

"Uh . . . yeah!" said Leslie with animated agreement. "And what are we thinking?" she continued. "We need to get pictures and start recording this stuff." She pulled out her cell phone.

Just then, they heard a trickle into the commode as Opie began relieving himself.

"Is your pee always that red?" asked Neil.

Opie answered, "Earthlings pee yellow if they're a healthy fellow. Dwovians pee red if they're far from dead." Opie turned his head and looked at Neil.

"You're rhyming now! That's just wrong," said Neil.

CHAPTER

13

Denko had just been informed about Hero's death.

"Holy crap! Well what are we supposed to do now? We lost communication with Colonel Skrako around the same time the commander and the earth woman arrived," said Denko. "Do we have any idea what happened? Did the commander say anything before passing?"

"Nothing. He was unconscious when he arrived and near death. But according to the computer, the cause of death was damage to the electrical part of his heart—most likely caused by a needle. There was also a lot of our strong sedative drug in his system. So it's a safe bet that he was injected," answered Grenko.

"I know there was a lot of friction between the commander and Colonel Skrako in recent days." Manko weighed in. "You don't suppose Skrako could be responsible do you?"

"No way! I would trust Skrako with my life—even more than the commander!" strongly answered Grenko. "No, I think the most likely scenario is they were caught by surprise and attacked. And at the hour of the day, it was most likely the mate of the Earth woman."

"She was calling out to a Neil a little while ago," offered Denko.

"Yes. His name is Neil. I remember that from our briefing," said Manko. "He must have been there."

"Well, what do we do now?" asked Denko. "The command chain puts you in charge now, Grenko, so what's the plan?"

"Well, we need to take good care of the Earth woman. That's first priority. Also, since we don't know what has become of Skrako and his mini jerblonk and crystals, we all need to be on high alert. We need to keep trying to raise Skrako, too. And there is one person who may know what happened—the Earth woman. So we need to do what we can to get information out of her," Grenko answered.

"I've already started building a relationship with Anna—the Earth woman. In fact, I was about to rout out to get her a steak, egg, and cheese bagel from McDonald's. That's what she requested, and I think she's testing us," said Denko.

"Perfect. You stay on that assignment, Denko. Keep in mind that she apparently doesn't know if we have her mate or not. Let's see if we can use that to our advantage. Manko, you guard the Earth woman while Denko goes to pick up the McHappy Meal. No, wait! Scratch that. Manko, you rout out to get the meal, and Denko you stay with Anna and keep trying to get information from her. Meanwhile, I will go let our engineer, Chenko, know what is happening. He will need to continually try to contact Skrako from the command center. Are we all clear?" Grenko's strong but calm leadership skills were already becoming apparent to his colleagues.

"Got it," said Denko.

"Right-o," answered Manko.

Opie was once again tied up to the chair and zip-tied.

"If you have some rusty steel around here, please rub some of the rust into my drink of water." Opie requested.

"Why in the world would I do that? This is clean filtered water. You can't drink that?" asked Neil as he finished filling the glass at the refrigerator door.

"I can drink that for a while, but the water on Dwovy has a high iron content. Rusty water on earth is similar. It helps me keep my iron levels up, plus it tastes much better," was the answer from the alien.

"Fascinating!" said Leslie. "So the oceans on your planet have iron in them instead of salt like we have here on earth."

"Yes. Exactly. Except the oceans on Dwovy are perfectly balanced for our bodies and we can drink them. It's a very peculiar situation you have on your planet. You have tremendous amounts of water, but the salt content would kill you if you drank it long term. I'm still trying to understand that—very weird," Opie said as he looked at Leslie. "You would think that all life on Earth would be able to use the ocean water, not just the ocean animals."

"Right. I've often wondered about that, too. This is so cool talking with someone from another planet. Unreal!" Leslie shared excitedly.

"All right, here's the deal. You're getting the plain water this time. If you keep cooperating and behaving, the next glass of water will be rusty," Neil explained. "Now please finish retelling me about the volcanoes. Listen carefully, Dr. McCabe and Dr. Duplay. You will want to hear this"

"When we arrived five thousand Earth years ago, our first task was to drill deep holes beneath some active volcanoes in the equatorial region of your planet," explained Opie. "We did this with a laser array on our spacecraft—it was specifically designed by Dwovian scientists for this purpose."

"That was first priority? Why did you do that? What's the purpose of it?" asked Chepp.

"It had two purposes. First, drilling deep beneath an active volcano allows us to access the heat energy of the magma flows. Humanity's understanding of crystals is still virtually nonexistent compared to the rest of the galaxy. To charge crystal transducers, it is important to have a natural electromagnetic spectrum that matches the specific natural frequencies of the crystal. We can use our ship's reactor to charge many of our crystals, but there are a few important crystals that require an infrared spectrum exactly like that radiated by liquid rock, like the magma in your volcanoes here on earth." Opie spoke with authority and intelligence that captivated all three of them.

"But doesn't the energy required for drilling make the energy you get back a moot point?" asked Neil.

"You're missing the point, Neil," answered Chepp. "The reactor has enough energy to last a very long time. The spectrum of the infrared heat available matches the specific resonances in some of their crystal transducers. And those are apparently difficult to reproduce by synthetic means. Am I understanding right?"

"Exactly, Dr. Duplay," answered Opie. "The reactor onboard our spaceship will last at least eight thousand Earth years, so we have a large supply of energy for our needs. But the second and more important reason we drilled these holes was so we could release the draminkos worldwide during volcanic eruptions. Volcanic eruptions spew ash and dust over an incredibly wide area and high enough into the atmosphere that within a year's time it is uniformly distributed. You may be aware that much of the dust on planet Earth is ash and dust from past volcanic eruptions."

"Volcanic eruptions would be an efficient way of uniformly distributing very small particles worldwide. I am guessing the draminkos must be very small and numerous. But what are they?" offered Chepp.

"Again you are on the mark, Dr. Duplay," answered Opie. "Draminkos are very small robotic devices capable of submicroscopic surgical procedures."

"Oh my god! You tinkered with our DNA, didn't you? You used nanotechnology to mess with our DNA!" burst Leslie as she had an epiphany moment.

"It was not my idea or my preference, Dr. McCabe." Opie was once again defensive, as he had been with Neil earlier. "But it was a key part of my leader's plan to save our race. We first had to make a way to experiment with potential genetic solutions. His plan with the draminkos has worked. The latest data we have shows that Neil's mate, Anna, is carrying the genetic cure in her body."

"Okay. So you programmed these little draminkos to surgically alter our DNA," said Chepp in a moment of clarity where it was all coming together.

"Wait! Wait! Wait! This is what he was telling me before. That seems unbelievable. You mean that's possible? They could mechanically alter our DNA with submicroscopic machines!" Neil looked like a modern-day child learning that people didn't always have telephones. He was in shock.

"Think about it, Neil. We have recently been able to do amazing genetic manipulations with our current technology. The Dwovians apparently are many generations ahead of us in technology and scientific knowledge. Their nanotechnology is probably incredible," said Chepp.

"The crystal technology is the main thing you are missing. Once you discover the amazing ability of crystals to act as transducers, things will take a huge step forward for Earth scientists. It will cause a paradigm shift in your nanotechnology," explained Opie.

"So the draminkos are submicroscopic, programmed machines that humankind breathed and ate? They invaded our ancestor's bodies and manipulated our DNA through mechanical, surgical techniques?" summarized Leslie while checking her hypotheses with the alien.

"Correct," answered Opie. "The draminkos only had an energy lifetime of two hundred Earth years, so all manipulations were completed during that time, finishing by roughly 4800 Bc in your calendar system. Since then, the DNA alterations have been passed on to future generations via natural human reproduction."

"You bastards changed what it is to be human, without even asking us if we approved," Leslie spouted off with a mixture of anger and disappointment. "Tell me, these genetic manipulations wouldn't happen to have also introduced sleep into the human race, say about five thousand years ago also, would they?"

"Yes. That feature of the manipulation was added to allow us to more easily perform genetic testing on your bodies without detection. Having Earth people fall asleep made it easier to operate in stealth mode. There are only a small number of us on this expedition. Remaining undetected was high priority. We had to stack the odds in our favor."

"What the heck are you guys saying? Are you saying these genetic manipulations have made human beings sleep longer than we are meant to sleep?" queried Neil.

"No, more than that, Neil. The Dwovians actually made us sleep for the first time. My research has produced evidence that sleep is basically an induced illness caused by genetic manipulation.

Humankind—in fact, most animals on Earth—are not meant to sleep at all!" Leslie was clearly animated with her speech as it was all coming together for her.

"The draminkos entered all living creatures on your planet over their two-hundred-year operational period, and any creature with similar coding strands in the DNA was affected—usually in a similar way. Unfortunately a couple of native species developed side effects from the draminkos' DNA manipulations and have gone extinct."

"This is totally unbelievable! Does anybody else feel outraged and violated by news of this!" Neil asked.

"*Yes!*" both Chepp and Leslie answered at the same time.

"So we sleep when we are not meant to sleep. There goes about one-third of our lives. I also heard you mention something about speeding up our life cycles. How much did this whole 'hack a human' mission shorten our lives, might I ask?" asked Neil.

"Just remember this wasn't my idea, and many Dwovians were against it. But we are a race on the brink."

"How long!" yelled Chepp as he stared at Opie.

"Well, when we arrived on your planet, humans did not sleep and your average lifespan was two thousand Earth years."

Anna was sitting up now. Most of her questions had been answered. But that didn't mean she was totally comfortable being the mother of a miracle child. She still was a bit wigged out by the alien's, and she would not rest easy until she was back with her husband.

She was not tied up or shackled in any way. In addition, the door to the room she was in was open. But every time she made a motion toward it in an attempt to go through, a door would materialize. It was an amazing technology, and it mesmerized Anna each time she saw it happen. Eventually she came to the conclusion that attempts to escape through the door were a waste of time. She was not going anywhere until she was released or until someone helped her escape.

Denko entered the room with a tall glass of beer on a tray.

"Here is your beer, Anna," he said.

She looked at him and derisively laughed. "I can't drink that!"

"I don't understand. You requested it," came the reply from Denko, who was legitimately confused.

"No, I said, 'I could use a beer about now.' I had no idea you would actually go get me one."

"Why wouldn't I? I explained to you that my orders are to properly care for you," explained Denko.

Anna actually found herself touched—albeit very slightly—by this little alien captor and his blind devotion to her care.

"It has alcohol in it, Denko. I can't drink it when I'm pregnant. It could harm the baby. That's probably why I want one so badly—precisely because I can't have one. Also, when humans are stressed, sometimes we like to drink alcoholic beverages because they help calm us down."

"Oh. I probably should have known that. Please don't tell Grenko." Denko looked nervously out into the hallway as he pushed a button on the wall near the doorway. A small section of the wall dematerialized revealing a chute in the wall, and he quickly disposed of the bottle of beer and the tray by tossing them into the chute. "Grenko is the one who is our expert on food and drink on this planet, but now that he has been pressed into a leadership role, I have been trusted with your care. Sometimes I can't remember all the things I'm supposed to remember." The small section of the wall reappeared, fading back into existence, and the opening to the chute was gone.

"Oh, I totally get that, Denko. I've forgotten far more than I've remembered in my lifetime. Now, when am I going to get to see Neil? I've told you everything I remember happening."

Anna was unaware that nearly two days had passed since she was abducted. Her interrogation was not hard once the Dwovians promised her she could see Neil afterward. But since waking up, she had not slept again. She still had a lot of adrenaline in her system. Also, it was practically impossible to sleep in the environment she was in, even if she wanted. The steady bright orange lights throughout the spacecraft were a bit annoying—an unnatural color of light for Anna. And the metallic floors and walls seemed to amplify all the clicks, whistles, rattles, and pops of these creatures strange language, not to mention the sound of footsteps. The ceilings were lower and the rooms smaller than on Earth, giving an uncomfortable, cramped feeling to her environment. It was also very warm, like a hot summer day, and the air seemed a bit thin.

"Wait here," said Denko.

"Yeah. Like I could go anywhere, Denko," Anna said sarcastically but with a sad tone and a downcast look on her face.

⁂

Neil, Chepp, and Leslie were finally on the same page regarding the Dwovians' presence on Earth and why they had an intense interest in Neil and Anna's baby. Well, that is if they could believe what they had been told. The whole story came from an alien who had worked with another alien to kidnap Neil's wife. Needless to say, Neil was still suspicious of Opie, and his instincts were to get Anna back ASAP. They stood in the dark hallway between the kitchen and front door to quietly discuss their situation.

"I still think we should call in Dr. Warstein," quietly said Neil.

"I think we should just force Opie to transport us to his spaceship and we use brute force to get Anna back," said Leslie in a forceful whisper. "If they need information from her baby, we can provide that for them. But we need to get her back as soon as possible."

"I get that, Les. We all are anxious to get to Anna. And if what we heard is true, then we will likely have to break Anna out like you suggest—using force. But we really can't be sure Opie has been truthful with us. Neil says Dr. Warstein can bring drugs to help us be sure we are getting accurate information from him. At that point we can develop a good plan," countered Chepp in a better whisper than hers. "Neil? What do you think? It's your wife, so you should make the decision."

The three confidants were standing together side by side as they kept an eye on Opie. They had been interrogating Opie all night and had learned a lot about the Dwovians and their plight—if it could all be believed. It was about 5:30 a.m. Neil had not shaved the past two mornings and a shadow of a dark beard and mustache were coming in giving him that rugged and sexy look some women love.

"Ugh. I'm absolutely beat, and we all are in need of some shut-eye—thanks to these Dwovians! So any rescue mission has to wait until our minds are alert and thinking clearly," answered Neil. "And while we wait, I *do* think we should call in Shelly Warstein. She is young, but my gut says we need to trust her. We will only get one shot at rescuing my wife, and the more information we can get out of Opie before going in, the better our chance of bringing her home."

"Okay then, that settles it. Call her in while I work out a schedule for guarding little Ronnie Howard out there," said Leslie.

CHAPTER
14

"Hey. It's Shelly. I'm just about ready to pull out. I should be there in about three hours or so, depending on traffic. I sure hope you're shooting straight with me about all this."

On the other end of the phone was Neil Reese, calling from his cell phone in his suburban neighborhood outside of Pittsburgh, Pennsylvania.

"Trust me. I'm shooting straight with you. I know it's all hard to believe, Shelly, but when you get here, you'll see. Just make sure you bring the drugs. My wife's life very well could depend on them."

"No worries on that! I've got a small suitcase full of various psychoneurotic drugs here that I'll be bringing," Shelly answered. "God, listen to me. What am I saying . . . This is freaking me out. I mean, I've never even met you in person. I have to be crazy to be doing this based on a telephone call from a stranger. But I'd give anything to meet a real alien, and there is just something about your voice that's believable and has me convinced that you really need my help."

The slightly overweight Dr. Shelly Warstein with the cute nose and brown hair was on a phone in her laboratory in Tech Station, Pennsylvania. As a scientist, she was mature and wise well beyond her age of twenty-six years. As a person, she was still prone to teenager-like, impulsive, misguided decisions, and she feared this might be another one.

"Well, I appreciate you trusting me. And I have my own worries, too, Shelly. Not only the worry about you actually bringing the drugs, but the worry of keeping this thing quiet. You didn't tell anyone, right?"

"Of course not."

"You see, we're both in the same boat on this trusting each other thing, because if this thing leaks out and authorities get involved, the aliens may just abandon their colleague and take off for their planet with my wife. So please, please, please, for God's sake—not a word to anyone."

"Don't worry. I didn't even tell my research partner or family about this. I just sent out an email to everyone telling them I have a migraine and will be holing myself up at home until it's gone."

"You sure that will work?" Neil asked. "We might need your help for a couple of days, you know."

"I have a history of migraines—I get one almost every month, unfortunately, and they know the pattern when I get one. They won't be suspicious for at least forty-eight hours."

"Okay. I guess that will work then. Listen, Shelly, I hate to cut this short, but I'm exhausted. As I told you, we've been up all night. So we are going to try to get some shuteye while we're waiting for you. We're taking turns guarding the alien, and I'd like to get some sleep before it's my turn."

"No problem, Neil. I totally understand. Go get some sleep, and I'll see you soon."

"Great. And thanks again, Shelly. I know this wasn't an easy thing for you to decide to do. Please drive carefully and we'll see you in a few hours. Call us if anything changes."

"You got it. Bye, Neil."

"Bye, Shelly."

Click. Neil set his cell phone down on the table next to the leather recliner he was stretched out in, and before his hand even fully released the phone, he was asleep.

⌘

Anna was finishing the last bite of her breakfast sandwich. She had been very hungry, and although it was a risk, she doubted it contained any dangerous drugs or poisons since she knew how much they cared about her baby's health. Of course, that was assuming they were being honest. At any rate, it sure seemed like an authentic steak, egg, and cheese bagel from McDonald's.

Denko walked back into the room with another alien. Anna soon learned he was the one called Grenko and that he was the alien currently calling the shots for the Dwovians. He delivered some unwelcome news to Anna.

"So Neil is not here! You bastards lied to me? You told me I could see him after I gave you the information you wanted. You need to take me to him—wherever he is—right *now*!" yelled Anna Reese as she got up out of her chair. The chair reminded her of those used in elementary schools. It was clearly designed for Dwovians and not adult humans. Her head was unusually close to the ceiling for a woman of her height. The gears in her head started to spin at high speed. "Think! Think! What can you say, Anna, to get some leverage over them? Come on, think."

Even though she was an impeccably honest person, she decided that if they lied, then she could lie, too. After all, she figured "all is fair in war and alien abductions."

"If you don't take me to Neil right now, the baby will die."

"What are you talking about?" asked Grenko.

"We Earth women have a special muscle in our womb that will contract and kill the baby if the woman doesn't have regular physical contact with her mate," answered Anna.

At that statement, Grenko and Denko quickly paced over to the jerblonk on the table near the door of the room. They began speaking in Dwovian to each other—which to Anna sounded like rapid, crisp pops, clicks, whistles, and clinks. Denko tapped a few strokes on the jerblonk's keyboard, and they studied the screen. After a few more clicks and pops of Dwovian communication, Grenko and Denko walked back over toward Anna.

As they walked, she couldn't help but think about how little and vulnerable their two bodies looked. For a moment she thought about how she might overpower them—a karate kick to the gut to send them flying or a kick between the legs—would that work? Then she remembered the magical door that appeared whenever she tried to go through. Until she understood how to get through that, she had better save her bush whacking. She decided to confidently sit back down and keep playing out the deception.

"We don't believe you," Grenko answered. "We have been on your planet for five thousand years and we have no records of such a muscle in your female anatomy. In fact, we have observed the protection instincts of Earth mothers, and we do not believe an Earth mother would risk losing her baby by being away from her mate for long if your claim were true. Additionally, we have observed many single mothers who spend considerable time away from—"

Suddenly Anna screamed as if in pain. Grenko and Denko stepped outside her room and quickly conversed. Anna was convinced they were buying her act. Hopefully they would rush her to Neil. She screamed again. Denko disappeared in the hallway for a moment and was quickly back in the room with Anna. He walked straight toward her and brought his face close to hers and looked into her eyes.

"Please stay calm and tell me what we can do."

"Ahhhhh! Take me to Neil!" Anna screamed again and closed her eyes. Suddenly she felt a sharp jab in her leg. She opened her eyes and looked down to the sight of a hypodermic needle rammed into her thigh by Denko.

"You son of a bit—" Anna's vision quickly became blurry and she lost consciousness.

Denko called for Grenko, who quickly entered the room.

"No problem. She never saw it coming," said Denko.

Grenko helped him move Anna to the exam table, then Grenko gave the orders.

"Strap her down and keep her calm, like we talked about. Above all, be sure you monitor that baby and keep it safe. I want verbal reports any time the status changes."

"Got it," replied Denko.

With that, Grenko was out the door and heading for the command center. He was calling for Chenko and Manko.

"Uh-ohhh! We may have a problem, guys! You're on TV, Leslie. No. Strike that. We're both on TV," called out Chepp. Again with a louder voice, he said, "Guys, wake up!"

Leslie rolled off the couch and came running down the hallway toward the kitchen. "What's going on??"

Chepp was sitting in the kitchen chair across the table from Opie, who was still tied up. Chepp held the gun in one hand and pointed with the index finger on his opposite hand to the small flat-screen TV mounted on the side of the kitchen cabinets.

"I guess that reporter you were supposed to meet with started talking with the other reporters about you being a no-show. They've been looking for you for the past day. I guess they found our marriage record from Vegas, and since they couldn't find me either, they are suspicious and are searching for us. They just said something about checking airports, so it probably won't take them long to figure out that we flew to Pittsburgh."

Neil was finally up and joined the group in the kitchen. They all stared at the TV and listened to the report on the local channel.

"At least they'll never think to look for us at Neil's. Should we let somebody know we are okay if we can, without giving them information about where we are?" questioned Leslie.

"I could call the university and check in. But they may be suspicious if I don't tell them where we are and what we are doing. Besides, the authorities are now involved. I guess I could make something up. How about visiting a sick friend in Pittsburgh?" asked Chepp.

"Sounds believable to me," said Neil, "But you do know you're going to have to face those reporters sooner or later, right, Leslie?"

"Yeah. Once we get your wife back and that crisis is behind us, then we can think about that," said Leslie. "But we probably should decide soon how much of all this we are going to document. Sooner or later the cats gonna bust out of the bag, and the evidence could either help protect us or get us in trouble."

This was the first time since Neil took Opie prisoner that he really reflected upon the consequences long term of what he was doing. Would the government come after him? Did the alien have rights that would be recognized by some US attorney, and could he be imprisoned for violating them? Neil believed he had no choice in what he had done so far, and he was just going to have to trust that his fellow human beings would agree with him.

"I hadn't thought about that," said Neil, "but now you have me thinking. I think we should document as little as possible right now. We need to make a commitment right now to stick together and cover each other's backs no matter what. We are in uncharted territory here."

"Well, let's see . . . We are dealing with live aliens, genetic manipulation of the entire human race from ancient days, the potential death of an entire race of intelligent beings, kidnapping, stealing drugs from a government funded lab . . . Yeah, this is uncharted territory for me. How 'bout you, honey?" Chepp quipped, trying to lighten the weight they were all starting to feel.

"Yeah. Probably at least one of those is a first for me." Leslie chuckled, playing along.

"But seriously, I need to know you guys have my back," said Neil nervously. "I invited you guys in because I need your help, but I need to know I can trust you."

"Neil, I'm holding a loaded gun that *you* gave me, sitting in your kitchen. I think you've already decided you can trust us. And if it helps to hear it said out loud—you can trust us," said Chepp.

"All for one and one for all," quoted Leslie.

"Thanks, guys. I really needed to hear that right now," Neil replied with a deep breath with some relief in it.

Suddenly the twangy voice from the other end of the table spoke.

"Believe it or not, I am on your side, too." Neil, Leslie, and Chepp all turned their faces to Opie. He continued, "I am hoping we can work out a mutually beneficial agreement to our current situation. This will depend on our convincing my commander to change his strategy in finishing up our mission. But I honestly believe it is more beneficial for the people of both our planets to be allies rather than competitors. Can I join your band of brothers?"

They were all caught off guard by these statements and looked at Opie and each other in silence for a few moments.

"I guess I'm the de facto leader of this group of Earth people right now, and all I can say right now, little Opie, is that we will see. We have a long way to go for that to happen. We need to first find out if you're being truthful, and then we need to know more about your plans. But hacking the life code of a race of people is a strange way to try to make friends."

"We had to do something, Neil. I hope you can eventually see that," said Opie as his lips curled slightly downward matching with his downcast face.

Dwovy may be many light-years away, and the Dwovians distant genetic cousins to humans, but the look of sadness and remorse on this little alien's face spanned those great separations. For a moment, all four intelligent beings shared in the emotion of disappointment communicated by Opie's face.

CHAPTER

15

A crowd of reporters sat in a small community room waiting for a press conference to begin. Ralph Stryker, a lead reporter from GN3, the Greater National News Network, was front and center.

Ralph craned his neck to look around the beautifully decorated second floor room. There were modern couches around the perimeter with a few tall wooden chairs, elevated tables, and stools in the back of the room. There was drop lighting, cork flooring, and contrasting earth-colored tones throughout. The room resembled a modern coffee bar or cafe in places, except there was a small stage, a podium and a projection screen at the front of the room. In front of the stage were several rows of wooden chairs arranged for the audience.

The left wall of the room was floor to ceiling tinted glass windows. They provided a spectacular panoramic view of the most beautiful part of the CUS campus. The dry, sunny California sky looked a deep blue through the tinted windows.

Ralph could imagine the room being used in many different ways—for screening movies, for public lectures, or even for small time musical or comedic performances.

Suddenly a burst of laughter erupted from a group of reporters in the back corner of the room. Apparently someone had been telling a joke and they finally reached the punch line. Ralph turned his head back around to face the stage, just in time to see a well-dressed, distinguished man with a recently trimmed white beard, deep bronze tan, and modern-style glasses. He was standing near the edge of the stage talking with a younger man dressed in a green polo-style collared shirt and tan pants. The younger man was apparently the audio visual technician, and he was going over some event details with the older gentleman. Ralph was guessing the older man was Dr. Dennis Richland, the dean of science at the University.

"You all right?" whispered Athena Kirkland who was sitting in the seat immediately beside Ralph on his right. She had been his faithful young sidekick for the past year.

"I'm better than fine, Theney. I think this is going to be the biggest news story of the century—hell, probably in the history of humankind—and we are going to knock this thing out of the park you and me. These other saps, they don't have a clue what we are dealing with here."

"Ya think?" asked Athena, better known to her friends as Theney.

"Yep! And with the leads we have, I think we should be able to track these two professors down within twenty-four hours—hopefully even less time than that. And once we find them, we are not going to lose them. I just want to hear this science dean confirm what we already know and see if there is any other information he has that could be of value to us. Then we are off to Pittsburgh, where we will use my secret weapon to track them down," Ralph answered.

Theney smiled. She had a short and stalky build, which humorously contrasted with Ralph's tall, thin body. In fact, they had won a prize at last year's company Halloween party for their rendition of Abbott and Costello.

Professionally they were an ideal fit for each other. They had worked some great stories together this past year, and lately could finish each other's sentences. Theney had a pretty face that could pass as a double for Halle Berry. With a great heart and a brilliant mind, Theney brought the research skills to the team, while Ralph brought the vision and tactical instinct.

Finally, there was the familiar click of a sound system and microphone being activated. The press conference being given by the science dean of CUS regarding the missing faculty members, Dr. Leslie McCabe and Dr. Cheppard Duplay had begun.

Dr. Shelly Warstein had arrived. Neil opened the door and invited her in. As if she wasn't nervous enough, she found Neil's dashing good looks caused her to question her own appearance probably more than necessary. After exchanging a few pleasantries and the obligatory handshakes and "nice to finally meet-you," Neil walked Shelly to the kitchen. She carried her little hardback briefcase of drugs with her.

The second she entered the kitchen, her eyes gravitated to the little alien. She could not take her eyes off him. Inside, her mind was racing and saying, "Holy crap! Holy crap! Holy crap!" She tried to play it cool and not overreact.

"Leslie and Chepp, this is Dr. Shelly Warstein, a chemistry professor from Keystone Tech. Shelly, this is Dr. Chepp Duplay and Dr. Leslie McCabe from the California University of Sciences," Neil said as both Leslie and Chepp stood up. Leslie extended a hand to Shelly while Chepp laid the handgun on the table and then extended his.

"Nice to meet you," politely responded Shelly as she shook hands. She noticed Chepp's good looks and felt the firm handshake from his toned, muscular body. She also noticed that Leslie was quite attractive herself. The whole thing was starting to feel odd to Shelly. She was not unattractive herself, but these three looked like a group of middle-aged cheerleaders or models, not scientists. She hoped she was not being duped for the drugs.

She looked back over at Opie and studied him. He looked like a cute little boy, just like Neil had told her, but his skin tone was a bit gray, his fingers were very long, and he had six fingers on each hand. His fingernails had an orange-ish tint, and he had only little pencil-sized openings where his ears should have been. He was bald. He did look like a bald Opie Taylor from the old *Andy Griffith Show*. If this was someone pulling a hoax, they were going to great lengths for a score of only a few syringes of drugs.

"And I am the one you have come to inject," said Opie in his metallic, Stephen Hawking-ish tone.

"Whaahhhh!" Shelly jumped back. "Is that his real voice or do you have him hooked up to some kind of computer?" She was clearly in a bit of shock and very nervous at the moment. Neil moved closer to her and laid a reassuring hand on her upper arm.

"That's my fault. I should have warned you about that. That's his natural voice," said Neil. Then he turned his eye to Opie and asked, "Now how in the heck do you know that? Why would you think she's here to inject you with a drug?"

"It's obvious, Neil, that you are not sure whether you believe me. Otherwise, I would not still be tied to this chair. There is a manhunt about to begin for your colleagues, so time is short. You are desperate to get Anna back, but as a good military thinker, you recognize the importance of having good intelligence before going after her. In the midst of this, a chemistry professor shows up carrying a small metal suitcase. She's here either to torture me or to drug me to get the truth out of me. Considering your dislike of violence thus far and the fact that you may need to use me in exchange for your wife, I'm betting it is drugs."

"You were able to deduce all that from what you've observed?" asked Neil.

"Well, that and the fact that I heard you three talking about the plan while you stood by the door earlier today." Opie smiled. "Dwovian ears are extremely sensitive. We hear at higher and lower frequencies than Earth people. The expanded range means that if we listen carefully we can hear the vibrations from your voices through the walls of your house."

"Well, I'll have to keep that in mind for the future. But unfortunately this is happening, little Opie. We have to inject you because we need to know the truth, just like you said. So I'd appreciate it if you could keep the struggle to a minimum."

"There will be no struggle, Neil. I will voluntarily submit to this process. I understand why it has to be done," said Opie.

"Whoa. This is a fascinating little alien you have here, Neil," said Shelly. "When would you like to get started?"

∽

"Ladies and gentlemen, welcome to Pittsburgh. The temperature outside is eighty-six degrees under partly cloudy skies. The local time is 3:14 p.m. On behalf of the captain and the entire flight crew, we hope you enjoyed your flight with us, and we wish you the best in your plans in the city tonight. You may now use your cell phones and electronic devices. Please remain in your seats until we've come to a full stop, and as always, we thank you for flying National Air."

"My buddy Jack said we could meet him at the TGI Fridays in the airport. Since we don't have to pick up luggage, I'm going to call him and tell him we'll meet him there in fifteen minutes. So as soon as we can grab our carry-ons, let's make our way there. We can stop and use a bathroom on the way there," said Ralph Stryker, looking over at Theney who had the aisle seat in the Airbus.

"Sounds good. So this Jack guy is your secret weapon, huh?" asked Theney.

"Yep. We go way back and I've used him before like this. It's gonna cost me a Ben Franklin for his time, but it's well worth it," answered Ralph.

The plane had finally come to a stop and the tarmac was moving into place. In almost no time, folks opened the overhead storage compartments, grabbed their belongings, and were exiting the aircraft. Ralph and Theney were about midway back in the plane.

Once inside the airport they looked for an electronic kiosk to find the location of the TGI Fridays. Theney was still feeling a bit nauseated from the flight, so she was happy to have her feet back on solid ground, and the cool, fresh air in the airport felt wonderful on her face, arms, and legs.

"Here it is," Ralph pointed on the display, "and it looks like we can stop at these restrooms on the way," he said as he tapped his finger on the bathroom location. "We can grab a quick bite in the restaurant while we get the details from Jack."

"Whatever you say boss." Theney smiled.

Ten minutes later, they were sitting in the TGI Fridays. The waitress had gone to get their drinks when Ralph's friend Jack came in and sat down at their table.

"Ralphie! Good to see you! You got it?" Jack said, getting right down to business. He was dressed in an airport security uniform and apparently was still on duty. He looked around in different directions as though concerned he was being watched.

Jack was a middle-aged ex-steelworker with a handsome mug except for a scar on his left cheek. He was clean-shaven and had short salt-and-pepper hair.

"Right here, just like always," Ralph said sliding the $100 bill across the table.

"Okay. I searched through the security footage and found that Dr. Duplay guy you sent me the photograph of. He rented a car at the Enterprise desk and drove off with the other lady, Dr. McCabe about"—he looked at his watch—"thirty-nine hours ago."

"Thanks, Jacko. Pleasure doing business with you, as always," said Ralph. Jack nodded and quietly got up and started walking back the direction he had come from.

"That's it? That's all he's going to give you?" whispered Theney. "That took like thirty seconds. How are we supposed to find them from that information?"

"Well, think about it. If they rented a car, my guess is they are still in the area. Ever heard of GPS?" answered Ralph.

"Huh? Ohhhhh. I follow you. We can locate the car and thus the professors," answered Theney. Ralph smiled and slowly nodded yes as a parent would to their child. Then Theney asked, "But how are we going to get the Enterprise personnel to share that information?"

"We don't. We look at it ourselves," said Ralph. "All we need to do is distract the Enterprise clerk long enough for me to get the routing number for the GPS in their car and another buddy I have in the New York Police Department can tell us where they are."

"But even if I distract them somehow, how will you know where to look?" asked Theney.

"Well, fortunately I worked at one of the airport car rental counters in LA while undercover once for a story. I know how most of these airport rental services work. Cars are coming and going all the time, so the clerk actually signing the cars in and out in the garage—the one handing over the keys—he or she keeps a clipboard near the key rack. That's where the information will be."

"Wow. You're scary good at this stuff, Ralph. You probably could have been a private investigator instead of a newsman."

"I was," he answered.

Ssspp . . . tk . . . tk . . . pip . . . tink . . . whuip . . ., came the clicks, whistles and pops from Opie's mouth. His eyes were open but glazed over like a person in a trance.

"What in the world are all these noises he's making?" asked Shelly. "I hope these drugs aren't frying his brain."

"I don't think so. I heard these aliens converse in what I suspect was their native language when they abducted my wife. It sounded a lot like that. I'm pretty sure he's just speaking his native tongue," answered Neil.

"That makes sense," said Leslie. "When a person enters the first stages of sleep—that very relaxed alpha state—the same communication centers in their brain light up on MRI machines as when they hold one on one conversations while they are awake."

"And so that would suggest that when we enter the alpha state, even if we are multilingual, we tend to think in our first language. Is that what you're saying, honey?" asked Chepp.

"Yes. That's what I'm saying. I think the medication is working, Shelly. I think you've put our alien here into an alpha state. That's what you said you wanted to do, right?"

"Yes, now that I have him in a stable alpha state, I can give him the truth serum."

The IV bag continued to drip medication into the alien's arm. Shelly nervously pulled out a small glass bottle—the kind used by doctors to hold injectable medications. She put her arm out and held it up to the light and turned the little bottle over back and forth a few times. The medication inside was a cloudy white translucent fluid.

Shelly had to stop and wipe the perspiration off her forehead. It wasn't overly warm inside the house, but Shelly was boiling over inside with nervousness. She was grateful that Opie had showed her where to insert the IV needle into his arm and had briefed her a bit about the similarities in Dwovian and human physiology and genetics. He also had warned her that his blood would have a brownish orange tint compared to human blood.

Now that the IV was established and Opie was into the alpha state, all she had to do was inject the truth serum into the IV line. But this was touchy business as far as dosage. The IV could be adjusted higher or lower to keep Opie in the alpha state, but the truth serum was given all at once. Too much and Opie could have a psychotic outburst of rage, like a person on bad crack, angel dust, or bath salts. If she were to give him too little of the serum, then combined with the sedative it could cause electrical disturbances in the heart rhythm, and sudden cardiac arrest would become a real possibility.

She double-checked her calculation on the dosage, then pulled a syringe out of her case and pulled the safety cap off the needle. She turned the little bottle upside-down and pushed the needle up through the soft, sterile stopper into the serum. Pulling down on the plunger of the syringe caused the translucent white fluid to stream in and fill the syringe. She yanked the needle out and flicked the side of the syringe with her finger to send any air bubbles to the top. Then she held the syringe up to the light to carefully and gently push the plunger. As the piston inside slid quietly upward a little of the serum spurt out of the needle tip.

"Well, here goes nothing," said Shelly followed by a long deep exhale in attempt to let go of her apprehension. Neil, Chepp, and Leslie creeped a bit closer, then leaned and moved their heads to get a good view. Shelly plunged the needle into the IV line and injected the full dose. They looked at each other, then back to Shelly. She pulled the needle out and put it into a safety bin, then turned toward Neil to report.

"Give it five minutes and his brain should be all yours, Neil. Let's hope we get the answers we need."

CHAPTER
16

Theney and Ralph had finalized their rental agreement and they walked out into the parking lot through automatic, sliding glass doors. The first thirty feet of the lot was under a steel and concrete canopy, which provided shade. There were three car rental companies that shared the parking lot. They looked to the right and found the Enterprise attendant who would show them to their car and give them the keys. He was standing behind a desk-sized kiosk on wheels outside the sliding glass doors.

"Good afternoon, folks. Enterprise? May I see your rental agreement?"

"Sure. Here you go," answered Ralph, looking back toward the parking attendant with a smile as he handed over the paper.

"Okay, so a luxury sedan. Good choice, good choice," said the attendant, who was a large, well-built African American man, Ralph guessed about 6'3" and about 220 lbs.

"You're a big guy. Did you play football?" Ralph asked.

"Yes, sir. Good guess, sir, I did. I played for Slippery Rock University, about fifty miles north of here. I was middle linebacker."

"I figured as much," said Ralph.

"Yes, sir. Thank you for asking, sir. I currently have three different model luxury sedans ready to go, sir—a Nissan, a Lexus, and a Toyota. Do you have a preference?"

"How about the Nissan?" answered Ralph. "Does that sound good to you, Theney?"

"Huh? Oh yeah. Fine," answered Theney, who was caught a little off guard by the question.

The attendant reached to the right and unlocked a cabinet in the kiosk, grabbed a key fob from the third spot down on the second column, and then relocked the cabinet. Then he looked at the tag on the key fob and began typing the numbers into the computer terminal at the kiosk. He continued looking back and forth between the tag and the monitor. Ralph yawned a big yawn.

Suddenly Theney began to stumble a little into the kiosk and bumped it noticeably.

"Uh-oh, Ralph, I'm getting really dizzy. I think my blood sugar may be too low again. Ooh . . . I really don't feel good." Before you knew it, Theney was leaning her back against the kiosk and was starting to slide to the ground.

"Oh my goodness. Will you help me with her?" Ralph said looking at the attendant. The attendant ran out to the front of the kiosk and crouched down.

"Are you okay, ma'am? Would you like me to call for help, ma'am?"

"No. I'm okay. If you could just help turn me so I'm laying down, and, Ralph, if you could run and buy me one of those sugary sodas from that soda machine around the corner, I'll be fine. This happens to me sometimes after a long flight."

The attendant stooped down further and helped Theney take her business jacket off and then lay her back onto the sidewalk. She asked him to fold her jacket up and put it under her head as a pillow.

"What is your name?" Theney asked.

"My name is Mike, ma'am," he politely answered. "You sure you don't want me to call for medical help?"

"No. Heavens, no. As long as Ralph comes back with the soda and I get a few sips into me, I'll be fine in like ten minutes," she answered.

"Okay. I'll take your word for it, ma'am," he said.

"My name is Athena, but everyone calls me Theney. You can call me Theney."

"Yes, ma'am. I mean, Theney. Would you like me to get any ice for you, or anything like that?" The attendant, Mike, was clearly concerned and apparently not used to attending to customers lying on the ground.

"No. I'll be fine once I get some sugar in me," she said. "Do you know anybody else like me, Mike, who struggles with hypoglycemia? That means low blood sugar."

"Well, I have a great aunt who sometimes has what my mom calls a spell. We usually run to the fridge and get her some orange juice, so maybe that's what it is," he answered.

As if on cue, out of the sliding glass doors came Ralph running with a cold can of Coke. He bent over and snapped open the can for Theney and handed it to her. She briefly sat up a little and guzzled a few big swallows. Then she burped into her closed mouth quietly and laid her head back down.

"Thanks, boss," said Theney. "Give me about five minutes and I should be good to go, right?"

"Yeah. I suspect that's right," said Ralph.

About five minutes later, Theney had made a remarkable recovery and she was able to get to her feet and walk while holding Ralph's arm. Mike the attendant showed them to the rental car, wished them the best, and then he hurried back to his kiosk to attend to a distinguished looking gentleman in a well-tailored suit who was quickly becoming impatient. As soon as the door to the vehicle was shut and Mike was jogging away, Theney looked at Ralph with wide eyes.

"Please tell me you got it!" she blurted out.

"Yep!" Ralph proudly replied with a smile.

"How did you do that? I never even noticed anything. You were back with that soda in no time."

"Well, our timing was perfect. He still had his screen open in the log file. I just quickly scrolled up several screens and found the last name, Duplay. Then I took a quick pic of the screen with my phone," answered Ralph. "Now. Let me see what we have."

Ralph opened up the photo album on his phone and looked. He used his fingers to zoom in and move the photo to reveal the rental vehicle's GPS code.

"Bingo!" Ralph playfully chirped out. "Now let's go find a comfortable coffee shop to sit at while I call my buddy in the NYPD."

⤴️

"What is your name?"

"Skrako. Colonel Skrako," answered the drugged Opie.

"Where are you from?"

"I come from God's favored garden of the galaxy. The home of the brave and the true, Dwovy! Hail Dwovy!" he answered with pride. His eyes were glazed over. He had been speaking monotone, but his love for Dwovy had come through with this answer.

"Why are you here on Earth?"

"We come here to save Dwovy from the curse of the Plinks. We are here to discover the solution," he said. "We come in the name of God to save the Dwovian empire."

"What is the Dwovian empire?"

"Our homeland. The United Planet of Dwovy. Success and health to Dwovy."

"What is the Plinks?" asked Neil.

"The Plinks is a destructive illness caused by alteration of Dwovian DNA. It prevents the birth of viable Dwovian offspring. We must cure the Plinks or the extinction of the Dwovian empire is assured."

"Is the Plinks contagious? Does the disease pose a danger to humans?"

"The Plinks was caused by an unusual, rhythmic pattern in the gamma frequency radiation from the variable star, Tenkor, which supplies the energy of life to Dwovy. All living Dwovians carry the cursed DNA alteration. It affects only Dwovians and is not communicable."

"Why are you on Earth?"

"To find the solution to the Plinks. Didn't we already talk about that?" Opie questioned in his dazed and half-comatose state.

"How?" asked Neil.

"By testing genetic solutions on the Earth creatures known as humans."

"How is the testing accomplished?" asked Neil.

"Through Hero's plan, the official plan adopted by the legally elected High Council of Dwovy. One, introduce the sleeping illness to humans through the release of programmed draminkos. Two, inject the individual DNA-altering draminkos into pregnant human females while they sleep. Three, monitor the results until a solution is found or until the mission is irreversibly compromised. Either way, we 'cry while we fly' on our way back to Dwovy. We cry either tears of heartache for the death of Dwovy or tears of joy for the solution to the Plinks," answered Opie. His voice struggled to speak as orange tears began to spurt out of his eyes. "Oh, Dwovy! My homeland! May God sustain you!"

Leslie looked at Shelly and quietly moved over to stand beside her. Neil continued his questioning of Opie.

"What do you think?" Shelly whispered to Leslie. "Do you think this sleeping illness is reversible? And do you think the testing process endangers human babies?"

"I have to think the sleeping illness would be reversible with Dwovian technology. But I doubt humankind could reverse it," answered Leslie quietly. She continued, "I'm sure the testing does pose some risk to human babies in that we do not know everything about human physiology. Now that we know this genetic testing has been going on, it may explain the slight increase in certain diseases through the years, such as autism."

Shelly looked back at Neil and Opie, deep in thought about what Leslie had just said.

"Why the special interest in Anna Reese?" asked Neil a little louder as he leaned a little closer to the alien. "Why did you abduct her?"

Shelly was monitoring the patient from a couple of feet away, standing out of the way of the light Neil had shining on Opie for the interrogation. She was standing by the IV bag, checking the drip rate. Leslie noted Neil's increase in intensity and wondered if her quietly talking with Shelly had upset him. So she tipped her head close to Shelly's, then cupped her hand around her ear and whispered very softly into it.

"Is this normal for him to be answering so clearly in English when that's not his native language? I mean, he looks out of it based on his eyes and face, but his answers seem like he's awake. He seems coherent like he's having a regular conversation with Neil. He couldn't be faking this, could he?"

Shelly turned her face and put her mouth to Leslie's ear now.

"Negative. This is totally consistent with previous hypnotic regression therapies I've been involved in. The part of his brain responsible for communication is wide-awake, and even his senses are continuing to register information in his short-term memory. But his conscious mind is totally asleep. That's why he looks like he's asleep. He will not remember this conversation at all when he awakes," answered Shelly.

Meanwhile Opie was answering Neil's questions. His answers under the influence of the drugs continued to be consistent with the explanations he had given previously while awake. It was the commander, Hero, who ordered that Anna be brought to the spaceship in order to protect her since her baby may verify the correct DNA repair to cure the Plinks. The DNA cure would keep the protein foyerik-bento from forming in the Dwovian fetuses. Anna could be the miracle mom who would save an entire civilization.

"Two more questions," said Neil as he boldly put his face right up next to Opie's. "First, should I trust you?"

"Yes. I am trustworthy," humbly answered Opie.

"Final question. Will you help me get my wife, Anna, off your spacecraft and back home?"

"Yes. I am sorry she was taken from you. Anna should be brought home, and I will help you," Opie answered.

∽∾

"Denko. What's her status?" asked Grenko as soon as he walked through the door.

"Well, take a look for yourself. She is calm but conscious, and she is resting easy. The biological readings on her and the baby are within normal ranges, although I think the warm temperatures on our spacecraft are causing extra perspiration," Denko said.

"Extra perspiration?" asked Grenko with a confused look.

"Yes, come look at this," said Denko. He led Grenko over to Anna and showed him her damp blouse.

"Why is her blouse wet, especially near her shoulders?" asked Grenko.

"That's the perspiration. Humans have glands in their skin that secrete this water-based moisture if their bodies become too warm. The evaporation of the moisture helps to cool their bodies."

"That's incredible," Grenko remarked.

"Yes, it is. It is a very ingenious mechanism. You may smell a peculiar odor near her as well."

"I was going to ask about that. I noticed it as soon as I walked in. What is that?" asked Grenko.

"It is the odor given off by the bacteria in the Earth woman's perspiration," said Denko, proud of how much he was learning and anxious to impress Grenko.

"Well, that's disgusting," proclaimed Grenko. "Is it harmful? Does it pose a risk to the baby?"

"Not so far as I can tell—other than the annoying odor. It appears that this is one of the reasons humans shower so often. A shower with soap and water harmlessly carries the bacteria away, and it is otherwise harmless and does not cause illness," explained Denko.

"Well, lower the temperature in here some more if needed. Otherwise, carry on," said Grenko as he turned to walk back out the door. He took a few steps and then abruptly turned around again as he remembered. "Oh. And just so you know, we have not been able to contact Skrako. As much as I hate to do it, I am working with Manko and Chenko on a search and recovery mission. The longer Skrako is out there, the more likely our mission is to be compromised. We have not seen any news reports that cause us concern, but we really cannot leave him out there. I will keep you informed."

"Thank you, sir," replied Denko.

Neil had just made another pot of strong coffee and was pouring himself a cup. Opie had his feet zip-tied to an old, green army cot as he lay unconscious sleeping off the barbiturate drugs. Shelly was sitting at the far side of the kitchen table and she lit up a cigarette and took a long drag. She exhaled and blew a cloud of smoke into the air.

"Oh my gosh. I'm sorry. Does anyone mind if I smoke? I'm so tired and so used to smoking in my own house, I forgot to ask."

"Anna does not like smoking, but she's not here right now, and I certainly could use the smoke to keep me alert," answered Neil. "In fact, do you mind me bumming one from you?"

"Sure, here you go," said Shelly, handing the pack of Marlboros over to Neil.

"We are both ex-smokers, so it won't bother us much, except, please, no matter how badly we may want one, please don't let us have any. We both struggled to quit before we got married, and we haven't smoked since," offered up Leslie as Neil lit up and the room began to fill with more smoke.

"Yeah. Tell me about that," Neil jumped in. "I thought you two were just colleagues, and then when you arrive I find out you're married. What gives?"

"Well, it's your typical story, Neil," said Chepp. "We secretly started dating and fell in love, unbeknownst to our colleagues. We made a spur-of-the-moment decision a little more than a year ago to get married in Las Vegas while there for a conference, then moved in together. After about six months, we split, and then this past week we fell in love all over again and realize life is better together. Like I said, a pretty boring twenty-first-century relationship tale."

They all laughed.

"Did he tell it about right, Leslie?" Neil asked, tipping his head toward her.

"Yeah. I guess. In a nutshell, he did. It sounds a bit odd, but that's been our path. I'd just add that most of our problems out of the gate were probably my fault. I think I loved my career path more than Cheppie, and that caused a lot of pain for him. But now I know what I really want. Life is pretty boring and sad without him in my life. And I truly understand how much he unconditionally loves me. I am madly in love with him now and forever more, with my whole heart, ready to grow old together, till death do us part." Leslie's voice grew softer and warmer as she spoke and looked into Chepp's face.

Chepp stood up and stepped one step over to where Leslie was sitting. Then he leaned over and gave her a kiss on the lips. It was not just a peck, but it was also not a long public display of a kiss. It was more the "wait until later" type of kiss, and everyone in the room knew it. Chepp's charm and unspoken communication owned the moment.

Then, in a purposeful way, so as to break the chain of romantic thoughts that Chepp and Leslie had brought to the forefront of everyone's minds, Shelly announced, "So what about this rescue plan? Shall we figure this out?"

CHAPTER

17

"Take a right onto Maple Syrup Road . . . Recalculating . . . ,"
announced the GPS system.

"Crap! That must have been it back there. I thought that was an
entrance to a farm," said Ralph.

"It probably was," suggested Theney. "A farm that produces
maple syrup would be my guess. A lot of these farms have through
roads cutting across them by the looks of it."

"Well, the new route on the screen looks like it will only take
us four minutes longer, so I'm not turning around," answered the
journalist.

"Uh-huh. Speaking of time . . . the Garmin says we're going to
arrive in about eighteen minutes, and it's getting dark. Any chance
you want to share your plan with me? I mean, being a black woman
in what I'm guessing is going to be a white neighborhood after dark
doing something shady is not something I really want to do without
a plan. It's not like I can claim to a cop that we were invited."

"Yeah, I guess it's time," said Ralph. "Okay. Open up my bag
on the back seat."

Theney unbuckled and reached around to the back seat and
grabbed Ralph's duffel. It was a typical roughly cylindrical duffel bag,
a black one. She sat forward and laid it on her lap. She unzipped it
expected to see clothes, and she did.

"What am I looking for, boss? Just looks like your clothes in
here."

"Reach down to the very bottom and feel for a couple of sheets of foam board taped together. Try not to bend them when you pull them out."

Theney reached down, through Ralph's clothes, underwear, toiletries, and all. At the bottom of the pile, she felt them. Carefully pulling the foam boards out, she found there were three stacked together and fastened somehow on the sides. She turned the stack and held the top piece so that the dusk summer light still leaking into the car hit it head on. There was something printed on it. She read the blue-and-red foam board. It said "Domingo's" and was a good representation of their logo from what she could tell.

"Domingo's?" she questioned as she looked over at Ralph driving.

"Yep! Open it up. It will fold open into a triangular sign like you see on the top of pizza delivery cars. I taped some magnets on the bottom piece."

Theney was ahead of Ralph and already manipulating the foam boards as he was explaining. Ralph had taped some of the sides together and he used a couple of tabs of Velcro to hold the three sheets into a triangular shape. It looked to Theney like it was just about the right size and shape.

"Okay. I'm guessing this is going on the top of our car, and we're posing as pizza delivery people. Am I right?" She asked.

"Mostly, my favorite protégé. But you are posing as the pizza delivery person, not me. That's why I told you to bring those black slacks and that blue oxford shirt I've seen you wear before. Did you bring them?"

"Uh-huh. I gots 'em, homeboy. But they ain't stylin' no way no how, so I was wondering whatchu asked me to bring 'em for. I'm gettin' worried—you into some kinda kinky role playing, ain't you, and you hopin' to get sumpin'-sumpin' off me on this trip."

"Good Lord. What in the world are you saying?" Ralph asked.

"Don't worry, boss. I was just getting myself into character. Thought maybe I'd play a woman with some street cred. Not all black women delivering pizzas are going to sound like me," she explained.

"Yeah. I guess that makes some sense, and I must admit you really had me going with that voice. But they equally well could sound like you naturally do, Theney, and the first rule of deception is keep it simple," answered Ralph.

"Got it. Now how's this going to work, boss? What are you doing when I deliver the pizzas?"

"I'll be right there with you. I'm going to hold a clipboard and pose as a Domingo's Pizza field trainer and investigator. Think about it. We have the coordinates of the car, but it could be hidden in a garage or parked on a side street or something. So we don't really know for sure what house they are in. We tell whoever opens the door that we have chosen their neighborhood as one of the test regions for a Domingo's Pizza initiative to improve the pizza delivery process. If the customer is willing to answer a few short questions about the delivery process, then they get the family pizza special for free. That way if we pick the wrong address, it won't look odd for us to go to the next door up. It keeps our cover until we find them," explained Ralph.

"Got it. But what if they don't open the door?" asked Theney.

"Well, we can't control everything, but I think they'll be more willing to open up for a pizza delivery person than a vacuum cleaner salesperson, don't you? I mean it's about 9:15 p.m. on a summer evening, and who isn't intrigued by a couple of pizzas showing up at their door. Right?"

"Yeah. I guess you're right. It's about as good a way to track them down as I can think of. In fact, it's kind of brilliant, boss."

"Well, thank you, Theney. Have I mentioned lately that you have been my favorite partner to work with?"

Theney laughed. "I'm the *only* partner you've ever had according to the GN3 network."

❧

Nightfall had arrived. The only lights on inside the Reese's home were a small lamp on an end table and the recessed light above the kitchen sink. Neil, Chepp, Leslie, and Shelly were sitting around the kitchen table. There were shadows, but they could see well enough.

The alien had regained consciousness about ten minutes ago but was still tied in his cot.

"We will eventually need to let people know what is going on," said Neil. "But once we do, we will have plenty of special government forces trying to get to us. I'm not sure which group it will be first, but we will probably be detained for interrogation somewhere. If it's all the same to you, I think we should try to avoid government involvement as long as we can."

"Agreed!" said Chepp.

Neil turned his head and looked toward the cot. Then back at the group sitting around the table.

"Well, we all heard his responses under the influence of the truth serum. Do you think we should trust him and bring him into this conversation?" asked Neil.

"You can trust me, and I will help you under two conditions. First, you must honor your commitment to keep your government and military out of this," said Opie. "It is the last thing our mission from Dwovy needs. And second, we would like your permission to follow up on your baby Neil, to see if it carries the cure. It is in no way dangerous to your baby at this point."

Neil looked around the room. Each person silently gave him the "your call" look. He looked back at Opie.

"We will do our best to keep the government and military out of this as long as possible. But the media will keep digging until they find Chepp and Leslie, and we will have to release some information. We can't keep this all secret forever," answered Neil.

"I understand. I am in risk of execution if I do not follow commands, Neil. I was ordered to help detain Anna," Opie replied. "But at this point, I believe my commander is not making wise decisions. He has jeopardized our mission by becoming too hands-on and aggressive in his decisions. I will assist you in the recovery of your wife, but I am risking my life. The only hope for me is that my colleagues will agree with me that the commander was derelict in his duties and my actions were justified. Finally, I still need an answer to the second part of our agreement, Neil. May we continue to track the protein developments of your baby if I get Anna back to you?"

Neil's mind raced. He knew he needed to answer, but the answer would carry consequences. He wished he could see the future and know which path to choose. He desperately wanted Anna back, but could he trust this little alien from Dwovy?

Two days ago, Neil had never heard of the place, and now he was being called on to make a spur-of-the-moment decision to evaluate the trustworthiness of an entire culture of aliens based on a few hours of interaction with one of them. Were they creatures who took their morality seriously and adhered to their commitment to truth, or were they liars, manipulators, and deceivers? Could he trust this little creature, so cute and innocent looking, all the while knowing he was a militaristic creature bound to duty in a command structure that approved the unannounced DNA manipulation of another race?

On one hand, Opie had been honorable, pleasant, and cooperative with Neil. On the other, his planet had been guilty of crimes that were not easily excusable. They were crimes that naturally made Neil think about the way extremist governments on his own planet had acted. Nazis, communists, and socialist dictators had brutally violated the rights of people throughout history. But would that be enough to condemn an entire planet of people and deem them all untrustworthy?

Neil asked for a moment and bowed his head and closed his eyes. He may have looked deep in thought to those in the room, but he was actually deep in prayer, asking God for guidance. In just a minute, he looked up and opened his eyes. He looked around the room and then back at Opie.

"I've decided to trust you, little Opie. And may my Lord and Savior Jesus Christ and his Spirit seal this decision and hold you responsible to it. I will trust you, because I trust him."

The room was silent for just a moment.

"Wow," said Chepp.

"Double wow," said Leslie.

Shelly stood with a blank look on her face as if caught off guard by the answer, while Opie smiled and nodded once in approval.

"It is settled. Now, can you get me moved to a more comfortable position so we can talk this through? I've had quite enough of this smelly army cot. And I am warm now, so this blanket can be removed."

Suddenly there was a knock on the front door, and the doorbell rang. Neil quietly ran up the hallway and glanced out the window and saw a car sitting at the end of his driveway. It looked like it had some kind of sign on it. Two people stood at his door, one of them holding two pizzas. Neil suspected the neighbor kids had messed up again giving their address to the delivery pizza place. His address number was 699 and theirs was 669. He wasn't sure if the kids were high and kept giving it wrong or whether the pizza people wrote it down wrong or had it in their computer system wrong. But this was not the first time this had happened.

"Uh-oh. Everybody stay quiet and out of view while I handle this," said Neil.

⌒✺⌒

The bright orange lights, the exposure to warmer-than-normal temperatures, and the drugs were beginning to take their toll on Anna's pregnant body. Fortunately, the Dwovians excellent scientific and technological abilities allowed them to recognize this, and they reduced the sedation, lowered the temperature, and dimmed the lights before any serious harm was done.

Anna was once again sitting up in a small chair but still lightly sedated. She felt very relaxed and very calm. She liked these drugs—they were good stuff, and she was quite happy at the moment. Her screaming concerns about the baby dying if she didn't see Neil were but faint memories that she didn't care about at the moment. In fact, she couldn't tell if it really happened or whether she had dreamed it. Even if she wanted to remember, when she tried, she couldn't. And quite frankly, she didn't really care that she couldn't remember. She was in a happy place and her mind was busy watching a television screen playing an episode of *The Big Bang Theory*. She was aware of some faint clicking, rattling, and whistling in the background, but it didn't disturb her.

"I believe we should leave her at this dosage. She is calm and stable. The addition of the Hollywood on their TV device is proving helpful as well," explained Denko.

"I think it is referred to as a Hollywood show, not just a Hollywood. But I could be wrong. Either way, well done, Denko," praised Grenko.

"What is the latest on Colonel Skrako?" asked Denko.

"We have not been able to contact him, so we have no choice. Manko and I will be routing out in zero point one Earth days in an attempt to retrieve him."

"Understood. What is my role? To continue to care for Anna?"

"Affirmative, Denko. You are doing admirable and crucial work here, and that's where I need you," explained Grenko. "Chenko will man the command center while we are out. If Manko and I fail to return, you should move to plan Z, and may the Master of the universe be with you and Dwovy if that happens."

"I understand, sir. But I am confident it will not come to that," Denko said with encouragement in his voice.

"Let us hope so, Denko. Very well. Carry on," ordered Grenko as he turned and *swhoosh*—he walked through the amazing Dwovian door, a door that quietly dissolved away into the ether and reappeared as a wall almost as quickly.

Denko turned, walked toward Anna, and sat down beside her. He looked at the television and then at Anna and then back to the television. He was amused at the ease with which human beings could have their conscious minds distracted by something as simple as a television.

"You're short. Ha!" Anna blurted out with a giggle, looking at Denko. "Either that or I'm a giant!" she said as she smiled ear to ear and stood straight up and attempted to hold her hands above her head. But the metallic ceiling was so low that Anna's hands touched it before her arms were straightened.

"Holy cow! I'm huge! I used to be 5'3", but look at me now! I must have grown a lot!" rambled Anna with childlike mannerisms, sincerely impressed with her newfound height.

"Hardly dear. You are still 5'3", but I guess by your standards I am short. And so are all Dwovians for that matter. Now, please sit back down and watch your Hollywood show." Denko smiled as he took Anna's hand and helped her gluteus maximus find the chair.

CHAPTER
18

Ralph and Theney had picked up two large pepperoni pizzas from the local Domingo's Pizza, and now they approached the area of the GPS coordinates.

The neighborhood they found themselves traversing was a bit classier than Ralph expected. The homes varied in architectural styles with large lots, well-groomed landscaping, and most having three car garages. It caused him to pause and reconsider his plan. But the Domingo's Pizza sign was already magnetically attached to the top of the car, and Theney had changed into her black pants and blue oxford shirt. No, the neighborhood was upper middle class, but not so high class that these folks would have full-time cooks. He could imagine families in this neighborhood ordering pizzas. Besides, the faux Domingo's employee badge pinned on Theney's left pocket looked terrific. Ralph loved to admire his work.

He looked around the neighborhood as he drove and followed the GPS on the car's dashboard. It was set to the last known location of the car rented by Doctors Duplay and McCabe. The neighborhood was quiet, and there was only one person currently outside even though it was a pleasant summer evening. It was a healthy-looking, tanned, elderly woman, probably in her midseventies, with wavy gray-and-white shoulder-length hair. She looked to be watering some flowers and was shaking out the last few drops of water from her watering can. She sat the can down on her porch as she headed back into her home and shut the front door.

"Arriving at destination," announced the GPS.

Ralph slowed and pulled over in front of a very nice stylish rancher that reminded him in size of the home he had seen on *The Brady Bunch* as a child. It was a relatively new home, no more than a decade old. The styling on the outside with its tan brick and stone gave it a comfortable suburban look, and it had a three-car garage with an asphalt driveway on the left side of the house. The driveway was attractively landscaped on the left side with flowering trees and ornate bushes, which helped provide privacy from the neighbors. The homes did not sit far off the street like they do in more rural areas, but Ralph suspected the backyards of these homes were quite stately.

There were attractive, matching lampposts along the street and in the yards of each home. The neighborhood looked well planned and designed, except each home was unique in architectural design. It was not a neighborhood full of cookie-cutter homes like you often see nowadays. Ralph was impressed with the neighborhood, and actually, if the truth be told, he was a little jealous.

"There it is!" shouted Theney with enthusiasm pointing in the driveway. "A Toyota RAV4." She looked down onto her iPad and continued, "The plate matches what you got from the Enterprise computer."

Ralph stopped the car at the entrance to the driveway effectively blocking it. He wanted to reduce the chances of anyone 'leaving' before he had his chance to snoop and find the doctors.

"Okay. Time to go to work, Theney. Just play the part we discussed and follow my lead. And don't use that 'hood talk'—just keep it simple," Ralph said as he opened up the car door and grabbed his clipboard.

"Got it. You think they're in there?"

"Oh, I guarantee they're in there. If not, the people in this house know where they are," answered Ralph. "The rental car is parked in their driveway, these people know *something*, Theney."

They walked up the driveway and along the short, but winding, nicely landscaped walkway that led to the front door. The flowering trees smelled heavenly to Theney on this comfortable summer night.

Upon reaching the door, Ralph quickly pressed the doorbell button—*ding-dong*—and he followed that with an aggressive knocking on the front door. It would be impossible for anyone to ignore his presence at the front entrance. Ralph was not timid; in fact, he was downright bold in just about everything he did.

Theney saw the curtain in the window near the front door move ever so slightly.

"Someone's definitely in there, boss," she whispered, trying not to move her mouth in the process.

Suddenly the door opened.

"May I help you?" said the tall, attractive, middle-aged man.

"Uh, yes, sir," Theney said with a smile as she stared at Neil Reese. "We are here on behalf of Domingo's Pizza. We have two hot free pepperoni pizzas for you right now if you are willing to answer a brief survey."

"Are you sure you're not supposed to be delivering those to the neighbors up the street? They are much better customers than us."

"No, sir, the idea is we want to get new customers, so somebody like you is exactly who we want to talk with," said Theney while Ralph stood observing.

Neil thought for a moment and realized they hadn't eaten anything in hours. He had opened the door in the hope of maintaining a "normal" presence with his neighbors who might be watching, and he figured he could quickly dismiss them. However, the smell of the fresh, hot pizzas began to make his mouth water. On one hand, he was anxious to get rid of these two pizza pushers and rush to get Anna. But on the other hand, his military strategy screamed out to leverage the situation he was presented. It made sense to eat something while they developed their plan for getting Anna back.

"All right, as long as it won't take more than a couple of minutes, step inside."

Once they crossed the threshold of the door, Neil immediately led the two toward the left, into his formal living room. He did not invite them to sit down, and he closed the glass French doors to the room for sound privacy.

Ralph spoke as soon as the doors clicked shut.

"The pizzas are yours, but we know that Dr. Duplay and Dr. McCabe are here."

Neil was caught off guard and he turned quickly and grabbed Ralph by his tie. Ralph was tall and thin, but Neil Reese was built with muscular tone like an ultimate fighter, and he had martial arts training in the military.

"Who are you, and what do you want? Are you government? Military?" Neil was in Ralph's face and his voice meant business. His heart this day had become laser focused on the thought of rescuing his beautiful, small framed Anna, and nothing was going to derail his plans.

"Whoa! Whoa! Whoa! Take it easy, pal. We're not government or military. We're just journalists trying to get the story," answered Ralph.

"Oh yeah? What newspaper?" barked back Neil. His grip on Ralph's tie was firm and their faces were inches apart.

"Not a newspaper. We're from GN3," answered Ralph. "I can pull out my credentials if you let me."

Neil pulled Ralph forward a few feet with him as he opened the French doors and yelled down the hallway toward the kitchen. "Chepp! Put Leslie and Shelly in charge of watching Opie and bring me the gun. We've got a problem here."

"On it, Neil!"

In a matter of seconds, Chepp showed up with gun drawn.

"Hey, mister, we're not looking for any trouble. We're just looking for a story," nervously said Theney with a bit of a stutter when she saw the gun.

"Well, you found one," Chepp answered in his matter-of-fact voice with a half smile, always looking for the humor in a situation. Chepp stepped into the living room and waited for Neil to tell him what to do.

"Hold them at gun point, Chepp, while I frisk them and empty their pockets."

"Right-o, Neil."

Neil first frisked Ralph. He immediately found and pulled a small pistol from Ralph's jacket pocket.

"Well, they're definitely not military or government," said Neil, "No self-respecting person in that line of work would carry a piece of crap gun like that." Neil checked to see if the gun was loaded, emptied the bullets and placed them in his pocket. Then he tossed the small pistol onto the coffee table to his right.

He finished patting down Ralph and emptied his pockets. Neil flipped open Ralph's wallet and found an ID from the GN3 network along with other press credentials.

"I'm sorry, lady, but I'm going to need to check you as well. I'll be as polite as I can."

Neil patted down Theney and found absolutely nothing on her other than a cell phone, which he confiscated.

"They appear to be media, just like they claim. Let's take them to the kitchen and tie them to chairs, Chepp."

Then Neil immediately turned to the reporters.

"You two. Here's the deal. I don't want to hear a word out of you for the next several hours. If you say a word, I'll shoot you myself. You may think you know what's going on here, but I guarantee you there's much more to the story. You sit and observe without a peep. If all goes well, in a few hours we can give you the story of a lifetime—one that will land you in the media hall of fame. Do we have a deal?"

"Do we have a choice?" asked Ralph.

"Does it look like it?" sarcastically said Chepp as he waved the gun around a little.

"We agree. Right, boss?" quickly said Theney as she looked at Ralph with wide, scared eyes. She was still just a kid, and she looked it right now.

"Your terms are acceptable . . . and . . . we don't seem to have a choice at the moment," answered Ralph.

At that, Chepp started moving them down the hallway toward the kitchen with a come hither motion of the gun. He carefully walked backward and sideways with the gun pointed at the detainees as he led them down the hallway. Neil followed up at the rear.

Upon reaching the kitchen, Ralph's and Theney's eyes darted around the room and they both stopped on the little, bald-headed alien wearing the dark robe. He definitely stuck out among these otherwise normal-sized and attractive humans.

"What's happening, guys? Talk to me," blurted out Leslie as Shelly stood up from the table.

"These two are reporters, Les. I'm guessing they tracked us here somehow. We're going to detain them while we go get Anna," answered Chepp.

"Holy crap! That's kidnapping, Neil," said Shelly. Neil walked over to Shelly and looked into her eyes and spoke with a strong, reassuring whisper.

"Settle down, Shelly. I've got an agreement with them, and besides, we are in uncharted territory as we talked about earlier. We need to stick together and get through this, first. Then we can worry about the aftermath."

"Well, if you're done with me, maybe I should just head out," whispered back Shelly.

"I can't let you do that, Shelly. Until we get my wife back, I can't risk any leaks on what is happening here. The government and media will be involved soon enough. We need to all stay on the same page and control this situation as best as we can. Besides, are you telling me that you have other scientific work to do that is more pressing than taking part in humankind's inaugural interplanetary event with intelligent extraterrestrials?"

Shelly stared back at Neil as she felt the humble pie Neil was serving crush into her face of pride and judgment.

"All right. I guess I deserved that," she said. After all, she thought, she was fortunate to have seen and interacted with an actual alien—something she had always wanted to do—and Neil was the one who had made that possible for her.

After a quiet nod of assurance toward each other, Neil turned and grabbed two kitchen chairs. He moved them out to the edge of the kitchen where Opie's army cot was still on display. Chepp and he secured Ralph and Theney to the chairs with some rope around their waists and feet. Their hands were left free and they were allowed only their notepads and pens for taking notes. Then Neil tossed the boxes on the table.

"Anyone want some pizza? Complements of the GN3 network," he spoke loudly.

"We're everywhere you want to be!" Chepp mocked the network's tag line with his best announcer's voice. Then he quickly turned toward Ralph and Theney, bent his knees a little, and opened his eyes and arms wide as he added with a Vaudeville enthusiasm, "Including your local pizzeria!"

Leslie giggled, and Shelly had calmed down enough that even she grinned.

❧

Back on the metallic saucer in Guatemala, Manko and Grenko were making ready to route out.

"You have everything I told you to bring?" Grenko asked Manko.

"Yes. I even have one of those god-awful killing machines."

"Hey! Keep in mind, we don't use them unless I give the order, Manko. Our mission is simple—find and retrieve Skrako as quickly and discreetly as possible. No evidence left behind."

"I understand, Acting Commander Grenko. I am clear on the mission. Long live Dwovy!"

Grenko and Manko stepped into the router. They each were strapped with multiple crystal sensors, a handheld jerblonk, syringes, and the killing weapon called a bleak. In Dwovian culture, they were prepared for war.

❧

"Then after we get Anna, we all teleport back here. Is that right?" said Chepp.

"Yes. That's what I am proposing," answered Neil.

Chepp, Leslie, and Shelly unanimously agreed. Then Neil turned his head and looked around the room until his eyes stopped on Opie. He was now ready for Opie's input.

"What do you think, Opie? You heard the plan. When we route into your spacecraft with guns drawn, will your commander be willing to cut his losses and let Anna go? What should we expect?"

In his typical, computerized-sounding, metallic voice, Opie responded.

"Hero has been tasked by the Dwovian High Council to bring home a genetic cure. They have given him all authority on this mission to make decisions and lead. His penalty for failure is public execution, including all his living ancestors back four generations. To say he is highly invested in seeing the potential cure protected would be an understatement."

"So you're saying we should expect him to pull out a ray gun and try to vaporize us or something?" asked Leslie.

"Yes. Something like that. But our so-called ray guns do not vaporize a person."

"Okay. But it sounds like you do have guns then. So what do they do?" questioned Chepp. "Are they lethal?"

"They shoot a nearly invisible, high-energy pulse of electromagnetic radiation that destroys the entire electrical system of any biological system it hits. It is merciful—so far as we know—but incredibly lethal. If you receive a full hit of it anywhere on your body, you will become 100 percent instantly paralyzed as every nerve in your body—both myelinated and unmyelinated—become nonconducting. Dwovians scientists speculate that you feel a very brief flash of warmth throughout your body, followed by nothing, a total loss of feeling—paralysis. So it apparently is not a painful process."

"You mean if this beam of radiation hits me in the foot, it will kill me!" asked Neil, clearly skeptical. "That seems hard to believe."

"Imagine a humongous lightning bolt striking a power line, Neil. The electricity surges through the power network frying everything. It's a bit like that, except this is a high-frequency electromagnetic wave packet that works through biological nerve cells. But it's a similar process. The weapon is called a bleak, named after the scientist who discovered the phenomenon."

"Is there any way to shield yourself from this bleak? Will a lead vest or some kind of shielding work?" Chepp asked.

"No, a lead vest will not help you much—not if the distances you are being shot from are so small, like they will be inside our flying saucer," answered Opie. "Speaking of which—because of the saucer shape and the height of Dwovians, the ceilings inside our spacecraft are lower than this," he said, pointing his long spindly finger up. "They are only two meters tall, or about six feet. Neil and Chepp, you will clearly need to be careful going through the interior, especially doorways."

"Seems like we need to refigure this plan a little bit, Neil," suggested Leslie.

"I concur," quickly answered Neil. "Let's start again—same objectives, same personnel, but let's replan the operation to better deal with an enemy that is encountered in a restrictive space with these lethal weapons. And then let's get rolling. I want my wife back before this night ends!"

"The router should be able to transport up to 3 humans and me at one time," added Opie. "Do not forget to account for that in your plan also, Neil."

"How do you know they plan on taking, you? They never mentioned that," asked Shelly Warstein.

"I am intelligent enough to understand the basic concept of prisoner exchange, Dr. Warstein," answered Opie. He was clearly annoyed by this question and frustrated in his efforts to prove his superior intelligence, especially after being confined to a kitchen chair, and then a cot, with simple zip ties.

Chepp chuckled. "Did any of you ever see that little black Martian dude on Looney Tunes? The one that wears that funky helmet, and he huffs and puffs and says to Bugs Bunny, 'You are making me angry . . . very, very angry' in that goofy voice?"

Leslie laughed out loud. "That's it! I knew he reminded me of something when he responded there. Oh my gosh, that's funny, Chepp."

"Yeah. I get it, Chepp. But can we get back to the plan for getting my wife and unborn baby back safely, please?" Neil snapped. He was clearly anxious, tired, and emotionally exhausted. Nothing would be right or funny until he had Anna back safe and in his arms.

"Sorry, Neil. I was just trying to keep our spirits up and keep us all calm," Chepp apologized.

"It's okay, Chepp. I'm sorry, too. In spite of my military leadership that shows on the outside, I'm a bit of a wreck on the inside," Neil said. "I want my wife back."

"We will get her safely home, Neil. Don't worry," answered Leslie.

Ralph and Theney, who were sitting side by side, glanced at each other's face, and then they glanced at each other's notepads. They took notes about all they were observing. Even though they were not being permitted to talk, they could discuss things with each other through notes they wrote. It reminded Ralph of study halls back in high school.

CHAPTER

19

"Hey! Dinatti! You get that update from Stryker and his toady?" yelled Don Smith, the chief of the GN3 twenty-four-hour news team. *Crash!* A huge lightning bolt struck outside, hitting a building across the street. A vigorous thunderstorm at the Atlanta headquarters of GN3 had temporarily knocked out power. The lights flashed briefly as the backup generators kicked on.

"Not yet, boss! I received a text from Ralph with GPS coordinates somewhere outside Pittsburgh, but nothing in the past four hours," yelled back Frank Dinatti.

"I'm assuming you haven't been sitting on your butt waiting for him, Dinatti!"

"Uh, no, boss, I tried him about thirty minutes ago," said Frank.

Don Smith opened his eyes wide and gave a death stare at Dinatti. He didn't need to say anything. The stare was enough.

"But I'm going to try calling him again soon—I mean now. I'll try calling him again now, boss," said Frank.

Don turned around and headed back to his office with a slight grin on his face. He loved the feeling of being in charge and watching his employees respond, especially when he could do it nonverbally.

He shut his door and mumbled under his breath, "These kids have no idea how to handle important news stories!"

He quickly curled around his desk, dropped onto his leather executive's chair, and pushed a button on his desk.

"Sally! Get me Mr. Jenkins at the *Atlanta Eyewitness Journal* on the phone, pronto!"

A feminine but teacher-like voice of a middle-aged woman responded, "Right away, sir."

"And I need more coffee!"

"On its way, Mr. Smith."

～◯～

Neil, Chepp, Leslie, Shelly, and Opie had worked their way through the details of their rescue plan and at the same time had worked their way through the two pepperoni pizzas. Now it was time for the energy of the pizzas to transform into energy for a rescue mission.

Neil and Chepp were currently shoving bullets into magazine clips for the semiautomatic Glock handguns that Neil had retrieved from his gun safe. They were each taking a fifteen-round clip with them in addition to the fully loaded one in their guns. That gave them a total firepower of sixty rounds which Neil believed was more than sufficient for any offensive the Dwovians could mount. Opie said there were six total on this mission, including him. He was hopeful Anna could be brought home without a shot being fired, but he had made it clear to the team that he would use force if necessary. Neil was anxious and a bit jumpy but otherwise prepared mentally for the mission at hand.

Opie found his mind gravitating toward his wife, Nori, and their hope of having children. He used his trained Dwovian mind to imagine her with him now. It was a way to calm and center himself. He could smell the sweet fragrance of Nori's skin and feel her long slender fingers on the sides of his face as her green eyes stared into his. The thought of an intimate moment like this in the complex neural network of the Dwovian mind made the memory as real an experience as a virtual reality machine on a human being. In fact, it was even more real than a virtual reality experience. All the sensory information from the actual event could be reproduced in the Dwovian mind, including odors and touch sensations—thus the origin of the commonly used Dwovian phrase "as authentic as a Dwovian memory." The crisp vision brought Opie temporary peace and calm, but it didn't last as his concentration was interrupted by chatter around him.

"Say your goodbye to Leslie, Chepp. I am going to my room to get the crystals and electronic mechanisms I stripped from little Opie," commanded Neil, "then it's showtime. Shelly, I'm going to have to ask you to cover little Opie while I go to my room." He handed the short, stalky Dr. Warstein the gun.

Shelly had never held a gun before, but she figured she could fake it for a few minutes. Not! As soon as Neil put it in her hand and let go, her arm fell from the weight of the piece and it slipped from her hand and dropped handle first onto her own foot.

"Ow!" she yelled in immediate reaction to the pain received by her left big toe, and she shook her foot a couple of times. She quickly picked it up with two hands and recovered, pointing the barrel at Opie. His eyes opened wide in horror.

Neil looked at him with a stern look and said, "Yeah, you best not mess with her—she could easily accidentally shoot you better than I could purposely."

Then he turned and ventured toward his bedroom to get the Dwovian devices that Opie had explained were necessary for routing to the flying saucer.

As the gun was once again pointed in his direction, it reminded Opie that his new friends still had reservations about trusting him. He was fairly certain Neil's biggest concern was that he would escape and not that he would hurt them. That was the reason he was still being held as a prisoner—because he was Neil's only lead to finding Anna.

Opie's mind now wandered onto more unpleasant thoughts. Even if the cure for the Plinks made it back to Dwovy with Opie, he would never have a child with Nori. His decision to assist the Earth men would surely be interpreted as treason by Hero, and it was virtual certainty that he would receive the death penalty along with the rest of his living ancestors and Nori before they could have a child. In fact, knowing Hero, he would court-martial and execute Opie on the journey home to Dwovy. He still held out hope that his colleagues would support a motion to relieve Hero of command.

Neil had returned with the crystals and jerblonk. He immediately took the gun from Shelly, who was relieved to hand it over.

"I'm glad to have that thing out of my hands," said Shelly. "I was worried I might accidentally shoot him and blow everything."

"Pretty unlikely, Shelly. I slipped an empty clip into it a few minutes ago before handing it to you. And the safety was on, too."

Shelly laughed. "Ha! You're always a step ahead, aren't you, Neil? You're like a real-life James Bond or something."

"I don't know about that, but I do try to stay a step ahead."

∝∾

Don Smith shut his office door and cracked the window in his office. "To heck with the thunderstorm," he thought. He needed ventilation so he could smoke his cigar without setting off the smoke alarms outside his office door. Don was running the station, and as long as he got results, the higher-ups in the network couldn't care less if he smoked in his office. Don was old school and the employees in the station knew that. He had been running the station for thirty-seven years now, from the time it was just a local station, and nobody had the guts to challenge his authority.

Beep.

"Mr. Smith, I have Mr. Jenkins on line number 2 for you."

"Got it. Good girl, Sally."

Don plopped into his seat, picked up the phone, tucked it between his ear and shoulder, and said, "Jenkins. That you?"

He stuck a fresh stogie in his mouth, lit up, and puffed as he listened to the response.

"Of course it's me. Who the hell else would it be! After all, you had your secretary call me, didn't you? And right in the middle of final call! I had to hand that off to my second-in-command just to take your call. You know better than to call me at this time of day, Don! This better be important!" Fred Jenkins was the head editor of the *Atlanta Eyewitness Journal*, the fourth best-selling newspaper in America these days, and he was not happy.

"Oh, it is," said Don as he finished, exhaling cigar smoke. It mixed with the warm, moist air coming in from the window and hung about midway between the floor and ceiling. "You know those scientists from California? The ones that say they've discovered proof of aliens or something and then went missing?"

"Yeah. That's the story I was waiting to finalize before we go to print. That's our front-page lead tonight. And I'd like to get back to it!"

"I got a hot lead for you, Jenkins, but you gotta act fast. I sent Stryker out after that story and he told me he'd have an exclusive interview with these missing scientists within twenty-four hours."

"Well, I'm guessing that son of a gun delivered for you—luckiest damn reporter on planet Earth the way he gets to these things first. You offering me some quotes or something?"

"No. And it isn't luck, Jenkins. That guy has contacts in every corner store and parking lot in America, I swear. And for twenty-five years he's reported in like clockwork for me until today."

"What do you mean? He's gone AWOL on you?"

"Yep, kinda. Knowing Stryker, he found those scientists, but he's not reporting in," said Don.

"So what are you thinking? You think he's in trouble?" asked Fred Jenkins.

"He had a newbie reporter with him and neither one is reporting in, nor are they answering their phones when we call. We have the last known GPS coordinates on the car they were driving, and it's in a populated area just outside of Pittsburgh. Last report was they were closing in on the scientists."

"So you think they're caught up in whatever is going on with this Dr. McCabe and Dr. Duplay?"

"Yeah, my gut says Stryker and his toady found these two, and they're into it thick. They're unable to respond for some reason. I can't possibly spare another reporter right now, but I can give you the last known GPS coordinates."

"Well, it's not like Christmas morning, but I'll take it. I can send a reporter up there pronto to see what's going on. I should have something for you later tonight. You got an extra camera guy you can send with 'em?"

"You're reading my mind, Jenkins. I can send a camera guy, and I was hoping you could send that cute redhead you have—what's her name—Candy Kramer. She'll make the TV camera smile if we can get a live feed at any point, and word has it she did a few live reports in Chicago before jumping to your ship. We got a deal?"

"It's a done deal, Don. Kramer was my lead reporter on this story anyway. Was giving her the big chance. So she won't even balk at my request. She will be happy to have this lead. Send your camera guy over here ASAP and I'll get them on a chartered plane in no time."

"Pleasure sharing business with you, Jenkins. You're still an ugly son of a gun, but you're a good newsman."

"Right back at you, old man."

Click. The two men simultaneously hung up without saying goodbye. This was not their first rodeo riding the same horse.

❧

Chepp grabbed Leslie's hand and gently pulled her with him as he went around the corner from the kitchen and opened the French doors to Neil's back patio. They were beautiful hardwood doors with solid brass hardware and a perfect array of glass windowpanes. Anna had them adorned with elegant pleated and ruffled sheer white curtains that stretched vertically from the top to the bottom of the windowpanes.

As they stepped out, the cool summer night air fell onto their faces and arms. It was dimly lit outside on the natural stone patio with only some short, decorative lights marking the boundaries of the patio and walkways. Some of the lights were partially under the beautifully green, flowering bushes that landscaped Neil's amazing home, and they cast a few shadows across the patio. The air was just beginning to get a little damp, and it was very quiet at this hour of the night; only the crickets could be heard.

Chepp leaned his head back and looked up as he slowly walked pulling Leslie along. Even though they were not very far from Pittsburgh, the air was clean and filled with the aroma of flowering bushes. The sky above them was a deep black so that the stars stood out bright and numerous.

"Look. The summer cross, and there's Cassiopeia," said Chepp quietly as pointed.

"Oh, Chepp, it's so beautiful. It looks like the stars we saw when we drove out into the desert outside of Vegas," answered Leslie.

It was a very romantic setting, and Chepp said a brief prayer in his mind, thanking God for providing such a beautiful place for them right now.

Chepp stopped walking at about the middle of the patio. He turned around and wrapped his strong arm gently around her back and pulled her into an embrace and kissed her in one fluid motion. It was slow enough to not startle Leslie but surprising enough to thrill Leslie as she suddenly felt the lips of the man she loved pressed against hers in a firm and deeply meaningful kiss.

Chepp was romantic. He had a way of reading the moment like this and taking charge of Leslie's insides without her being aware that he had done it. It was at these moments she had no doubt that he was the most perfect man walking planet Earth.

Chepp inhaled gently as they finished their perfect kiss, and then they stood eye to eye with the tips of their noses just barely touching. Leslie's toes curled as her heart pounded faster, and she felt weak in her knees. Chepp let go of her hand and wrapped his other arm around her as if he knew what was happening inside her, and he steadied her with a firm but gentle uplift. His warm arms felt good touching her cool bare skin as she snuggled under his manly embrace and wrapped her arms around his thin waistline. Chepp stared deeply into Leslie's eyes. Every so often, his eyes magnetically danced around her face in order to capture every beautiful feature.

"Leslie McCabe. As beautiful as these surroundings, and as spectacular as this night sky, I believe your beauty overwhelms them all."

"Why, Dr. Duplay, are you trying to woo me?"

"Oh, I'm just getting started. I'm saving the best for later."

Leslie giggled and leaned her head forward so their foreheads were now touching and their eyes literally were an inch apart.

"Chepp, promise me you'll be careful tonight. I never thought this whole thing would lead to you going on a risky rescue mission on an alien spacecraft."

"Don't worry, Les. Now that I have experienced you again, there are no forces in this universe—alien or otherwise—that could keep my arms from finding you to hold or my lips from finding you to kiss. I promise—in the words of Arnold Schwarzenegger, 'I'll be back.'"

Leslie giggled again.

"You better. I just recently discovered the man that I need in my life forever, and I can't go back to doing life without him. There's just nobody quite as good as you, Cheppie. So I'm sorry, but I'm afraid I'm going to have to hold you to that promise."

Chepp and Leslie found themselves once again in the middle of a deeply tender kiss when the glass paneled door opened. It was Neil sticking his head out.

"Ready when you are, Chepp."

Chepp and Leslie reluctantly broke away from their kiss.

"Yep. Be right there, Neil."

Chepp looked back at Leslie.

"Pray for us, Les."

"Yep," she replied, "I can't imagine what Neil is going through."

Chepp and Leslie walked back inside. Opie, Neil, and Shelly gathered together. But Chepp ran off toward the garage.

"Hang on, Neil. Give me like five more minutes and I'll be with you, I promise."

"Can't it wait?"

"Nope! I'll explain later."

Neil looked toward the garage with questioning eyes but didn't follow Chepp.

"I bet he's going through my knives one last time," he said. "He didn't seem perfectly happy with the one he grabbed earlier."

Leslie was not paying much attention because she was busy pulling a Bible out of her duffel bag. Neil looked toward her.

"Once we route out, you and Shelly can release our two reporter friends over there and allow them to interview you about all that is going on. I'm sure they have lots of questions, and it will keep your mind off things while we are gone," said Neil. "After all, there's going to be no way for you to contact us a mile underground in Guatemala, and even if you could, there would be nothing you could do to help us. Either we will return or we won't. All you will be able to do is pray for us."

From across the room, Ralph Stryker boldly spoke up.

"Thank you, Neil. Yes, we indeed have many questions," he said.

"In good time, sir. In good time they will all be answered," replied Neil.

Neil looked down at his watch and moved over beside Leslie to be sure she had the same time. He was not sure why he was doing that. There was no need to have synchronized watches for this mission, but it was a habit he picked up in the military and it fit his obsessive personality quite well. He did not like to leave things to chance.

"What time will it be in Guatemala, little Opie?" asked Leslie.

"It is one Earth hour earlier in your system of time," came the metallic, computer-sounding voice emanating from the throat of Opie. "I believe you refer to it as Central Daylight Time."

Chepp hurriedly bust out from the garage door buttoning the top of his shirt. Neil's forehead wrinkled slightly as he cocked his head sideways and gave Chepp a WTF look.

"You finally ready?" he said.

"I hope," replied Chepp.

Leslie had her Bible opened to a particular page she had bookmarked, and she suggested they join hands and pray. Everyone agreed, so Shelly joined Chepp, Leslie, and Neil in the circle. Then even little Opie politely snuck into the circle between Neil and Shelly. His hands felt particularly odd. They were warmer than human hands and the long, spindly fingers felt peculiar as they wrapped the entire way around Neil's large hands.

Neil told Ralph and Theney they could pray from their chairs if they wanted to join in, but he did not want to release them until they had left.

"But how are you leaving? We have your car blocked in the driveway?" asked Ralph.

"No talking!" commanded Neil. Then in a quieter tone, he said, "Just like a reporter to grope for information at a moment like this."

They all bowed their heads and Leslie led them in a beautiful heartfelt prayer. She asked for success in bringing Anna home, for protection and safety, for a peaceful resolution to the current issues, and for a cure for Dwovy. After she had said "Amen," she spoke one more time.

"I wanted to share this scripture with us all before you route out. It is one of my favorite passages and speaks to how we must approach what lays ahead. It comes from Proverbs, chapter 3, verses 5 and 6: 'Trust in the Lord with all your heart, and lean not on your own understanding. In all your ways submit to him, and he will make your paths straight.'"

Neil and Chepp hugged each person, except the reporters, and moved to stand with Opie at the far end of the kitchen. Left to right it was Neil, Opie, and Chepp.

"All right, little Opie. We're ready. Now how does this work?"

"We only have one routing crystal and one jerblonk, so we all must touch to transport," explained Opie.

"Do we need to be touching skin against skin?" asked Chepp.

"No. As long as we are physically touching, we will all transport together. Because I am short, might I suggest you each put a hand on my shoulder? That way you can quickly be in a position to defend yourselves," he answered.

Chepp and Neil complied with the suggestion. The scene looked to Leslie like two teachers steering a student toward the school's Halloween parade.

"Neil, if you would hand me the clear crystal and the jerblonk please."

Still not totally understanding the subtleties of human timing and goodbyes, as soon as he had the items in hand, Opie activated the crystal and shouted, "Geronimo!"

There was a sudden flash of blue light that filled the room and they were gone. Then about a blink of an eye after that, there was another bright blue flash.

"Oh my god! What is happening! Where did they come from!" screamed Theney.

Leslie and Shelly turned around to see the backs of two aliens dressed in dark robes.

CHAPTER
20

Suddenly Chepp saw blue all around him, wrapping and enveloping his face. At the same time, he had a feeling of his body and head quickly shrinking down to nothing and then every bit as quickly reexpanding. It was an unsettling feeling, but it did not hurt, and it only lasted a fraction of a second. The next thing he knew he was standing in the middle of a very small room, about the size of an elevator, maybe slightly wider. It had no door or wall in front of him and looked out into the metallic spacecraft that Opie had told them about.

Instinctively, Neil and Chepp did a quick 360 spin move to check for threats behind them. They saw the walls of the router covered with crystals. The crystals also covered the ceiling above them and floor below. The crystals were small and aligned geometrically. Chepp was fascinated by them, but he knew now was not the time to get sidetracked.

Very quickly, their exit from the router was blocked by Chenko as he jumped in front of it holding a charged bleak aimed directly at Neil. He immediately began speaking Dwovian; clicking, whistling, and metallic rattling noises came forth from his throat. Chepp and Neil did not understand the language, but the rate and loudness of the sounds made it clear that Chenko meant business. Opie immediately gave a response in Dwovy, then turned and walked backward to stand beside Chenko facing Neil and Chepp.

"I'm afraid the plans have changed, gentlemen. Raise your hands and do as Chenko commands you," he said.

Chepp and Neil raised their hands. Things had been going as expected up to this point. Opie rightly predicted they would be cornered in the router immediately upon arrival. But Opie stating that "plans had changed" was not part of the plan. Chepp had an uneasy feeling in the pit of his stomach.

Chenko handed the bleak to Opie, who aimed it directly at Neil.

"One wrong move and I will fire," said Opie. Chenko began taking all the weaponry off the men. This was definitely not part of the plan. There was no need for Chenko to perform a full-body frisk. Opie had full knowledge of where they had strapped each weapon to their bodies, and he guided Chenko to everyone, including the knife Neil had sheathed under his pant leg.

Next, Chenko grabbed another bleak from a custom slot in the reactor wall. Neil and Chepp took note of the wall, which was filled with all kinds of devices in similarly designed slots and holes. Neil was not sure if the wall was an arsenal or a sort of charging station. He was guessing the latter because he saw some slots that had glowing crystalline wands inserted into them. Neil suspected these were removed from the wall to be used in devices, like we use batteries.

The bleak looked similar to the proverbial ray gun often shown in sci-fi films. In fact, it reminded Neil of the original phaser used on *Star Trek*. It had a shape somewhat similar to an Earth handgun, but the handle was wide and had some holes for accommodating the long fingers of the Dwovians. The trigger mechanism was just like the Earth handgun. You could fire the bleak by pulling the trigger. The top part of the bleak, which fired the beam, was generally cylindrical in shape and was roughly the diameter of the cardboard tube inside a roll of paper towels. On the firing end of the cylinder was a small array of crystals, which blinked and glowed green when the bleak was fired.

Chenko corralled the two Earth men using his bleak as a tool to silently guide them. After exchanging a few more clicks, whistles, and rattles with Opie, he forced them "at the aim of a bleak," as they say on Dwovy, through the command center room, past the reactor wall, and finally into the crew quarters. The ceilings in the flying saucer were indeed barely high enough to clear Neil's head. It reminded Chepp of walking in the basement of his grandparents' old farmhouse, except for all the metal and the annoying orange lights.

The sound of walking in the metallic shell of a hallway reminded Neil of the sounds he had experienced once while locked in a metal wardrobe cabinet during a basic training prank. The floor felt incredibly solid under his feet, almost like concrete, but it made a sound like you might expect sheet metal to make if you walked across it. Very odd.

Finally Chenko stopped in front of Opie's private quarters. He waved his hand and the door to Opie's room quickly de-materialized.

"Holy crap! Did you see *that*, Neil!" blurted out Chepp.

"Uh-huh," replied Neil, but not in his normal tone. Somehow Chepp could sense through that short reply that Neil was boiling over inside and about to blow a gasket.

Chenko walked them into the room. Both Neil and Chepp had to duck to get through the doorway.

There were several chairs lined up against the far wall. As he pointed his bleak at the chairs, Chenko spoke his first English words for the men, "Sit!"

❧

Back at Neil's house, Grenko and Manko immediately saw that Ralph and Theney were restrained, so they rapidly turned and aimed their bleaks at Leslie and Shelly. The ladies recognized the gun-like devices that Opie had told them about.

"Everybody remain calm. Those weapons are highly lethal!" warned Leslie.

"You are correct," answered Grenko. "Now tell me where I can find Colonel Skrako, our colleague." Like Opie, his voice sounded metallic and computer generated.

"I assume you're talking about a little bald-headed guy about this tall?" Leslie slowly held her arm out with her hand about chest high.

"We call him Opie," blurted out Shelly Warstein.

"He was just here a minute ago. Please don't hurt us. This guy and I don't know anything about what's going on here," quickly added Theney. "Please don't hurt us." Theney was just a small click below hysterical.

"Who is in charge here?" asked Grenko.

Shelly looked toward Leslie. Leslie took a slow deep breath before responding, "I guess that would be me."

Leslie's hair had not been washed in a couple of days now, and it was beginning to show the signs. And the lack of sleep was beginning to bother both her and Shelly.

"Move over and sit down, both of you," ordered Grenko, pointing at two kitchen chairs. Shelly and Leslie complied, turning the chairs to face away from the kitchen table and toward Ralph and Theney.

Leslie was surprised the Dwovians were allowing such an arrangement. Unless these aliens had eyes in the back of their heads, which Leslie highly doubted, the Earth people had a distinct tactical advantage with this geometrical arrangement. The Dwovians were essentially surrounded, and the humans were facing each other allowing easy nonverbal communication if they so desired. As she considered these things in her mind, she also thought to herself, "I've clearly been influenced by Neil's thinking." Leslie was rarely concerned with military strategy. On a typical day, she would be more likely mentally critiquing Shelly's or Theney's hairstyles.

"For what reason was Colonel Skrako delayed in his return to our ship? What has happened?" asked Grenko.

"Would you like a drink of rusty water? I could fix you up a batch. You must be thirsty," replied Leslie. She was trying to stall for time. If Grenko and Manko returned to the flying saucer now, it could mean disaster for Neil and Chepp, and perhaps even little Opie, too.

Grenko turned to Shelly.

"Our commander returned injured and has since died. Our second-in-command, Colonel Skrako, never returned. I want answers."

Shelly had picked up on Leslie's lead. And her cute little personality played into it perfectly. She had a naturally happy, bubbly personality and liked to talk. Feeling a bit overwhelmed by the circumstances, she had been mostly quiet the past day or two. But being held hostage herself now by these little bald-headed alien's using surrealistic ray guns caused her to snap into silly mode.

"Oh my gosh. You had a commander and he died? You poor thing. You are probably devastated. You probably should let us fix you a hot cup of tea and you can talk it through with us. Bereavement meals are one of my specialties. This reminds me of when I lost my grandpa. I was a little girl, only about eight years old, and my grandpa was my hero. He served in the military, so he had a strong way about him—very steady—probably a lot like your commander—"

"Enough!" said Manko. "You will answer the acting commander's question."

Shelly looked at Grenko with sad eyes and a pouty mouth.

"Oh my. You are the acting commander now? How does that feel? You are probably very emotionally vulnerable right now. Dr. Phil would encourage you to get counseling to help you transition to your new position, and guess what, you're in luck. I was a psychology minor in college. Quite an odd combo, huh? Chemistry major and psychology minor. Not a lot of college students taking that combination, I can tell you. I thought about starting a special student club, but I realized I would probably be the only member. Ha! Anyway, if you . . ."

This back and forth continued for at least ten minutes as Leslie and Shelly masterfully played the aliens with the proverbial dumb talkative blonde earth woman routine. Then finally—"Stop! Quiet!" yelled Grenko. "No more talking!"

Leslie was surprised and impressed by Shelly's performance. Inside she was giggling, so it was challenging not to smile or laugh. What did they have to lose?

"When you say no talking, does that mean all of us or just her?" chimed in Leslie.

"We will get nowhere with these humans. I think there is something wrong with them, Commander. They are perhaps of lower-than-average intelligence," Manko said.

Leslie actually let out a small snort of a laugh. She then covered for it by coughing a little as though it were part of an involuntary cough. Shelly turned her head toward Leslie and winked with her right eye so that the Dwovians could not see it.

The clicking, whistling, and rattling began again.

"Why are you speaking to me in the Earth language, Manko? Please be smarter than that."

Manko looked down at his handheld jerblonk and his eyes grew concerned.

"Oh, Commander. I am so sorry," said Manko. "I am so truly sorry."

"It's not that big of a deal, Manko. Calm yourself. Your speech gave no secrets away," replied Grenko.

"No. That's not what I'm sorry for, sir. I mean, I'm sorry for that mistake also, but I just looked at my jerblonk and I realize I should have looked at it much sooner."

"What is it? Quickly!" asked Grenko.

"Well, I routed us to the last known location of Colonel Skrako's crystals, figuring that he would likely be close by them. I checked the location of the crystals shortly before we routed and they were right here near where we are standing. But now they no longer register at this location. They have changed location very recently."

"Where!" shouted Grenko.

Manko pressed a few keys on his jerblonks and his eyes grew wide as he looked up at the commander.

"Our ship, Commander! They are now on our ship!" answered Manko.

"Damn it! We're being invaded, Manko! Set your bleak to high power and route us back immediately!"

Suddenly, as before, there was a blue flash of light and all the air in the entire room suddenly glowed as if it became a blue neon light for a blink of an eye. Theney let out an involuntary shriek and momentarily shut her eyes. When she opened them, the aliens were gone.

Chenko eyed the two Earth men as he invisibly held them in their chairs with the business end of a charged bleak. Suddenly a crystal on his bracelet glowed. He waved his other hand in front of a spot on the wall. *Whoosh.* The door to the room suddenly dissolved. Chenko touched another crystal on his wrist and began chattering in Dwovian. He backed out of the room and looked at Neil and Chepp with squinted eyes. Then he said, using that computerized-sounding voice box that every Dwovian had apparently been blessed with, "I'll be back."

Neil and Chepp both let out a single, involuntary laugh at this little childlike creature saying the iconic line from *The Terminator*. The contrast in body size and physical threat between this little alien and Arnold Schwarzenegger made it impossible not to laugh. Chenko couldn't have been funnier if he had planned to be, but clearly he hadn't. Chenko briefly looked back at them with a confused look on his face, as if doubting his understanding of the English language, then suddenly the door rematerialized.

About five seconds after he had left, Neil and Chepp looked at each other and immediately got up out of their chairs as if thinking the same thing. They moved toward the spot on the wall where Chenko had waved his hand. They moved their hands along the wall looking for some sort of aberration in the surface—a ridge, a bump, anything. The wall appeared perfectly smooth. They could not identify any type of mechanism that would help them open the door. If only it was a door with a hinge, handle, or lock that they could manipulate. After a few minutes of silently searching, Chepp spoke up with his hypothesis.

"Shucks. There must be some kind of scanner that checks a biometric. You know, like facial recognition . . . or maybe it works on those long, creepy hands. I suppose with this level of technology, the scanner could even see fingerprints or some other unique DNA-coded feature."

"Well, if that's the case," said Neil, "I guess we're stuck here for a while."

Candy Kramer, the sexy, up-and-coming reporter from the *Atlanta Eyewitness Journal,* and the cameraman from GN3, Tim Thickett, quickly boarded the SkyBus and stowed their carry-ons in the overhead bins. Tim could not help but notice the drop-dead good looks of his colleague with the dark red hair. It wasn't very often that you saw a redhead with such a smooth, silky tan complexion. Many redheads have fair skin and some freckles. Not her. Tim wondered whether the red hair was natural. He doubted it. But either way, the look she was going for worked. As a young single man, he found his mind fantasizing about the possibilities of this cross country assignment with this bombshell.

Unfortunately for Tim, he was a tall, scrawny, awkward-looking twenty-four-year-old cameraman with a crooked nose and long greasy black hair he kept in a ponytail tied with rubber bands. This was not the look Candy Kramer went for—at all. She was interested in powerful, wealthy businessmen in suits. Men who looked like they could do a photo shoot for *GQ* but who had enough wealth and power to buy *GQ.* She was about as stuck-up and shallow as a woman could get. But she had learned to cloak it well when working for people who mattered. Unfortunately, Jimmy was not one of those people. When she was around her mother or girlfriends, she especially became a truly ugly creature. They would regularly scoff and laugh at the riffraff while admiring the tall, dark, and handsome wealthy men with the soft hands.

Tim sat down next to Candy. Soon enough they were buckled in, the plane was speeding down the runway and their flight was in the air.

"I'm glad we're on a commercial flight instead of one of those dinky charter planes," said Tim as he looked over to Candy. He continued, "So do you like flying?"

Candy very, very slowly turned her head to look at Tim with cold eyes that could have shot darts, but she didn't say a word. It was a clear to Tim that she was not interested in any kind of conversation. This was going to be a long red-eye flight.

It had been at least ten minutes since Chenko left them, and Neil and Chepp were still trapped in the room, trying to strategize.

"It's pretty hard to come up with ways to open a door that doesn't have hinges or latches," ruminated Chepp. "It blows my mind how there was a door here and in a matter of one second the wall just rematerialized."

"Yeah, it is hard to get a grasp on how far ahead of us they are technologically. But they must have a foolproof door opening protocol built into this ship in case of emergencies," said Neil. "Now, what would trigger it?"

"I don't know. The air is so thin on this ship and it's so warm in here that I'm having a hard time thinking," answered Chepp.

"Aha! That's it Chepp! The air. No matter how advanced a civilization becomes, there's probably always the necessity to monitor the air in an enclosed space like this flying saucer. After all, they breathe like us."

"Yeah . . . so what are you suggesting?"

"Well, if we can get some smoke going, that door may automatically open via some automated safety protocol. At the very least, it should set off some kind of warning in this oversized tin can and cause them to return and open the door."

Neil quickly pulled off his right boot and removed the insole. Then he reached down inside and pulled out a small, thin piece of steel about the size and shape of a popsicle stick broken in half. He also pulled out a small black metal rod about the size of a nail, like a carpenter framing a house might use.

"I've heard of having a trick up your sleeve, but this is my first experience with a trick down a boot," Chepp quipped.

"Yeah, this is an idea I came up with when I was in the Boy Scouts, learning survival skills, and I continued using it up through my years in the military. Always keep a small piece of flint and a striker in your boot. I actually cut out a small custom spot for them under the heel of the insole. The soles on the heel end of boots are nice and thick, and it's amazing what you can hide in them."

Chepp took a small piece of paper out of his pocket. He had used the paper earlier in the day to doodle a few scientific calculations. He also pulled a Kleenex out of his other pocket. He began tearing the Kleenex and paper into small strips to use as kindling for their fire.

"Where should we start this thing?" asked Chepp.

"How about on top of this computer-looking device?" suggested Neil as he grabbed a laptop-sized jerblonk off Opie's desk. "Maybe if it overheats that will trigger something, too. But let's place it on the floor in the center of the room," he said as he placed it down, "because I really have no idea where a smoke sensor might be located in here."

Chepp piggybacked on Neil's thinking by saying, "And if they come back, their eyes will be drawn down toward the smoke from the fire. The diversion might give us a chance to jump them."

"Well, if we jump them, go for the bleak first! Remember, according to our 'used to be alien' friend, supposedly if any part of that beam hits you, you're dead. So we don't jump them unless we know we can get control of the bleaks."

"Right-o, Neil. You just give the go signal when you think we have our best chance."

The paper was piled up on the jerblonk, and Neil began striking his flint with the piece of steel. A shower of sparks sprayed down on top of the paper. After several tries, a small ember began to persistently glow on the piece of Kleenex and it started to smoke. Neil very gently blew on it with an open mouth, and in a few seconds, there was a small flame. The fire slowly grew to about an inch high as it began to consume the paper. But the air was so thin that the combustion was slower than it would have been in an Earth atmosphere. There was a lot of smoke as the fire smoldered along. The thin atmosphere actually was working to their advantage—slow burning and lots of smoke—just what they needed considering their lack of fuel.

After about thirty seconds, their small fire was stable and the air at the top of the room was beginning to cloud up from the smoke. Neil and Chepp bent over to keep from choking on it as they each took a position on opposite sides of the door.

A loud, high-pitched, shrill whistling sound began blaring throughout the metal ship. The reverberation of the sound off the walls was painfully difficult for Neil and Chepp to bear. On the other side of the ship, Anna covered her ears with her hands and began to struggle against the sound as well.

The door dematerialized with the *whoosh* sound. A small, fragile, gray arm holding a bleak projected out from a dark sleeve and through the opening. Neil did not hesitate. "Now!" he shouted as he grabbed the arm and struggled to wrestle the bleak away from Chenko.

Chepp went low and pulled the legs out from under Chenko in a two-leg wrestling takedown. He firmly held onto his lower legs with his arms wrapped around them in bear hug fashion. Chepp rolled hard to the right while pivoting his head to see if there were any more Dwovians in the doorway. It was only Chenko. Suddenly the physical struggle caught up with Chepp, and his body cried out for oxygen by forcing his diaphragm to inhale deeply. He took in a waft of smoke and began to cough, but he continued to concentrate and held firmly to Chenko.

Neil had a firm grip on Chenko's forearm and wrist and was applying pressure with his thumb in a spot that would cause a human being to writhe in pain. But Chenko's grip was surprisingly strong despite his size. Neil looked. His long Dwovian fingers were wrapped firmly and completely around the bleak handle and through the small holes in it. His hand was interlocked with the weapon. Even in the midst of wrestling for the deadly weapon, the vision caused Neil to imagine the huge hands of a professional basketball center palming the ball. Finally, after a few more seconds, Chenko's energy began to wane, and Neil's pressure took its toll. The bleak fell out of his gray hand, and in one smooth motion, Neil quickly picked it up and was on his feet pointing the bleak at Chenko on the ground.

"Freeze!" Neil yelled.

CHAPTER
21

Chepp breathed in and out hard as he "helped" stand Chenko to his feet while simultaneously yanking his one arm behind his back and torquing it upward. Apparently, this move was just as persuasive to Dwovians as earth men because Chenko cried out in pain with a shrill, high-pitched clicking sound that reminded Chepp of a small dinosaur from *Jurassic Park*. "Such weird sounds," thought Chepp. As if performing, Chenko then coughed the strangest sound as he reacted to the smoke in the room. It sounded as if there were a miniature machine gun in his throat.

Suddenly a small round area on the ceiling dematerialized and it suctioned the smoke from the room almost instantly. It felt odd to Neil and Chepp as most of the air was temporarily pulled from their lungs. The suction pulled some smoldering paper ashes up through the air and they spiraled like a tornado toward the opening. Just as quickly, though the flow reversed, and the paper blew back downward as a yellow haze filled the room. The remaining paper debris that was charred—whether it was lingering in the air in the wake of the suction or laying on the jerblonk—rapidly dematerialized. But it was only the edges of the burned paper that dissolved. The yellow haze was dissolving only the portions of the paper that had been blackened by fire.

In just a few blinks of the eye, all the charred paper in the room disappeared and the yellow haze went with it. The room smelled clean again. There was not even a hint left of a smoky smell. Any remaining flakes of paper in the air snowed downward. Both they and the paper pieces left on the jerblonk were pristine. Not even the slightest sign of black or brown char remained on the torn edges. Amazing. No evidence of a fire remained. The ceiling rematerialized and the hole was gone.

"Okay. We're impressed, but enough of the parlor tricks, little alien," said Neil. "Take me to my wife—the Earth woman. Now!"

"As you wish," answered Chenko.

With hands raised, he walked in front of Neil down the hallway back toward the command center of the flying saucer. Chepp trailed shortly behind Neil.

As they emerged into the command center, Neil saw Opie standing at the command console with its shiny, glass-looking top. He instinctively grabbed Chenko and put him into a headlock with his left arm and held the bleak to his head with the right hand.

"Don't even move, little Opie! Where's Anna?"

"Neil, I have not betrayed you. Things are not as they seem. Our commander, Hero, is dead. I am now in charge."

"Then why have we had bleaks pointed at us from the moment we arrived on this overheated sardine can? Wait. Don't tell me. This is some weird Dwovian way of welcoming a guest aboard, right?" Neil said with sarcasm.

"No. It is not. However, Dwovians do have rigid protocol for transfer of authority. Until I could authenticate my leadership with the onboard genetic identification system, both the crew and the computer system are obliged to follow the previous commander's orders. It is a great sign—a very *great* sign—of disrespect, bordering on depravity, for this protocol to not be followed. I guess the closest human analogy in terms of behavior would be for someone to force you to watch your wife be raped by your enemy. It is unthinkable in Dwovian culture to disregard the protocol for transfer of power. I had to do this right."

Click-click-click, whistle, click, pop, whistle, click, twang, clink, clink, click. Chenko and Opie began speaking Dwovian to each other. Chenko struggled to get his clicks out as Neil continued to hold his neck in his arm.

"Knock it off. No more talking unless it's in English. If you're in charge now, then take me to Anna."

"I will, Neil. I just got done explaining to Chenko that the transfer of power is complete. I am now the commander of this mission. But first, for our peace of mind, you need to put the bleak down and release Chenko. To show you I am being truthful, I will return your weapons to you first."

Opie waved his hand over a counter to his right and an opening appeared in the counter surface. A small storage area about the size of a drawer was now apparent. The fading in and out of these surfaces and doors reminded Neil of the screen fade transition in computer presentations. The technology was very smooth, making only a light *whoosh* sound when particles in the air quickly moved during the transition. "The Dwovians apparently have found a way to adapt the technology to just about any application," thought Neil. He guessed that even the router transport system was related in technology.

Inside the drawer were all the weapons Chepp and Neil recently had removed from their bodies. Neil released Chenko and pushed him with a slight spin toward Opie keeping the bleak pointed at them both.

"Both of you, back up," Neil ordered. Opie and Chenko complied. They backed up and stood facing Neil about seven feet away. "Chepp, step up here and grab our stuff."

Chepp bent over sharply and reached into the drawer, which was at the same height as a kindergartener's school desk. He pulled out the two Glock semiautomatic handguns, the ammunition clips for them, and a couple of hunting knives with sheaths. He checked the clips to see if they were still loaded. They were. He loaded both guns and handed Neil's to him.

Neil quickly holstered the gun on his waist as did Chepp. Chepp then slid his knife into the sheath on his belt. Neil lifted his pant leg and stowed his blade away in a sheath on his lower leg.

Fully armed again, Neil and Chepp were breathing a little easier. All the while Neil kept the bleak pointed at Opie and Chenko.

"When you are ready, I will take you to Anna. I assure you the bleak is not needed. We are on the same team here."

Suddenly there was a flash of blue light that reflected off the metal walls. Bursting out of the router in an aggressive fashion were Manko and Grenko. Grenko saw Neil holding a bleak at his two colleagues and he immediately took aim.

"Look out, Neil!" screamed Chepp as he jumped forward toward Neil to push him out of the line of fire.

There was a brief sound like an electronic slide whistle rapidly making a glissando from a low pitch to a high pitch, then back to a low pitch, and a momentary green beam of light about the width of a dime could be seen extending from Grenko's bleak to Chepp's right arm. It all happened in the blink of an eye, and Chepp silently collapsed to the floor.

"Chepp!" yelled Neil as he dove behind the short command console. As his body was flying forward toward the floor, he stretched out his left arm and grabbed a handful of Opie's dark robe. His muscular arm, then pulled the sixty-pound Dwovian to the floor and slid him over. He quickly crawled on top of Opie and moved his left arm and hooked it around his neck to place him in a headlock. All the while his right hand clung to the bleak, which he now pointed up against Opie's head. Opie did not struggle against Neil.

"Drop your weapon, you gray bastard, or I'll fire this bleak right at your new commander's little head!" yelled Neil.

As Neil focused his attention on grabbing Opie as his hostage, Chenko had instinctively run and hid around the corner in the hallway leading to Anna.

There were three hallways that led away from the central command area. One went to the living quarters, the other to the medical sector of the ship where Anna was and the third to the research and engineering wing. The router was the first room on the right as one headed down the research wing. When the shooting began, Manko had doubled back into the hallway to the engineering wing to take cover. It was now Neil and Grenko in a standoff.

Neil glanced back at Chepp lying motionless on the floor with a blank, lifeless stare on his face. Neil was experiencing shock. He had never lost a friend in combat, and even though he had only known Chepp for a couple of days, his heart ached as he thought about how quickly Chepp had been taken. No blood, no scream, no suffering. Just alive one moment and gone the next. One thing was sure. These bleaks were as lethal as Opie had warned.

Opie plied the fingers of his hands up under the chokehold to buy a little space against his throat and he struggled to yell to his colleague Grenko.

"Cease-fire, Grenko! So says the commander!"

Grenko dove across the room and crawled on his hands and knees toward the command console. Neil could hear the soft metallic clinks on the floor as Grenko made his way over and ducked behind it on the opposite side of Neil. Only a couple of feet of high tech Dwovian cabinets separated the two.

Grenko carefully reached his hand to the top of the command console. The computerized command console came alive and began clicking and whistling and popping in the Dwovian language. Grenko responded with his own clicking metallic sounds, and again the computer spoke back to him with clicks, whistles, and pops.

"Enough!" Shouted Neil. "I don't know what you're doing, but I'm going to give you to the count of three to surrender or I'm going to blast your new commander and turn him into neurological pudding like you did my friend. One . . ."

"We surrender," answered Grenko as he tossed his bleak over the command console to Neil. "Forgive me, Commander. I could not obey your order to stand down until confirming your authority with the command console."

"Well done, Grenko," Opie struggled to answer.

Neil released Opie and used his left hand to push him hard and thrust him away. Opie slid on his stomach about five feet over the metal floor. Neil was strong and powerful when he was focused on a goal and his veins coursed with adrenaline.

With his free left hand, he grabbed the second bleak, and with one in each hand, he stood up quickly, nearly hitting his head on the ceiling of the command center.

Denko had now appeared in the research hallway beside Manko. He was unarmed as far as Neil could tell.

With laser focus and intent, Neil aimed the bleaks back and forth between the 5 aliens and yelled,

"All of you, toss over any weapons you hold, and put your hands on your heads!"

Manko tossed over his bleak and came out from behind the corner of the wall with a quizzical look in his eyes as he put his hands on the sides of his head, covering his small ear holes. The other alien's saw what he was doing and did likewise. Clearly they had not watched enough cop shows in the last one hundred years on Earth because they did not properly understand the "hands on your head" command. They currently resembled a group of kindergarteners afraid of a loud sound rather than a band of interplanetary soldiers being taken captive. Neil remained laser focused,

"Anna! Now!"

෧

Back at the house in Western Pennsylvania, Leslie and Shelly untied Theney and Ralph. All had grown mildly concerned about Theney's mental state. She seemed to be experiencing psychological shock, and releasing her was probably a good idea. Besides, both Ralph and Theney were due a bathroom break.

Leslie looked in Neil and Anna's refrigerator and found some glass containers with lids. One appeared to be half-full of homemade baked beans, and the other contained Waldorf salad. She found some bologna and salami in the bottom drawer and a frozen loaf of bread in the freezer. Leslie continued digging and working until she had found everything she needed to prepare a simple picnic-style meal on paper plates.

Meanwhile, Shelly spent some time with Theney. As a postdoc student, Shelly was only slightly older than her, but she was clearly handling the shock of watching real-life aliens materialize and dematerialized better than Theney. So Shelly tried to make small talk with her. Everyday topics, like favorite television shows, were the conversation fare.

Ralph didn't say it out loud, but he was grateful that Shelly was chatting with Theney right now. The everyday conversation was a soothing balm to her anxious spirit. Ralph sat quietly at the table with them—at least physically. His mind was already thinking about how he would present this story to his readers. For this perennial star reporter, his job always came before relationships.

Leslie carried the plates and drinks over to the table where the three were sitting and talking, and she sat and joined them. Leslie offered a prayer on behalf of the group, giving thanks to God and asking the Lord to watch over Chepp and Neil and to bless the food. Ralph, Theney, and Shelly politely participated in silence. They were not believers and did not understand the importance of what Leslie was doing. For them, prayer was silly.

In time, after enjoying their lunch and some more small talk, the conversation turned toward the elephant in the room.

"I know everyone is tired, but I doubt any of us will be able to sleep right now. So if everyone is feeling up to it, I'd like to interview you about everything that has been happening," offered Ralph.

"That's probably as good a thing to do at this point as anything," answered Leslie, "considering more reporters are eventually going to find us and start asking questions. I'd just as soon the first interview be with a small group like this where we can get the information right. Is everyone feeling up to it? Theney, are you feeling better?"

"Uh, yeah, I guess so. I mean I don't feel like running out the front door, screaming and waving my hands above my head any-more. I think I'm okay now. This whole thing has just been much different from what I expected. I mean, somebody please tell me. Is planet Earth in danger? Are these aliens invading? Shouldn't we be contacting NORAD or something?"

"That's a great question, kid. How about it, ladies?" support-ively asked Ralph. "It seemed to me as though these little creatures were looking for something."

"I was the last one to join this crazy story in progress, so I don't think I should say much right now. I think Dr. McCabe is the one to whom the questions should be addressed. I only know a fraction of what's happening," said Shelly.

The group simultaneously turned their heads and eyes to Leslie.

"Okay. I guess the best thing for me to do is start from the beginning, but before I do that, to put your minds at ease, yes, I believe we are safe, relatively speaking," said Leslie. "These aliens apparently are here on a mission to save their planet, not to invade or destroy ours. However, it will take me a while to explain, and I'm guessing you all will have plenty of questions. So, first, does anyone want more coffee or tea?"

Quick replies came back.

"No, I'm fine."

"No, thank you."

"Actually, I'll take some."

"Dr. McCabe, why don't you start and I'll make the coffee for our reporter. As a grad student in chemistry, I'm pretty much an expert at making coffee."

"Why, thank you, Dr. Warstein."

"So you are both doctors? Your doctorate is in chemistry, I'm presuming, Dr. Warstein? How do you spell your name?" Ralph grabbed his pencil and pad of paper and he began taking shorthand notes.

Shelly spelled her name as she started making the coffee. The secret knowledge of the mission from Dwovy was about to spread outside their little band of four human beings for the first time.

CHAPTER

22

The five remaining crew members of the Dwovian mission team led Neil down the medical wing of the ship. Neil followed them with a bleak in each hand. Finally, after about a thirty-foot walk, Grenko stopped the group and waved his hand. *Whoosh*—a door opened. Neil and Anna's eyes fell upon each other for the first time in three very stressful days since her kidnapping.

"Anna!" said Neil in an emotional outburst as he ran to her and leaned over and wrapped his arms around her. "Are you okay? Are you all right? Have they hurt you in any way?"

"Oh, Neil! Neil!" she simultaneously responded as she wrapped her arms around his neck and sat up from the examination table that she was lying on. "Thank God you're here! I'm okay, darling, especially now that you're here. How did you find me? Are you okay? I've figured out that we're on their flying saucer," she said, "but I have no idea where we are. Are we in space? How did you get here? Can we go home?"

Anna was rambling. She was overwhelmed by seeing Neil, but she was anxious and her thoughts were still scrambled from the sedatives she had been receiving.

"Shortly, you will both be free to return home along with Chepp," answered Opie.

He turned toward his crew with purpose.

"There will be no more arms lifted against the Earth beings. Period. Now that I am commander, we are going to do things differently."

He looked Grenko, Chenko, Manko, and Denko in the eyes to be sure they had received his command. He had spoken it in English for the benefit of Neil and Anna. The crew responded with an enthusiastic "Yes, commander," apparently as happy to have Colonel Skrako as their new commander as he was to embrace the new leadership.

"Manko. Take the body of the Earth being named Chepp and cool him in the pod to help preserve the body," said the new commander. Manko, quickly obedient, exited the room and walked down the hallway toward the command center.

"The body of Chepp? Who is Chepp? Why would the body of Chepp come with us? My mind is so mixed up right now. Honey, I'm scared." Anna anxiously looked at Neil.

"It's okay, sweetheart, Chepp is with me . . . or was . . . It's a long story. It will take some time. Just relax. We're going home," reassuringly answered Neil.

Neil turned to Opie with the bleak still pointing at the Dwovians.

"We are routing back to my house, Opie. Once we get there, I'll entertain the notion of putting the bleak away and honoring what you say. But until I have Anna and my baby off this craft and safely into my home, I'm not taking any chances. And *you* are coming with us to assure there is no routing us into a locked room somewhere. I know how much this baby means."

"I understand, Neil. You are a wise military strategist, one of the many qualities I've admired in you. Three adult humans plus me will be close to the energy limitations of the router, but I believe we will all be able to route together."

"Understood. If we must route twice, you, Anna, and I go on the first trip. Chepp's remains can follow on the second transmission," said Neil.

"Very well. It would be wise to allow Anna's head to clear from the sedatives before routing. She has been through a lot. She is also due for nourishment. Won't you both please accompany me to the conference room where we can strategize and talk things through while Anna eats her Subway sandwich? I would like you to join us also, Grenko."

"And what if I say no, we're leaving now?" defiantly questioned Neil.

"Then I'd say, good luck trying to use the router and getting yourself home, Neil. You seem to think you are in charge, but you go nowhere from here without our assistance. We are nearly a mile deep under a volcano in Guatemala. I don't know how you think you are getting your pregnant wife back to her bed in Pennsylvania without my assistance. I suggest you recognize these facts and start working with me as a partner rather than an adversary. Or perhaps you're not as intelligent as we thought."

Neil stood for a moment considering the situation and then somewhat reluctantly he lowered the bleak and tucked it into his waistband.

"We are only staying until she eats, then we are leaving," said Neil, "so the meeting better be as short as you are, Commander."

⤳⤳

Candy Kramer lit up, inhaled on her cigarette, then turned her head and blew smoke out of the partially opened window of the SUV. Tim kept one eye on the road while glancing over at her. The interior of the vehicle was only dimly lit by the dashboard displays.

"Keep your eyes on the road, Tim, and drive faster," she commanded without even turning her head.

"Oh, sorry," answered Tim. He was uncertain how she knew he was looking at her. "She must have eyes in the back of her head," he thought.

"And no, I do *not* have eyes in the back of my head," she quipped as she turned her head back toward him and stared while taking another drag from the cancer stick.

Tim was a bit freaked at how she was doing that. There was something spooky, almost otherworldly, about this woman. But for the moment, he was glad to have her actually talking with him saying anything. The first several hours of the trip were excruciating for a "talker" like Tim as she sat in silence like a cold stone wall.

The rental vehicle, a Cadillac Escalade, was comfortable and fun for Tim to drive. It was probably the nicest vehicle he had ever driven in his young life. His vehicles were usually decade old Hondas or Toyotas that had seen better days.

"When we get there, I want to do an intro piece standing in front of the house. I hope you're good with a camera, Thickett," she said condescendingly. "This is my big chance and I don't want some rookie camera action to blow it for me."

"Yes, ma'am!" said Tim with a bit of an attitude. Candy Kramer curled the corner of her mouth in a smirk. It was amazing. She was getting less attractive by the second for Tim—such physical beauty on the outside but a miserable wretch on the inside.

"Don't worry. I'm experienced enough. I'll give you good lighting and steady camera work," said Tim.

"That's what I want to hear. How long until we get there?"

"The Garmin says we will arrive at the last known coordinates of Stryker in twenty-two minutes," answered Tim.

"I need to use the little girls' room. Find me a late-night Starbucks or coffee shop, and hurry it up. You drive like a grandma." she commanded as though Tim were her personal slave.

"Hmmh! What do you know," said Tim Thickett in a surprised and amused tone.

"What!" Candy barked.

"Well, you wouldn't know it from your attitude, but apparently you pee and poop like the rest of us."

"Watch it, you son of a bitch!" yelled the redheaded Kramer.

"You shouldn't talk to your cameraman that way," said Tim shaking his head slowly in a "no" fashion. "I can adjust the camera to make you look green and fat."

"You wouldn't!"

"Keep up the prissy attitude, and oh yeah, you betcha I will," said Tim with a slight nod. He was wise enough to realize the kind of woman he was dealing with, and pushing back against her inflated ego felt good.

Candy opened her window a bit wider. In a display of disgust but also intimidation, she used her fingers to angrily flick what was left of her cigarette out the window as she squinted and stared at Tim.

≈

Opie, Grenko, and Neil had finished their discussions. The warm, thin air was getting to Neil, but he was glad they had talked. Anna and Neil would return home with the promise of no more secret visits from the Dwovians. Neil and Anna agreed to allow weekly collections of data by the Dwovians, provided they were scheduled, noninvasive, and did not endanger the baby or mother in any way.

As far as press conferences and release of information to the media, they would play that by ear. However, Neil had agreed that the location of the Dwovian flying saucer would not be disclosed. Commander Skrako was risking a lot by taking this new transparent and collegial approach to the mission. Neil appreciated the courage and integrity of Opie. The talk they had just finished helped to reestablish Neil's trust in Opie.

Anna finished her sandwich and glass of milk. She remained quiet while sitting closely next to Neil. She was perspiring a bit, but her color looked better now that the sedatives were wearing off. With Neil beside her, her nerves were calming, but nothing would feel better than returning to her own home.

The meeting was indeed short, lasting no more than twenty minutes, and the time had come for the trip back to Pittsburgh. Unlike an airport flight, this trip required no security scans, explanation of boarding procedures, or checking of luggage.

Neil, Anna, and Opie stepped into the crystal-lined router and then turned around to face the open side. They backed in, as one would do in an elevator, to make more room for Chepp's body, which laid in a supine position on one of the hovering Dwovian medical gurneys.

Grenko gently pushed Chepp's body toward the group as Opie grabbed the gurney and silently pulled it into the router and oriented it sideways in front of him. It was as tight fit, but they were all finally squeezed into the router. On a whim, Opie scanned the body with his handheld jerblonk. As he looked at the readings, he gently squinted and furrowed his forehead with a look of curiosity. Nobody noticed the look, however, because Grenko had turned to walk over to the command console, and Neil and Anna were standing behind him. Grenko quickly turned to stand over the command console.

"Tallyho!" he yelled, and with no further warning, he engaged the router by pressing buttons on the smooth, dark, glass command console. Neil rolled his eyes and gently shook his head sideways while exhaling in a quiet, very small chuckle. Their attempts to blend into earth culture were somewhat comical at times.

The crystals blinked, then suddenly there was a flash of blue light and Neil experienced the head shrinking feeling once again.

Ralph and Theney were receiving an education. Even Shelly was learning information she didn't realize. Like Chepp, Leslie, and Neil, they felt violated and angry when they learned the truth about sleep and the shortened lifespan of human beings.

Leslie explained how the Dwovians were desperate for a cure and that their civilization would disappear from the galaxy without massive testing of genetic alterations. This softened the blow but only slightly.

Ralph was particularly interested in the small nano robotic devices called draminkos. He wanted to better understand the technology and was hopeful that the technology could be shared with Earth scientists to cure diseases.

Ralph's mind drifted back to his late teenage years when he had lost a younger brother to an inoperable brain tumor. His brother, Jack, began to experience dizzy spells at the age of twelve, and he was gone before he could turn fourteen. The best radiation and chemotherapy treatments could not even extend his brother's life by two years. The draminkos could perhaps be used to destroy cancerous tumors and provide a true cure.

Ralph and Theney were a bit overwhelmed at how their world had changed in the past twelve hours. They each had to take deep breaths on occasion and calm themselves. It was not easy for the human nervous system to receive and process the significant changes happening in their environment.

It is not just the physical environment, like the temperature or air quality, that affects our physical health, Leslie and Shelly explained. The information gathered and processed by our brains about our perceived reality can negatively affect our body's physical health, especially when the changes in our reality are large and sudden.

Leslie reminded them of the common phenomenon of people passing out upon learning of the sudden death of a loved one, or post-traumatic stress syndrome experienced by those who simply see a horrific accident.

"In fact," explained Leslie, "the reading of Orson Welles's *War of the Worlds* on the radio in 1938 had led to widespread panic based solely upon what people heard and thought was real. They had personally experienced none of the events of alien invasion they were hearing on the radio, yet the information their brains were processing as reality led them to physical actions, such as rushing out of their homes to escape impending gas attacks by invading Martians."

As if on cue, suddenly there was a blue flash of light. Neil, Anna, Opie, and the levitating gurney with Chepp appeared before their eyes in the area between the dining room and the doors to the back patio.

The briefing at the table ended abruptly as they all quickly stood when the flash happened. Theney, who was facing them when they appeared, almost fainted as quickly as she stood. She felt week in the knees, let out a quick groan, and fell forward toward the floor. She held herself up in a crawling position initially, then quickly turned herself around and sat down on the floor hard. For a second, the attention in the room was split equally between this sudden band of space-time travelers and the fainting Theney. Then Shelly rushed over to assist Theney.

"I got her," she yelled to everyone as she encouraged Theney to stretch out and lay down. She quickly slid her small drug suitcase, which was sitting on the floor next to her, under Theney's feet to elevate her legs.

After the initial disruption of Theney going down, Leslie was immediately drawn to Chepp lying on the levitating stretcher. She ran over.

"Chepp! What happened? Is he all right? Was he injured?" asked Leslie as she quickly came toward him.

"Don't touch him! Not yet!" yelled Opie. He immediately moved between Leslie and Chepp's body. "I was picking up a faint heart beat on my jerblonk before we routed."

Opie pulled out a tapered red crystalline wand from his robe and began to wave it over Chepp while looking at his handheld jerblonk.

"He's still alive!" yelled Opie. "Impossible! We saw the beam from the bleak hit him!"

"He's alive?" loudly questioned Neil.

Leslie battled her way past Opie and began cradling Chepp's face between her hands.

"Chepp! Chepp! Are you there? Chepp, wake up! Speak to me, Chepp! Don't you dare die on me, Chepp!" Leslie was now gently slapping him on the cheeks trying to rouse him.

Chepp's eyes slowly began to open. He blinked and his eyes struggled to focus.

"What? . . . Oh yeah," softly said Chepp as his eyes focused on Leslie. He was still groggy and tingling all over. But he slowly was gaining strength and consciousness.

"Chepp! You're alive!" said Neil loudly with enthusiasm and joy as he moved to the side of the gurney.

Chepp began to sit up a little propping himself up on his elbows.

"Apparently, yeah. I guess it worked," he said. He looked around. "Wait, we're back at your house. Did we get Anna?"

"We got her, Chepp. In fact, here she is." Neil wrapped his big hand around Anna's, and he gently pulled his delicate beauty up beside him. "Anna, this is Chepp, a friend. A very good friend. Chepp, this is the love of my life, Anna."

"A pleasure to finally meet you, Anna," said Chepp. "You are even prettier in person."

"Dr. Duplay. How did you survive the bleak? Nobody survives the bleak. Your nervous system should have been electrically destroyed," said Opie.

"What's he doing here?" asked Chepp, looking to Neil.

"He's the new commander of the Dwovian mission, and we've come to an agreement," explained Neil. "I'll debrief you later."

"I'd like to be part of that debriefing, Dr. Reese, if you don't mind," requested Ralph Stryker, still focused on the story for his news network.

"You have not answered. How did you survive?" insistently asked the new alien commander with his metallic voice.

Theney was doing much better now, and Shelly helped keep her calm by encouraging her to breathe slowly and deeply. She fanned her with a newspaper she found lying on the kitchen table as Theney sat back up in a kitchen chair.

"Never underestimate an Earth man with a physics degree, Commander," answered Chepp. He slid up his shirt to reveal a long wire spiral wrapped around his muscular torso and held in place by duct tape. "I've got it on my arms and legs as well. It's from one of Neil's old extension cords," he said.

"Wait. You had protection from the bleak and you didn't give the protection to me?" asked Neil.

"Well, I wasn't sure it was going to work, Neil. I was concerned it could actually attract the beam from the bleak and make us even more susceptible. I know how fearless you are and how emotionally charged you were. I thought you might get a little careless if you thought you had protection from the bleak, and I was personally only giving this idea about a 5 percent chance of working."

"You do know me now, don't you? Well, thank God for the 5 percent!" said Neil as he gave Chepp a thumbs-up.

"I understand now. Your device is ingenious," said Opie. "Dwovian scientists have not worked with actual wire for thousands of years—not since the revolution of virtual wire. Sometimes the obvious answers remain elusive—or as you Earth folks say, we Dwovians couldn't see the threes for the fourzess."

"What!" laughed Leslie.

"Ha-ha," softly chuckled Chepp as he sat up all the way and turned to dangle his feet off the edge of the stretcher. "I think he means they couldn't see the trees for the forest."

They all laughed out loud, except Opie.

"I guess we still have much to learn about Earth people," said Opie.

"But I still don't understand," said Neil. "How did my old extension cord protect you against an alien ray gun?"

"Are you familiar with electromagnetic induction?" asked Chepp.

"A little," said Neil.

"When Opie explained how the bleak fries the nervous system with electric current, I immediately googled information on nerves and did some calculations. The main nerves run through our body in straight lines, which means they are perfectly arranged to create induced currents in loops of wire. I calculated the amount of induction required to counter the sudden current through our nerves and dissipate the energy. Then I created that amount of induction by wrapping the wire around my arms and legs and torso with the right spacing."

"Oh, Chepp! You're brilliant! I love you so much, honey! Thank God it worked," Leslie said emotionally as she hugged him and laid her left cheek against his right cheek.

"Chepp, all I can say is, you're the man," said Neil. "Oh, that and you owe me for an extension cord."

CHAPTER

23

"This is it," said Tim as he pulled the Escalade up along the curb a few houses down from the stylish home of Neil and Anna Reese.

"Finally!" replied Candy as she flipped down her visor and opened the lighted vanity mirror.

The drive to the last known GPS coordinates of Ralph Stryker and Athena Kirkland was a bit much for a city girl like Candy. She was not fond of the summer smells of the suburbs with their occasional field full of livestock.

"Give me a chance to freshen myself up, Thickett. Then we are going to go get famous as the news crew that bailed out the famous Ralph Stryker."

"What's your plan?" asked Tim.

"Well, the front of the house looks dark. I think we sneak around to the back of the house and see if we can see anything through the back windows," answered Candy as she flipped open a compact and applied some powder to her face. Next she scrunched her hair a little bit while looking in the mirror.

"Roger that," said Tim as they got out of the vehicle. He quietly opened the back of the SUV and began the work of pulling out a portable, shoulder carried television camera with an attached light.

Candy put on some red lipstick and snapped shut her compact. Then she hopped out of the vehicle with purpose.

"All right. Let's go!" she said.

They walked around the left side of the house through the grass, being careful to use the flowering bushes and trees as cover.

Fortunately, it was a dark night and the neighborhood was quiet. Almost everybody was asleep. The cool, damp well-tailored grass felt a bit funny on Candy's toes as she worked slowly around the house with her open-toed shoes. They came around the corner at the back of the house and worked their way onto the back patio. The blinds were drawn shut on the windows, and the sheer curtains on the French doors prevented anything but moving shadows to be seen behind them.

Candy crept close to the doors and found a small crack between the ruffled curtains and the wooden frame of the door. She peered in and looked.

She could just make out what appeared to be a man sitting at a kitchen table. All she could see was a right shoulder and back, but she knew it was a man by the thinning salt-and-pepper hair. He also appeared to be wearing a dress shirt with a collar. "Looks like Stryker," she thought to herself.

Suddenly there was a flash of blue light that filled the air inside of the house. Everything turned blue for a second—even the air itself. It was as if there were a blue glowing fog that filled the dining room. And then it was gone.

Her eyes adjusted quickly to the flash, and immediately she saw Dr. Reese, his wife, Anna, Opie the alien, and Dr. Duplay on a stretcher.

"Oh my god! Get over here, Thickett!" said Candy in a yelling whisper. "You aren't going to believe this. What the hell is going on here?"

Tim was a caught off guard as he fumbled with the camera. He had his back turned to Candy when the flash occurred because he was trying to use the light available from the small decorative lights around the perimeter of the patio to adjust his camera.

"What do you mean? What do you see?"

"People appeared out of a flashing blue cloud. Holy crap! There's a lot more going on here than missing professors, Tim. We need to get inside and find out what's happening."

"What do you mean 'they appeared out of a blue cloud'?" asked the cameraman.

"Just like I said, you dolt! They weren't standing there, then a glowing blue cloud flashed, and then they were standing there."

"No way!"

"Yeah way! And we gotta get in there. Let's get back around to the front. We need to contact GN3 and see if we can get something about this situation on the air ASAP. Give your boss a ring and get us permission to move forward in an aggressive manner. Then we are bustin' in there and going all Geraldo on them to get this story."

"Roger that," said Tim as they turned and made a beeline up the side of the house back to the driveway.

Tim set down the camera in the driveway and pulled out his cell phone. He pressed speed dial, and in almost no time, he was connected with the smoky office of Don Smith. He handed the phone off to Candy Kramer, who brought the news chief up to speed. Don Smith was not thrilled about being woken up, but for big stories, he knew it happened. He was usually pragmatic and did not chase stories that seemed outlandish like this, but he decided to go out on a limb and believe what Candy said she saw. His gut told him that something significant was going on—an experienced star reporter had failed to check in, two missing PhD scientists had gone missing and had been tracked by the reporter to this location, and now this fantastic story from an up-and-coming investigative journalist. He threw his full support behind Candy's idea for a surprise interview if they could get their foot in the door. He promised GN3 legal protection if the reporters should get themselves into trouble.

"We are a go on our enter-and-engage plan, Timmy-boy!" said Candy. "Whatever we get we send the raw footage immediately to Don Smith at GN3. His team will edit as necessary and get it on the air."

She continued, "We may not have much time, either. He says he's under obligation in the morning to report back to a special agent from the Department of Defense who is looking for Dr. McCabe. Apparently the announcement about her scientific evidence of extra-terrestrials has drawn the attention of the government as well."

In the Pentagon, the directors of several clandestine intelligence organizations and their teams gathered at 0500 to debrief each other and share information. From the moment her abstract entered cyberspace, the sophisticated government computer robots had identified the significance of Dr. Leslie McCabe's research. The US government had long been concerned about the potential presence of extraterrestrials on planet Earth and the threat of an invasion from space. Before covert surveillance could begin on Dr. McCabe and Dr. Duplay to better access the matter, the media had been drawn into the mix. From a publicity standpoint, it was a disaster.

"Damn it! How in the world did this happen? Who the hell dropped the ball on this!" screamed the director of Extraterrestrial Surveillance Program (ETSP), Roger Dagman. He picked up his cup of coffee and took a swig.

"Our job is to prepare contingency plans for the intelligence data we receive, Director. We had no indication from either ETSP or the Bureau of Extraterrestrial Science about this issue," said Frank Bodemeider, the director of the Department of Space Invasion Defense (DSID).

"The media just moves too fast nowadays. And usually they don't even wait to get the story right. With all the technology available, they sometimes know things as fast as we do," said a senior level field agent.

"Well, it doesn't much matter now, does it, gentlemen? We have no choice but to let the media chew this up and spit it out now. We are preparing to come clean on the Roswell incident anyway. The cat is coming out of the bag. The American people are about to learn that we are not alone," announced Roger.

"No choice there. A cover-up on this is virtually impossible at this point," agreed Bogart Goldstein, the director of BETS. "But we need to get McCabe and Duplay in here pronto. And be sure to take one of our ADP with you when you have them picked up, Dags. You never know."

"An ADP? You mean one of those alien cages?" an agent from ETSP asked.

"Yes. Of course that's what I mean. It stands for *alien detainment pod*. You need to keep your agents up to speed, Dags," responded Bogart.

"Don't worry about my team. You just line up the ADP, Bogey. And you guys better stand ready in case he's right, Frank," said Roger. "We'll pick them up as soon as we let the media break the story open. While they chew on that and have all their expert panelists on their talk shows, that will buy us time to question McCabe and Duplay."

"I'll make arrangements for the trip to Pittsburgh and have the team gear up. You just send word when you want them picked up, Director," said Jake (a.k.a. Q), the senior field agent for ETSP.

"Make it so, Q," said Roger Dagman as he exhaled cigarette smoke and simultaneously grabbed a cheese Danish from the center of the conference table.

⌒♋

The sun had just risen as Tim fired up the battery-powered transmitter in the SUV. His camera was linked properly now, and they could begin the interview. It had been almost two hours since he and Candy had shockingly been invited inside the house by the infamous Ralph Stryker. "Damned if Stryker didn't go and get the story of the millennium before me," thought Candy Kramer.

While Candy and Tim amateurishly stood in the driveway, planning a way of getting inside the house, Ralph had professionally interviewed all five human beings and the alien commander in what was bound to become the biggest story in human history. He was good. No, he was extraordinary. Not only did he get the story but he convinced them that this news needed to be released accurately through him as soon as possible.

When Neil and his makeshift team finally allowed Ralph Stryker to report in to Don Smith, Ralph was surprised to learn that two young media personnel had been dispatched to track him down. But that was nothing compared with the surprise of learning they had found him and were already there. Ralph laughed when he looked out of Neil's front windows to find them standing in plain sight in the driveway. So he simply opened the door, called out to them, and invited them in.

The surreal happenings of the last several days were about to travel out on radio and television waves to forever change the world. Everyone was incredibly anxious and excited. Only Candy was struggling with it all. She was happy that Ralph had agreed to allow her to be the field reporter who introduced the story, but she was jealous and bitter that Ralph was the newsman who was going to be the one to get credit and be remembered for cracking the story. Still, she would hopefully be picked up by a major network somewhere because of her proximity to this story and for being the face that interrupted life around the world with the shocking news.

Tim walked in the front door of the house carrying his camera on his shoulder, then he turned left and walked through the beautiful French doors into Neil's spacious and stately living room.

"Any time you guys are ready we can get started. I've got good signal," said Tim. "Once I let GN3 know we are a go, we'll get a thirty-second countdown. Then they'll interrupt the Gary and Dave morning show with this."

Chepp, Leslie, and Ralph, comfortably seated on a sofa, looked at each other, then toward Candy. Candy was sitting with good posture in a separate wingback chair to the left. The plan was for Candy to introduce the story and then turn it over to Ralph who sat on the end of the sofa closest to Candy. He would deliver the story to America via a live interview of Dr. McCabe and Dr. Duplay.

"I think we are good to go. Right, Candy?" answered Ralph.

"Yes. I absolutely agree, Ralph. Go ahead, Tim. Let them know we're ready," agreed Candy. She was being particularly respectful and kissing Ralph's butt. It was like she morphed into a different person around the great Ralph Stryker. Tim turned and secretly rolled his eyes at the behavior of Candy. "Such a fake," thought Tim. But he couldn't hate her too much. She was part of the story of how he came to be standing in this soon to be infamous room as the cameraman for a paradigm-shifting story in human history. Tim signaled the local network that was relaying the feed to GN3 to let them know they were ready.

Neil walked over to Chepp and bent over to whisper in his ear.

"The SUV is loaded and in position. Remember, as soon as this interview is over, we bug out. Pronto."

Chepp nodded that he understood and leaned over to Leslie. He quietly passed the message along.

"Everything is ready to go."

"I'm nervous, Chepp," she whispered back.

"Just relax. You can do this, Les. Just speak the truth and let the Lord lead you through this," quietly encouraged Chepp.

Chepp gently kissed Leslie on the cheek.

Tim received his go signal.

"Thirty seconds, everybody! Take your positions and get ready!" confidently announced Tim.

Candy scrunched her hair and cleared her throat. Then she adjusted her earpiece with the microphone. Leslie took a deep breath and gently exhaled out of her mouth through rounded lips to calm her nerves. Opie sat in a wingback chair at the other end of the sofa. Ralph leaned forward a little and said to Opie,

"Remember, not too much. People will be in shock when they first see you and hear your voice. We can follow up on things at a later time."

"Ten-force," said Opie.

Ralph had a confused look on his face.

"I think he means 'ten-four,'" said Leslie looking back at Opie.

"Whatever, dude," said Opie.

Leslie actually laughed out loud, and everyone chuckled a little. It was probably just what everybody needed to relax a bit. She wondered if Opie knew that and was so doggone smart that he did that on purpose, or whether they had just been blessed with one of those random acts of comedy at the right time.

"Ten, nine, eight . . ." Tim began counting down out loud. Then he got quiet and held up his right hand to indicate five more seconds. Of course, Opie interpreted that as the Dwovian hand signal for everything was "Okay to proceed."

The GN3 news flash music began, and Brian Smith, the lead news anchor for the network, interrupted the Gary and Dave morning show to send it to guest correspondent Candy Kramer in the Pittsburgh area.

"Thanks, Brian. What you are about to hear is astounding and life changing for all human beings. I encourage those watching to take a seat. We are here outside of Pittsburgh in the home of a pharmaceutical executive where we arrived late last night. Sitting to my right is the great, Ralph Stryker, who can tell you more."

"Thank you, Candy. What you are about to hear and see will change your view of what it means to be human. As many of you know, a few days ago news broke that a California University of Sciences professor Dr. Leslie McCabe had evidence that intelligent extraterrestrial life exists. Her research, which has not yet been reviewed by the scientific community, led her to this location where her research was confirmed in the most unlikely of scenarios.

"Dr. McCabe and her husband, Dr. Cheppard Duplay, disappeared from CUS shortly after this news broke, and many people have been looking for them since. Following an unnamed informant's tip, my colleague, Athena Kirkland, and I arrived here about a day and a half ago to find Dr. McCabe and Dr. Duplay along with the residents of the home whom shall not be named at this time."

Ralph turned toward Leslie, and Tim zoomed the camera out and panned to bring Leslie into the picture with Ralph.

"Sitting to my left is Dr. Leslie McCabe, a tenured professor in both biology and chemistry at CUS. Dr. McCabe, I know I'm putting you on the spot, but can you explain for the viewers in a nutshell this astounding discovery you have made."

"Well, I will do my best, Ralph. First, let me thank you and GN3 for this opportunity to share with the American people."

"Of course," answered Ralph.

"In a nutshell . . . okay . . . here we go. For the past number of years, I have been researching sleep. I have been interested in the genetic development of sleep, that is, the evolutionary reason we sleep. There has been much speculation that it is necessary for the body to go into this dormant, unconscious state so the body can heal and recover from the rigors of life, or so the brain can work out problems through dreaming. However, I have always found that idea a bit odd. The body is able to rest and heal even while awake, and certainly I do my most efficient solving of problems when wide-awake. I think if you interview college students, they will tell you that studying while sleepy is not very efficient. And further, there is nothing more susceptible than a sleeping animal. Predator animals should have long removed this via the evolutionary process. Animals that only catnap, like, well, for instance, the cat, should be much better able to survive. So I became fascinated with this idea."

"Basically you are saying that someone who sleeps a lot is not at an advantage as far as survival in the world," said Ralph.

"Exactly. And through some groundbreaking equipment developed by my research team at CUS, including the hard work of many talented graduate students, I was able to finally isolate the genes that cause humankind—in fact, most every animal on Earth—to sleep," shared Leslie.

"That's remarkable. That would be a groundbreaking discovery on its own, would it not? But there is more that you discovered, isn't there?" interrupted Stryker to help highlight what people were about to hear.

"Yes. I was pleased enough with that discovery as you elude to. But upon further investigation of the DNA from human mummies, and even animals, that lived several thousand years ago, I found that there was an abrupt change in the sleep genes in the DNA of all life on Earth. It happened about three thousand years ago."

"So let me get this straight. Some kind of genetic mutation happened on Earth that affected how long we sleep?" questioned Ralph, keeping the interaction between them going.

"Well, yes and no. There was definitely a genetic change, but it was not a naturally occurring mutation as it turns out. The genetic change was very specific and in a precise pattern in our DNA to introduce sleep to the human race."

"Okay. Wait. Are you saying that several thousand years ago, human beings did not sleep? That we were wide-awake around the clock? And then some kind of illness entered into the world that caused our genetics to change and we began to sleep?" asked Ralph.

"Well, that's what I initially thought. But the change happened quickly enough and in such a statistically unlikely way that I could not find a naturally occurring phenomenon to explain it. The human race, indeed most animals on Earth, changed over the course of about two hundred years at most. Our records of human history from that far back are not good. But yes, I am confident that we went from no sleep to an average of eight hours of sleep a day in a matter of about two hundred years. And I could not find any naturally occurring biological, chemical or physical phenomenon to explain it," calmly and professionally explained Leslie.

"And so you approached your estranged husband, Dr. Cheppard Duplay, with your hypothesis, and how did you react, Dr. Duplay?" asked Ralph as the camera panned over to Chepp.

"Well—ha!" Chepp chuckled. "I was actually a bit concerned for the health of my wife, to be quite frank. We had been separated for a little less than a year, so our contact with each other had been less frequent. When she contacted me and shared this . . . well, what I thought was an outlandish story, my first concern was that she may have a brain tumor or a mental illness or something. I'm guessing folks listening right now may be tempted to think that."

"I confess that was my first reaction as well, until I saw the proof sitting right in the room with me," shared journalist Stryker.

"Exactly. But as we came back together as husband and wife and I looked at her data and checked the physics—physics is the only scientific area where I am more knowledgeable than Dr. McCabe, by the way—she is quite brilliant. Anyway, when I checked the physics for her, it became clear to me that she was right. The only logical explanation for this sudden and specific genetic mutation would be if some intelligence purposely caused it. It became clear to me, like it first was to Dr. McCabe, that someone had purposely monkeyed with our DNA."

"It really is astounding. My mind is still trying to wrap itself around all of this," confessed Ralph. "It sounds like science fiction, but it's not—it's reality."

"Yes. Exactly."

Stryker turned, facing back toward the television camera.

"Now, folks, listen carefully. We have reached a critical mile marker in human history today. I'm sure we will all be hearing much more about everything presented here in the days and weeks to come. But for now, I am going to ask Dr. McCabe to finish giving us a rundown on what she believes history will determine to be the most significant discoveries of the past few days, and then we will provide astounding proof of Dr. McCabe's theories," said Stryker as he turned back to Leslie.

"Okay. I suppose the most amazing discoveries we have made in the past few days are, first, we are *not* alone. Intelligent life, similar to humankind, exists in our galaxy, and they have visited us. Second, these extraterrestrials have tinkered with our DNA, for reasons that will become clear in future news releases, using nano machines released into the environment about five thousand years ago. The results of the genetic alterations introduced sleep into the circadian rhythm of human beings causing us to be unconscious in REM sleep for eight hours per day on average. Additionally, the average lifespan of human beings was shortened from approximately two thousand years to the seventy-five-year lifespan we presently experience."

"Excuse me!" asked Ralph, convincingly shocked. "Could you repeat that one more time?"

"I know. It's shocking. The lifespan of our ancestors a several millennia ago was about two thousand years—and they didn't even have to sleep."

"Two thousand years! How did their body's hold up to that? I mean, most of us have broken-down bodies by the time we hit retirement age of sixty-five," asked Stryker.

"As far as we can tell, the genetic alteration increased our rate of aging and metabolism," answered Leslie.

"This really is historic—legendary—literally life-changing information—for every single person on this planet! Life for humankind will never be the same again, will it?" asked Ralph.

"No. I don't see how it can be," answered Leslie.

Ralph Stryker turned in his seat and faced forward toward the camera now.

"Well, folks. I know what you're thinking. This story is too far-out. It must be some kind of fake out or joke—a modern-day *War of the Worlds*. It is not. We now offer you the proof of what Dr. McCabe has been speaking about." Ralph's face turned very somber and serious as he felt the weight of the situation. "Here in the room with me is an intelligent extraterrestrial—an alien life-form from a faraway planet. I have spent the last half day in his presence, and I am absolutely convinced he is who he says he is. He is certainly not human. He has corroborated the facts that Dr. McCabe has just shared with us. He is highly intelligent and has been able to learn the English language in his time on the Earth, so we are privileged to let him speak a few words to you. Ladies and gentlemen, allow me to introduce to you, Commander Skrako from planet Dwovy."

The room was filled with tension and was absolutely silent as everyone turned their heads and Tim panned the camera to land right on Opie. The bright camera lights shined in his face as the camera revealed the small, child-sized alien sitting on a wingback chair wearing a dark-colored robe. The robe was nearly black, but it had some strange properties about it that caused it to randomly flicker small blue sparkles as the camera lights hit it. His gray legs dangled over the front of the chair and did not reach the floor. His feet were adorned with his favorite green Croc shoes. His hands, with long, spindly fingers, laid in his lap as he nervously twiddled his fingers up and down. Tim's camera work was spectacular. He framed the entire body of Opie from the green shoes up to the top of his gray bald head. Then he began slowly zooming in toward Opie's upper body. Opie did his best to smile, and again trying to use the appropriate human mannerisms as he raised his right hand up and twisted it back and forth in an attempt to wave hello.

"Howdy, Earth people," he said. "I greet you in the name of my planet, Dwovy. We want very much to have a good relationship with the people of Earth." His twangy, metallic voice was being broadcast around the country live. People all across the nation were calling each other on their mobile phones and telling each other to tune in to the broadcast. The bandwidth of the cable TV companies, internet providers, and phone lines was quickly becoming saturated as the people were becoming aware. Opie continued.

"We have much to discuss. My leaders ask for your patience and calm restraint as we speak to your leaders regarding how our people can best cooperate with one other. Until then, I wish you my best. Thank you."

Tim quickly panned the camera back to Ralph who looked directly into the camera and said, "And there you have it. With those words, the planet Earth has been ushered into a new era of interstellar communication and relationship. Now, back to you, Brian."

The feed switched back to Brian Smith, the GN3 anchor in Atlanta. He looked pale and in shock as the headline text rolled across the bottom of the screen: "We are not alone. Intelligent extraterrestrial speaks to humankind from suburban home in Pittsburgh." He was not prepared for the gravity of the report he just heard. For a brief moment, he looked like a deer caught in headlights with wide eyes and no motion. Then he suddenly snapped out of it and began speaking with urgency.

"Ralph, this is Brian Smith back in Atlanta. Thank you for this report which is . . . staggering in importance . . . monumental in importance. I'm still trying to wrap my mind around what I just heard and saw as I'm sure many of viewers are. Ralph, I must ask you a question that is on my mind, and we are currently receiving a lot of phone calls asking the same thing. You've just spent some time around this extraterrestrial colonel. Do you believe we are in any danger of an alien invasion or takeover? I mean, if I understand this right, these aliens have already interfered with human life by rebuilding our DNA. Do you believe these extraterrestrials are dangerous?"

"Great question, Brian. Based on my interaction and observation of the alien commander, I do not believe he is dangerous or that we are in any immediate danger. However, that being said, as you mention there has already been astounding damage to human life through the actions of Commander Skrako and his expedition to our planet. We are going to have to wait for the world leaders to speak officially with Colonel Skrako and to determine where we go from here. From what I understand, the GN3 network has—"

An alarm on Tim's equipment began to sound and blink.

"Crap, we lost our connection," announced Tim.

"What? Did they get the last part? My answer to Brian's question?" anxiously asked Ralph Stryker.

"Yeah. I'm pretty sure. It just went out about five seconds before you stopped speaking. The alarm doesn't sound until connectivity has failed for a full five seconds," answered Tim. "It may have been a bit intermittent, but the quality was still good enough that your main answer got through."

"Thank God," said Candy. "We could have a real panic on our hands if people think you were cut off by the alien before you could answer."

"No, we're good. But this interview is definitely over," said Tim. "My network traffic monitor shows absolutely *zero* bandwidth available. The last time this happened was 9/11. I'm guessing communications everywhere are being overwhelmed. So you guys were a definitely a hit. You rocked it. But I doubt with this equipment we will ever get a live feed backup. We can definitely pack it up at this point."

CHAPTER

24

Within minutes, the media and government would surely be gathering at the Reese household like turkey vultures on roadkill. In fact, some neighbors who had seen the live television news report were already out in their front yards talking to each other and pointing at Neil and Anna's home. A few groups looked like they were about to walk over at any moment. One could only imagine the circus that was coming, and nobody, especially Leslie, liked the thought of being trapped in the house.

So the plan was for Shelly to stay behind to help what Chepp was calling the "ET News Crew"—Ralph, Theney, Candy, and Tim—out of the Reese's home and to lock the place up as quickly as possible. She would try to shoo the others away as she did her best to discreetly return to her lab as quickly as possible to resume her work there.

The ET News Crew promised to not divulge Shelly's identity or her whereabouts. In return she would serve as the secret liaison between them and the Alien Five—Neil, Anna, Chepp, Leslie, and Colonel Skrako. If at any time Shelly's identity was compromised, then the Alien Five would stop contacting her, and the flow of information to this special news team would stop.

Additionally, Shelly would never know the true location of the Alien Five or how to contact them. This arrangement kept not only the ET News Crew highly motivated to keep Shelly's identity secret, but also Shelly would be motivated to stay anonymous as well or she would lose contact with her new friends.

As Tim continued to wrap up cords and stow equipment away, the faint sound of a helicopter could be heard in the distance. It was a cool summer morning with a perfectly clear blue sky, and it was apparent from the increasing loudness of the chopper that it was approaching.

"We aren't sticking around for that. Let's go. Let's move, move, move!" yelled out Neil.

Chepp, Leslie, Anna, Neil, and Opie quickly exited through the side door in the house and entered into the attached garage. A nearly new Jeep Cherokee was fueled and ready to go. With Anna being pregnant and such a small-framed woman, Neil did not like her sitting in the front seat with the airbag. So Neil and Anna got into the back seat and Opie joined them. Chepp jumped into the driver's seat and Leslie hopped in shotgun.

Chepp pushed the garage door opener, turned the keys that were already in the ignition, threw it into gear, and stomped the accelerator. The jeep SUV squealed its tires on Neil's asphalt driveway and jumped forward. Chepp quickly steered around Shelly's car in the driveway by going into Neil and Anna's front yard. He hopped the curb and swerved around Ralph and Theney's car at the end of the driveway and floored it once the jeep was pointing the right direction on the road.

The helicopter was nearly at the house and hovering lower.

"We should have gotten out faster. That doesn't look like a news chopper to me," said Neil as he leaned to the right over Anna and focused his eyes skyward through the tinted window.

"Maybe that helicopter is for something else. It could be unrelated to us," said Chepp.

At just that moment the helicopter turned the direction, the jeep was traveling and swooped down near them.

"Uh . . . ya wanta rethink that one, Doctor?" said Leslie looking over at Chepp.

"Such marvelous flying machines—based on ancient Dwovian technology. I am so glad we shared that idea with that nice painter who helped us a few hundred years back," said Opie.

"Holy shit! Da Vinci, right? That's why there's a flying saucer in his painting of *The Last Supper*!" said Chepp as it suddenly dawned on him that the Dwovians had interacted with Leonardo Da Vinci.

"You can deal with that later, Chepp. Right now you need to do your best to elude this chopper—for all our sakes, but especially Opie," Neil barked.

Without stopping or looking Chepp hung a sharp right out of Neil's neighborhood onto the main road and gunned it. The tires squealed as the jeep leaned to the left and everyone tried to grab hold of something. A car that Chepp had pulled out right in front of screeched its brakes and blew his horn.

"Apparently the person flying this helicopter has an interest in us, I gather," said Opie.

"Uh . . . ya think!" said Neil sarcastically. "They're some kind of government or military is my bet. Somehow they traced the source of the television transmission I guess."

"Opie, do you have any magical powers that could help us avoid them? You know like invisibility or something?" asked Anna as she leaned her head forward and turned it to see the little boy alien. "In the movie *ET*, the alien could make the bicycles fly."

"Not really. I also know I cannot breathe immersed in a tank of formaldehyde," calmly replied Opie. "But I do have my jerblonk and the routing crystal."

Opie reached into his robe and pulled out a long cylindrical crystal that glowed a sky blue color. It looked a bit like a glass stirring rod from a chemistry lab, but it was clearly glowing and not of this world.

"What's that do?" asked Anna.

"This will allow me and anyone touching me to route to our spaceship."

"Could it handle all of us routing at the same time?" asked Leslie. "I thought you said it had a limit."

"Considering Anna and I are small in size, it may manage routing all of us at once," he answered.

The black helicopter swooped low and turned back toward the jeep. It was heading directly toward them and was only about ten feet off the ground.

"Be careful!" yelled Leslie.

Chepp turned the steering wheel hard to the right and the jeep temporarily careened off the asphalt and into the drainage shoulder of the suburban road. The side of the SUV made a rhythmic thudding sound against the tall, thick weeds off the side of the road. Pieces of the weeds broke off and flew up around the side of the vehicle. The chopper blew by the left side of the vehicle at a height just above the roof. Anna screamed. Chepp turned the wheels hard now to the left, and the SUV leaped back onto the road surface with a screech. The vehicle danced and rocked a bit back and forth before Chepp finally got it stabilized again.

"Uh-oh," said Opie.

"What. What's the matter?" asked Leslie as she turned around to look in the back seat toward Opie.

"My crystal broke," he said.

"The crystal thingy that would allow us to transport to your ship?" asked Anna.

"Yes," said the commander.

"Are you telling me you can't route us out of here?" questioned Neil.

"That's affirmative," answered Opie.

The black helicopter was quickly back over them and swooping past. This time a gunshot rang out.

"Holy crap! Are they shooting at us!" blurted Chepp as the ladies screamed. Neil leaned over and caught a glance at a rifle with sniper scope sticking out the side of the chopper.

"They're going for the tires. Apparently they are going to force us to stop one way or the other," answered Neil.

"Oh, Neil, what are we going to do?" anxiously whined Anna.

"I know what I'm going to do!" blurted Neil as he reached over and put his hands around Opie's neck and began squeezing the life out of him.

"Oh my god, Neil, what are you doing! Let him go! That's not going to solve anything!" passionately yelled Leslie as she turned and reached over the center console in the car and lunged to help Opie. Opie was struggling to breathe and had his hands up at Neil's trying to pull them away from his throat, but the muscles in Neil's arms had well defined ridges in them as he squeezed hard.

"Neil! No, honey!" pleaded Anna as she unbuckled and reached over as best as she could to try to help pull Neil off the Dwovian commander.

The helicopter banked sharply as Chepp did his best to stay on the road but provide a moving target by swerving back and forth on the road. Fortunately the two lane undivided road was fairly flat and straight along this stretch and Chepp could easily cross back and forth over the double yellow line. But that option was about to run out. A pickup truck loaded with furniture was coming the opposite way. Chepp pulled the jeep back onto his side of the road and glanced at his speedometer. Ninety miles per hour! Suddenly a shot rang out from the helicopter, and it hit the road in front of them, quickly sparking and deflecting past the vehicle. The pickup truck blew his horn and zoomed past the jeep in a blur with the driver, clearly oblivious, screaming at Chepp. Quickly another shot rang out from the sniper as the helicopter cut across the road banking in a tight leftward turn. Immediately the front right tire of the jeep blew out in a loud explosion and pieces or rubber tire tore off the fast spinning wheel and hit the right side of the car. Chepp grabbed the steering wheel tight as he began losing control of the vehicle. The jeep began darting off the road heading for the drainage ditch.

"Hold on!" he screamed as he instinctively let go of the wheel with his right hand to reach back and hold Leslie in place to keep her from flying out of the car when they crashed. His left hand held firm to the wheel as muscles in his arm flexed to try to gain some control over the vehicles path.

The jeep dipped hard into the drainage ditch and rebounded out on the other side and became airborne. Still moving at seventy miles per hour, it landed hard on its driver's side. Glass shattered as it hit. The windshield tore loose and flew over the top of the vehicle.

The jeep continued sliding on the driver's side toward a small electrical substation—about the size of a backyard shed—that sat in the corner of the lot for a small grocery store coming up on the right. The left front wheel hit a small ditch and the vehicle had enough momentum to flip up over itself and began rolling end over end as the hood popped open, side view mirrors flew off, and various pieces of glass and broken debris sprayed outward from the jeep.

As if the hand of destiny were guiding it, the battered SUV slammed directly into the side of the electrical shed and tore through its sheet metal wall like a fist punching through newspaper. But a blink after that it was stopping as if it hit a brick wall. The metal of the jeep screamed as it hit into a massive transformer in the middle of the shed, and the frame bent into the shape of a boomerang around it. Simultaneously, sparks flew out of the transformer contacts and showered down onto the deluged scrap of vehicle that remained. It only took a fraction of a second for the gasoline to ignite, quickly followed by a huge explosion as the rest of the fuel violently erupted. Glass debris and metal strips were propelled up to 150 feet away as a giant yellow ball of flames grew to a forty-foot diameter and extended upward in a plume. Dark smoke began to pour forth from the wreckage.

The black helicopter descended and quickly landed in a clearing across the road. "You idiot!" yelled the man in the copilots seat of the helicopter. He turned his head toward the sniper behind him. "We were supposed to take them alive!"

He hopped out of the chopper and for an instant thought about trying to help the passengers in the wreckage. But the heat from the burning vehicle across the road could be felt, so he did not even venture over. He just stood still for a minute staring in disbelief. On a typical day, this man would have been quite the spectacle. After all, he was standing in a country field scattered with cow patties while wearing a designer black suit, white oxford shirt, and sunglasses, and he had a custom black helicopter whirling its blades beside him. But the large plume of black smoke and fireball burning across the street was what drew most everyone's eyes on this particular day. The man hopped back into the chopper and pulled his door shut. He pulled his phone out to pass along the bad news to his boss but thought better of it.

Sirens were barely audible in the distance as cars began stopping and drivers and passengers alike hopped out of their cars looking to each other for suggestions of what to do. One man began pointing at the chopper and then back to the burning wreckage.

"We will need to get out in front of this story," the man told his crewmates. Fly me over to the parking lot across the street—near that grocery store—so we can establish a media center before all the news trucks get here."

⤜✥⤛

Fire trucks continued to work on securing the scene. Hoses sprayed water and chemical foam to reduce the chance of a reignition of the fire—not that there was much left that could burn. The hot twisted metal wreckage was a mere skeleton of what it previously had been. There was hot, gooey, black, synthetic material clinging to hot beams of metal. The stench of the recently burning rubber tires was over-whelming as steam continued to rise upward around the twisted wreckage.

One of the men from the helicopter—the one wearing a black suit with a white dress shirt, no tie, and black oxford dress shoes—stood still about twenty-five feet away with a blank face staring at the wreckage. His right hand and thumb gripped his chin and he was clearly deep in thought when his phone rang. He pulled his vibrating phone out of his suit pocket and answered. Before he had a chance to say hello, the gruff voice of Roger Dagman, the director of ETSP, came on the phone screaming.

"What the hell is going on? I got a call from Homeland that there was an explosion at a grocery store nearby? You got them!"

"We lost them, sir. We had positive visual on them in the vehicle just seconds before the crash. But as far as we can tell at this point, there are no bodies in the wreckage. No unusual materials found in the vicinity either. It's like they evaporated."

"That makes no sense. Was there any possible way they could have survived the crash and run off?"

"Negative, sir—unless they somehow bailed out of the SUV just before the crash."

"Find them, Q! They couldn't have gotten far."

Immediately as he got off the phone with Director Dagman, the senior agent going by the alias Jake Nollman, was seized by a group of local reporters and asked to make a statement about the event. Jake was a tall, dark-haired man of age thirty-six years old. He had a joint assignment with both the ETSP and FBI, but of course, the existence of the ETSP was not public knowledge. It was the FBI ball cap that he wore that attracted the reporters, and of course, that was all part of his plan. It was critical to control the story, and it always worked better when the reporters came after him. The arrogance of most reporters is such that if you go to them with a statement, they feel they have not done their job and they move to a tangent point. But if they come to you, they think they invented the story and will go with it.

"Jake" spent the next thirty minutes making statements and answering questions for the reporters. He did his best to reassure people that a thorough investigation was underway and that there was absolutely no threat to national security. Jake simply repeated the following story over and over.

"Dr. McCabe and Dr. Duplay were registered as high profile missing persons with the FBI. In the midst of our investigation and in an attempt to recover them, a high-speed chase pursued. In the midst of the pursuit, a front tire on the Jeep Cherokee blew, and the driver of the vehicle lost control and crashed. There were no survivors recovered. The investigation continues."

No matter the question asked, Jake skillfully returned an answer of "I cannot answer that or tell you more at this time. Our investigation is ongoing."

This put the fire out, so to speak, on the story for a day or two. But reporters are reporters. Once they investigated and realized there were no bodies from the accident in the local morgues and as local EMTs confirmed they removed no bodies from the wreckage, the shit hit the fan and Jake found himself in the hot seat. The days following were embarrassing for the FBI, and they simply had no explanation about what became of the bodies. But that would not last, because the Alien Five took actions of their own.

CHAPTER

25

One half of an Earth year later . . .

Leslie could not help but sit and think about how much had changed on planet Earth in the past six months. The world was abruptly awakened to something it had generally resisted since the flying saucer crash near Roswell. And that was the fact that human-kind was not alone as the sole intelligent species in the universe.

She took a bite of her bagel with cream cheese, then washed it down with a sip of hot tea. The reality of the Dwovian empire on a distant planet shocked the people of planet Earth more than anything in human history had. Accepting the reality of hydrogen bombs capable of vaporizing entire cities? Accepting the reality of scientists cloning a person who was already dead? That was child's play for human emotions compared with accepting the fact that lit-tle gray-skinned aliens truly existed and had flown many light-years through space in a flying saucer over five thousand years ago to alter the DNA of nearly every living animal on Earth such that it greatly shortened their lifespans and caused them to sleep about one-third of their lives away. That was emotionally overwhelming for many people. And the Alien Five realized they had a divine call to lead at this time. If they did not, who would?

Even though the world still had no idea where the Alien Five were, Opie and Leslie appeared on television regularly over the past six months—about once per week on average—to explain as much as they could. They would record and edit a short informational video about fifteen minutes long each week. They used a blank green screen backdrop and then filled in the background scenery electronically. This was to reduce the risk of someone tracking them down based on clues in the video. Sometimes they used photos of Dwovians on planet Dwovy—provided by Opie—as he explained about his people and their predicament with the Plinks illness.

Then, each week, Opie took the video when it was finished and routed to the flying saucer. He sent the video to Shelly Warstein through an anonymous, untraceable electronic transmission. Shelly would contact Ralph Stryker and pass the video to him.

Ralph aired the video on GN3 almost right away as part of his new weekly show, *ET Update*, which spent two hours each Friday evening discussing the latest information related to the extraterrestrial presence on Earth. He had a guest panel each evening, which usually included scientific experts, a UFO or alien abduction expert, and sometimes even a science fiction novelist. It was amazing to watch the UFO crowd, who had been mocked as crazies and wackos for decades by the media, become the most sought-after guests on television. They appeared on news programs as well as the popular talk shows, including the late-night talk shows.

The other news networks picked up the video released by Ralph Stryker and GN3 to rebroadcast it. So nearly every person on planet Earth heard from Leslie and Opie every week. Generally speaking, it was every Friday evening—or Saturday morning, depending on where in the world you lived—that the video clip was aired and made its way around the globe. It was *the* important issue of the week for citizens of Earth, and the topic dominated conversations in homes and businesses all around the world after being released and played.

There was a general sense of anxiety that had developed among the average person because of the newly discovered inferior technological position of the human race. People were clearly concerned about invasion, especially world governments. But worse than that, there was also a hatred that had been ignited in many human hearts. "The hatred of the masses is almost primal in nature," Leslie thought. Perhaps most people were not really mean and hateful, but rather there was a natural, evolutionary instinct to dislike these extraterrestrials as a legitimate threat to humankind.

She thought about the fact that she had initially been outraged over what the Dwovians had done to planet Earth, too. So she could relate. But as she took time over the last six months, to consider things from their perspective, her anger became more tepid. She still didn't approve, but she realized Dwovians had an administrative order on their planet as well, and they were subject to their high leaders just like human beings on Earth. Opie's pictures, stories, and explanations of Dwovian life helped to calm some cohorts of Earth citizens. They began to understand that, just like on Earth, those in charge on Dwovy are imperfect beings who sometimes make decisions that are not the best.

In addition, hindsight is always 20/20. There was no way they could know that tinkering with the genes to make people sleep was going to shorten their lifespans so drastically. Nor could they accurately predict the effect on the rest of the animal life on Earth. After all, some animals' lifespans, like the giant tortoises for example, were relatively unaffected by the Dwovian's alteration to the sleep genes. Giant tortoises on Galapagos still have a lifespan of nearly two hundred years—almost the same as before the Dwovians messed with us.

They only wanted us to sleep so they could carry out their mission without disrupting human life and culture more than necessary. That was actually a considerate motivation.

As far as the main part of their mission, there was no way they could know ahead of time that their genetic tests on our in-vitro children would cause autism in some cases. Generally speaking, the alterations were harmless to the babies, usually only affecting a few background proteins in human physiology that were not critical to our health. Above all of these considerations was the tremendous weight they carried of knowing their race would soon be extinct if they didn't find a solution to the Plinks illness.

Yes, Leslie's heart had softened somewhat toward their decisions, and she had come to terms with it. She had become quite good friends with Opie and his colleagues over the last six months. At times, Dr. McCabe's scientific mind wondered whether she was experiencing something like a Stockholm syndrome or if something different was happening. She had been confined to the same location for months, and she was in near continual communication with these aliens. "I should talk to Shelly about this sometime," Leslie thought. "She is as close to a shrink as I have in my network."

The morning sun shined through a clear blue sky onto Leslie's face as she sat at the kitchen table in the safe house. It was freezing cold outside and the fresh snow from last night covered the pine trees and sparkled in the sunshine.

The safe house was deep in the mountains of western Wyoming, not far from the Teton mountains. It had been home for the Alien Five since the day of the newsflash and car crash. Thank goodness Neil had a friend with this remote hunting cabin he hardly ever used. He had given Neil a key years ago and told him to make use of it whenever he wanted. His friend was getting older now. His wife had passed and he had no children. It was sometimes hinted in conversation that he would leave the cabin to Neil when he passed since Neil often commented about how much he loved the cabin and how grateful he was to be able to use it for solitude and hunting. Anna had been to the cabin a couple of times before, but most of the time Neil came to the cabin to escape day-to-day life with his one hunting buddy, Jimmy. Unfortunately, Jimmy had been killed in Afghanistan a couple of years ago while serving on a tour there.

It was a rustic log structure made of light brown wood and was just large enough for their group of five people. It had only two bedrooms, but since there were two married couples among them and one littlest creature who came and went regularly with a flash of blue light, it was perfect.

The cabin had modern luxuries, but was off the grid. It had well water and a private septic system. Outside there was a large propane tank that was used for the gas stove, the domestic hot water, built-in propane lanterns throughout the home for light at night, and even a gas powered refrigerator that had been salvaged from Neil's friend's (the owner's) first home. The propane could also run a generator for producing electricity on demand. The main source of heat in the winter was the centrally located fireplace, which almost always had a fire going in it due to the cold mountain climate.

There was plenty of chopped wood out back thanks to Neil's and Chepp's hard work, but there was also a small, undersized gas furnace that could be used if need be. Neil's friend told him that it was expensive to refill the propane tank, so he always suggested they use the fireplace as much as possible. It was far cheaper to pay for a good chimney sweep than fill the propane tank. After all, the wood fuel was free—other than the price of some physical labor—since the cabin sat on fifty-five acres of heavily wooded land. Much of it was covered with fast-growing mountain pine trees, but there was still plenty of hardwood to be found, too.

Leslie loved the fireplace. It was made of beautiful natural stone and had glass doors and small convection blowers to help distribute the heat. It worked great. The small living room area had a large window that framed a gorgeous view of the next mountain over. The cabin was very relaxing and provided a feeling of seclusion and peace.

Leslie reflected on how fortunate the group was to be here. Of course, the entire Alien Five was fortunate to be anywhere. They had escaped the horrific fiery crash by the width of a gnat's eyelash. Thank goodness Neil had thought to choke enough oxygen out of Opie's bloodstream that the bee-bee-sized physical monitor activated the router on the Dwovian ship moments before the crash. They were all touching when the router activated, so all five of them were instantly transported to the flying saucer right before the jeep had smashed into the transformer and burst into flames.

When Neil interrogated Opie in his kitchen, back when they first met, he was glad he had asked how Hero and Anna had disappeared. Opie had explained how the miniature health-monitoring device was implanted in all Dwovian astronauts and was a proud achievement of Dwovian engineers. He explained how it automatically activated the router if their signals indicated a life threatening condition. That short verbal exchange had saved the lives of four human beings and the current Dwovian commander.

Leslie was grateful for how God watched over them during that unexpected scramble in the SUV. Had they known it was going to be such a perilous trip, they could have used the Dwovian router to begin with. But Neil wanted to avoid the router since Anna was still recovering from her captivity and he was concerned about the psychological effect it may have on her. In addition, he was uncertain about the effects the router was having on his unborn child, in spite of the assurances Opie had made that it was harmless.

Leslie chuckled inside as she thought about the confusion of the FBI and government officials on TV when they could find no bodies in the wreckage. The media kept pressing them for an explanation, but of course, they had none, so they just kept using the buzz line "This is an ongoing investigation by the FBI, and at this time, I cannot reveal details that could jeopardize the investigation." But people knew that was nonsense. They could tell the officials had no clue. So they came up with their own stories and explanations. Eventually Leslie and Opie revealed the truth about that day in their video broadcasts.

The Alien Five were in communication with the necessary clandestine US government departments now via their newsflashes. The media still wanted answers about why the crash happened, suspecting the government was to blame. But since finding out that the Alien Five were still alive and producing videos, the hype was now focused on more important matters than the chase that led to the crash. And thanks to Opie and his routing to the Dwovian flying saucer beneath the volcano in Guatemala before communicating, nobody on Earth had any idea where the Alien Five were staying. The cabin was remote and Opie was able to route food and supplies to the cabin with him. So until the propane tank ran dry, there was no need for them to even start a vehicle or travel anywhere. They were, metaphorically speaking, a needle in the haystack of the world.

The six months in seclusion had been hard on Neil and Anna, as well as Leslie and Chepp. The first month was okay, but months 2 through 4 had been hell. Cabin fever erupted for sure during that stretch, and the four were short with each other and restless.

But the last couple of months were much better as the Dwovians established a way for the four to secretively communicate with their relatives and to receive virtually every television broadcast around the planet. It provided a sense of connectivity with other human beings that had been missing. Now the couples had settled into their lives and the isolation had actually pulled them closer together not only as spouses but also with each other as friends.

Anna's pregnancy was nearing its conclusion, and all indications were that she would be having a healthy baby girl in a matter of a week or so. In the meantime, Leslie had conceived and was four months along in her pregnancy. It gave Anna and Leslie plenty to talk about, and they enjoyed looking at women's magazines together which Opie routed in for them.

The weekly videos released by Opie and Leslie had explained the Dwovians recent plans to reverse the genetic alterations to the DNA of humans and other animal life. Draminkos programmed to restore the DNA would be released in a volcanic eruption again, and within about two hundred Earth years, all life would be restored to its previous condition. This was little consolation to those alive right now though. And there was division among people as to whether they even wanted the Dwovians to genetically mess with life on Earth again.

Polls showed that about 54 percent of people on Earth wanted the correction made, saying "it would simply restore things to the way they naturally should be" and that "humankind will move forward much faster if amazing people like Albert Einstein were to live for two thousand years." On the other side of the argument, people simply pointed out that "the Dwovians didn't accurately predict what the genetic changes would do the first time, so why should we believe that their attempts to undo them won't cause worse problems?" This side, which included many esteemed human scientists, also made a lucid argument that "we do not know the Dwovians well enough to trust them" and "this could be their attempt to weaken us further in order to invade our planet."

Yes, the Earth had dramatically changed in the past six months. There was a lot of unrest and uncertainty. Even the stock markets were volatile, rising and falling by as much as 10 percent a day on a regular basis. There was a resurgence in spirituality as people had a desire to make sense of it all. It strengthened some people's faith in a supreme being and weakened others'. Wearing tin foil hats had become controversial. Some people who wore tin foil hats before had recruited others, convincing them that the aliens could not read their thoughts if they wore the hats. Others felt they were offensive. They felt they were insulting to the Dwovians and upsetting to those who were struggling to cope with the reality of aliens on Earth. It was indeed strange days for planet Earth. A sharp turn in the path of humanity.

CHAPTER

26

"Okay. Push. Push, Anna, push! A few more seconds. Good! Okay, take a short break, and then one more hard push and your baby will be here," said the middle-aged doctor with her ponytail tucked up under her surgical cap.

The room was your typical modern-day birthing room in a city hospital. The lights had been dimmed comfortably low for most of the labor, but now a bright light shone in the direction of the important action so the doctor could see what she was doing. There were two nurses in the room assisting. The orderly who had helped place plastic on the floor had just left. The heart monitors beeped and the IV dripped pain-relieving meds into Anna's epidural anesthetic tube.

Anna was in the final stages of delivering her baby. Soon there was the final push and the sound of a healthy baby girl's lungs filling with air and crying was heard. There was a tired smile and simultaneous tears on the face of Anna and happy commotion in the room as the nurses congratulated the new parents and carefully cleaned off the baby. They weighed and measured her, gave her the shot of vitamin K in her thigh, swaddled her, and handed her over to Anna.

"I love you, honey. You were wonderful. She's so perfect. Look how cute," Neil said as he and Anna looked in to the eyes of their firstborn child.

There were crowds of media personnel just outside the front of the hospital waiting for the announcement that the baby was born. The hospital had set up a podium for the official announcement, and the media all had their lights and microphones set up and ready.

The hospital had provided a spokesperson—the head of neonatal medicine—who wasted no time getting to the spotlight to make the announcement to the media. The world's eyes were on this birth because they knew it was the main reason the Dwovians had come to planet Earth—to save their people. With the birth of the baby, people wondered what would happen now. Will this baby's birth truly confirm the answer that the aliens were looking for? Would they have to take the baby with them? People anxiously awaited to see what would happen next. There had been plenty of discussion regarding this topic for the last month or so in the media, but the Alien Five had not provided detailed information about the plan for the Reese baby. Neil and Anna had done their best to remain anonymous and out of the spotlight. They worked to shield any attention toward their baby. But of course, once the media learned of the Dwovian mission with the DNA alterations to babies, and after Leslie and Opie had shared that a baby with a potential cure had been discovered, it did not take long for the media to narrow in on Anna. The home in Pittsburgh belonging to Dr. Neil Reese, and his pregnant wife, Anna, was probably more than just a random location to hold the worldwide, earth-altering newsflash. So Anna and the birth of her baby were now the focal point in the entire surrealistic events of the past six months.

Neil stepped out of the birthing room and into the hallway for a breath of fresh air. Even though he was trained military, the smell of the blood and having just viewed the trauma of childbirth left his stomach a bit queasy.

"Dr. Reese," said the well-built man in the black suit as he held out a paddle scanner that looked something like the TSA uses. He waved it around Neil, front and back, as he continued.

"Congratulations on the birth of your daughter, Abigail."

"What did you just say? Who are you? How do you know all of this? I haven't even called my friends yet," said Neil. "You're government, right?" Secretly Neil already knew about this man and his alias, Jake Nollman.

"My name is Allesandro Quenos. I am from the Department of Homeland Defense. I know this is an exciting time for you and your

218

wife. However, for national security reasons, we will need to ask you both some questions and soon. The United States is in need your help, Dr. Reese, and we hope we can count on an honorable veteran like you to assist your nation in its hour of need."

Neil took note that the man had called him Dr. Reese twice in a very short period of time. He had learned from Shelly Warstein that using titles, and names can be a powerful technique of influence.

"What kinds of questions?" responded Neil.

"For reasons I cannot divulge, we need to engage in conversation with the Dwovians. As you can likely appreciate, having worked in extraterrestrial drug research with the military, our technology is extensive. But it is not yet able to track the location of the Dwovians. We know, Dr. Reese, that you've been in close communication with them and we are hoping that we will receive your cooperation in getting us in touch with the Dwovians."

"I appreciate you asking, but at this time we simply want to be with our baby. Perhaps we can talk at a later date," answered Neil.

The tall Mr. Quenos forced an insincere smile and blinked his eyes twice quickly. Clearly, he did not appreciate Neil's quick attempt to blow him off.

"Please understand that this is a matter of national security. I'm sorry to say, but until we get the required information from you and your wife, we will need to hold you in isolation. I will be posting armed guards outside of your room. You'll be isolated in this room until we have a chance to properly debrief you or transport you, your wife, and daughter to another location for interrogation."

"Like hell!" said Neil. "I suspect we will not be able to help you much, Q."

Mr. Quenos raised his eyebrows at Neil calling him Q. He did an upside-down smile with a smirk to let Neil know he was mildly amused at Neil knowing his nickname. "I wonder how he figured that out," thought Q.

Neil continued. "Our communication with the Dwovians has been only superficial. Other than the brief encounter with the Dwovians when they entered our home about six months ago, we have not spoken to them, and we have no idea where they might be," answer Neil.

"Dr. Reese, I can assure you lying is not going to work. We know for a fact you've been in close communication with the Dwovians and are likely one of the Alien Five. With support from the Department of Homeland Defense lawyers, we attained a search warrant to search all belongings of the Reese household. We already ran tests on some of your wife's belongings in her overnight bag and found DNA evidence that indicates you've been in direct contact with the Dwovians recently. We are counting on you to be more forthcoming and provide the truthful answers we need."

"And if we don't?" asked Neil. Mr. Quenos chuckled softly and lowered his voice a bit as nurses behind the nurses' desk had already taken note of the man in the black suit and his security scanning paddle.

"Well, Dr. Reese, we have already taken the precaution of classifying you as a potential national security threat. It would not take much effort on our part to have you and your wife held in an undisclosed detention center and your baby, Abigail, turned over to child protective services under our supervision. I hope that will not be necessary."

"Boy, you people are something. You can't even let us enjoy the birth of our baby for an hour before you're in here using her as leverage to get the answers you want. Well, I can tell you something, Mr. Quenos. We will hold out as long as possible before we provide you the answers you want. We have concerns about any government that would chase down and risk the lives of American citizens by shooting out the tires of an SUV traveling down a public road," answered Neil.

"It appears we've reached an impasse, Dr. Reese. We will make arrangements to transfer you and your wife to a detention center, where you will be held in safe and comfortable conditions. Your wife will receive the post-childbirth care she needs, but neither of you will be released into the public before we get this information from you. You can think what you want of us, but yes, we will use your child as a leverage point since this is a matter of national security with hundreds of millions of American lives at stake. We know how important your baby is to the Dwovians. We will use her as leverage if we must. If you should change your mind, just let one of the armed guards who will be posted at your door know you'd like to speak with me."

Mr. Quenos quickly turned before Neil had any chance to respond and walked down the hall toward the waiting room.

"Unbelievable," Neil said quietly under his breath as he opened the door to go back in with Anna. Actually, thought Neil, it *was* believable. The things that had happened for the past six months on planet Earth made almost *anything* believable. And in this case, thought Neil, from the government's point of view, they simply had no other choice. Neil and Anna were their best hope of finding the Dwovians.

As soon as Q reached the waiting room down the hall, he pulled out his cell phone and communicated with his boss.

"Reese is resisting. Plan B will be necessary," he announced into his phone. He quickly hung up and pressed another speed dial button. "Get things ready. As soon as we know the mom and baby are stable, I want transportation available on the helipad. And where are the guards? Get them up here." He hung up and pressed another speed dial button. Plan B was being quickly put into motion by Q.

Neil was resistant enough with Mr. Quenos that he had little doubt Q was putting his plans into motion. In fact, he knew two things for sure: First, Mr. Quenos's threat was not a bluff. And second, there was no way he would let Abigail be separated from Anna. Neil knew himself well enough to know the limitations of his inner being. He knew he would break down and give up the entire Dwovian mission and spacecraft if it meant safety and well-being for his wife and daughter. Neil knew this was his Achilles's heel, and Q knew it as well.

So Neil took advantage of the moment, one in which no government officers were breathing down his neck. Almost immediately, as he entered the room and saw Anna, a nurse entered directly behind him to give Anna some fresh ice water and graham crackers. Neil asked her if he could borrow her cell phone because he had left his at home during their rush to the hospital. It was only a half lie. He *had* left it at home, and they *were* in a rush, but it was not by accident. He and Anna had come to the hospital with as little as possible to reduce the chances of anyone tracing them back to the safe house or the Dwovians.

"Of course." She smiled. "You're not the first first-time dad to forget a cell phone." The chubby blonde middle-aged nurse chuckled at her little joke and pulled her phone from the right pocket of her nursing jacket. She handed it to Neil.

"I'll be back in about ten minutes to check your bleeding, honey. If you need anything in the meantime, just press your call button. I'll dim the lights for you. Try to rest. With a new baby you need to take advantage of time to sleep when you have it," the nurse said to Anna as she left the room.

Anna was exhausted and looking forward to eating her grahams and drinking some water. She looked at Neil and smiled and then opened her mouth wide and stuck her tongue out in an expression of exhaustion. The newborn, Abigail, was lying in her clear plastic hospital bassinet and two nurses were getting ready to transfer her to the hospital nursery for the rest of the routine testing they did on all newborns. Neil was very careful to check out the nurses before allowing them to take his daughter. He was walking a fine line. He needed to cooperate with the official hospital personnel for the sake of his wife's and baby's health. And when he put on his strategic, military-thinking helmet, he realized he may need some hospital employees help in the near future in order to resist the government. Being extra cooperative and polite to the right folks could go a long way.

Neil kissed Anna on her cheek and told her how much he loved her. He recounted to her how amazing she had been during the delivery and how incredibly blessed they both were. Then after encouraging her to eat her grahams and rest, he quietly dismissed himself into her bathroom.

As soon as he was in the bathroom and the door was locked, he took out his Swiss Army knife and flipped out the small screwdriver. He removed the screw from the cover plate on the outlet above the sink in the bathroom. Inside was a small crystal that had a short cord hanging from it. At the end of the cord was a mini audio plug—the kind that would fit into the small earphone jack on a smartphone.

"Thank God," said Neil and he reached in with his fingers and carefully pulled the crystal out of the box. He plugged the device into the nurse's cell phone and then quickly replaced the outlet cover and screwed it back tight. Next he dialed the phone.

The Alien Five had done extensive research on area hospitals in the last couple of months. Neil had decided that his baby would be born in a hospital. He did not like the idea of bringing doctors and equipment to the cabin. There were too many things that could go wrong with that plan. And even though he was amazed at Dwovian technology, he was not comfortable with the idea of Anna delivering the baby on the flying saucer either. So the only remaining option was to have the baby in the hospital.

But of course that was problematic because they knew the government and media would be all over Neil and Anna within hours, maybe minutes, of entering a public hospital. The whole world continued to talk about the Dwovian "savior baby" that Anna carried in her womb. So they needed to plan ahead and be sure they had control over the situation as much as possible.

As they researched hospitals, they analyzed the rooms and looked at patterns in the hospitals operations. They also checked the track records of doctors. They settled upon Lincoln Hospital in Lincoln, Nebraska. It was one of the only hospitals in several states around them that met all their criteria.

So once Anna was full term and ready to deliver, the Dwovians hacked the hospital computer system and chose one of the open birthing rooms for Anna to occupy. Then they entered her information into the hospital computer system, transferred her medical records, and even listed the best obstetric doctor in the city as Anna's doctor. Hopefully hospital personnel, and even the doctor, would just go with it when they showed up at the hospital in labor.

Then Opie gave Anna a dose of medication to induce labor. While Anna's contractions began, Opie routed into the bathroom in the birthing room at the hospital and planted the crystal device in the outlet box for Neil. They anticipated that Neil and Anna would be under close supervision, so they planned a way for them to privately communicate with the Alien Five with the crystal device. There was no telling how quickly the government would arrive at the hospital or what technological tracking devices they would have with them. But the bathroom was an interior room with no windows and no escape, so they guessed that they would be able to duck into the bathroom without much scrutiny. In hindsight, Neil was glad Opie had come up with this plan when Mr. Quenos showed up with the paddle scanner.

The ringing sound began to quietly be heard by Neil as he held the nurse's cell phone to his ear.

"Chepp!" said Neil in a soft voice as soon as he heard the phone answered on the other end.

"Hey, Buddy! Great to hear from you. What's the latest? Are you a dad yet?"

"Yep. Everything went as planned. We are the proud parents of a little baby girl. She was seven pounds, fifteen ounces and nineteen inches long. Mom and baby are doing well."

"Woohoo! Congrats, Neil!"

"Hey, I can't thank you enough, Chepp, for yours and Leslie's support over these past six months. By the way, there's a cigar in the end table drawer at the end of the sofa opposite the fireplace. That's for you."

"Found it. That's awesome. Hey, give Anna a big hug for us, would you?"

"Will do. But that's not the only reason I'm calling. As we suspected, the government is here. That guy named Q is the one who is leading the charge. They're going to hold us until we provide information about the Dwovians' whereabouts."

"Ugh. Are you okay? Are you sure you can talk freely? Could Big Brother be listening in?" wondered Chepp in a concerned voice.

"No worries there. Opie hooked me up a Dwovian crystal that plugs into the phone. The moment the phone is activated, the crystal activates and the phone call is made using quantum cryptography. Only your phone on the other end has the quantum key. The cryptography is foolproof and untraceable according to the Dwovians. In addition, the crystal sends out a jamming signal that mimics natural atmospheric disturbances and makes any electronic bugs or listening devices in the vicinity nonfunctional."

"So cool! I wish I could spend more time playing with their technology," said Chepp.

"Me, too. Anyway, like I was saying, they are going to hold us. You may even hear rumors that Anna and I have been classified as national security threats."

"You mean these guys would be willing to destroy you and your family just to get to the Dwovians?"

"We're going to hold out as long as we can but the creeps are using our baby girl against us. By the way, we named her Abigail Leslie. I'm guessing you know where the Leslie came from."

"Oh my goodness. She will be thrilled to hear that," said Chepp.

"We hoped as much."

"I'm outside right now getting more firewood, but I can't wait to tell her everything," excitedly proclaimed Chepp.

"Anyway, they are threatening to isolate us from our baby to leverage us, and they are even willing to use her as bait to attract the Dwovians. Let Opie know, will ya?"

"Will do, Neil. Ugh. That really could become a mess," said Chepp.

"We will hold out as long as we can, but it's probably a good idea for the Dwovians to speed up their work. They need to finish releasing the draminkos if they are going to do that and get back to Dwovy as quickly as possible. The thought of our friends floating in formaldehyde makes me sick to think about."

"Ditto. I'll let them know."

"I am uncertain of what techniques the government has developed that will press the truth out of us. But I am certain at some point or another we will not be able to withstand the separation from our daughter and any other pressures they apply. Warn Opie that they will eventually close in on them now that they have us in custody," reasoned Neil.

"We all agreed this was the best route to take, Neil. Don't be tempted to blame yourself," reassured Chepp.

"Thanks, Chepp. I am so sad that our baby's genetic alteration did not provide the answer the Dwovians were looking for. It is crushing for me to think about the thousands of years of efforts on planet Earth by the Dwovians and the sacrifices that we've personally made in our own lives and careers was for nothing. I hope the Dwovians can enjoy what's left of their time. And who knows, perhaps a cure will be developed back on their own planet."

"Yep. I feel the same way. But there's certainly no sense in them staying on planet Earth any longer. They would just risk being found. As you say, they may as well enjoy what's left of their days with their loved ones back on Dwovy. At any rate, I'll pass the word along to Opie. I'm hoping he will get to see you again before he departs. It would be sad after all this time if you were not able to say goodbye to the Dwovians since you were a focal point in this whole interplanetary event."

"Yeah, me too, Chepp. But apparently, the suits are able to recognize the DNA of the Dwovians. And with all the security cameras around, and with the technology getting better even as we speak, they may be able to eventually track him if I have contact with him. And that would threaten all of them. It's just too risky."

"Right-o, Neil, that makes sense. Perhaps in the future, they could come back and see you and Anna maybe for Abigail's wedding some day or the birth of her child."

Neil was hopeful about the possibilities even in the midst of the current uncertainties.

"I gotta go, Chepp. Do not contact me. I'll contact you when I can."

"Got it. Godspeed, my friend. And, Neil?"

"Yeah?"

"It's been an honor. You take care of Anna now, and remember, we are with you in spirit no matter what happens."

CHAPTER

27

"Neil, who are these men? Where are they taking us? What is going on? Where is our baby?"

Anna was panicked as two men in suits forced her to get into a wheel chair and began to wheel her out of her room. Quenos, the third man, grabbed Neil by the upper arm and forced him to walk out of the door behind his wife. Neil shrugged his arm away, clenched his jaw, and with steely eyes let Q know that he best not touch him again.

"It's okay, honey. I will explain in a little while. For right now just go with the flow. Everything's gonna be okay."

"But, Neil . . . our baby . . . Where's Abigail? Do something, damn it!"

"Trust me, Anna. I've got this under control."

The agents surrounded Neil and Anna as they led them down the hallway. This caught the attention of nurses and doctors, who tried to explain to the agents that Anna had not been officially discharged yet and they could not leave until they cleared her. Mr. Quenos simply flashed his badge and told folks it was a matter of national security. Stunned, they didn't know what to do and grudgingly cleared out of the way.

Quenos led them toward a dark colored SUV in the hospital parking garage. Neil could see down the hallway through the open doors. The SUV had two agents around it, one of them female with a medical kit, presumably to tend to Anna. Before they could get to the garage, they needed to pass through the lobby of the hospital.

There was a huge mass of reporters and cameras and microphones shoved into their face as the government security agents made a path through the crowd. The reporters yelled questions,

"Are they being charged with a crime?"

"Where are they being taken?"

"Do you have representation, Mr. Reese?"

"What about the baby?"

"Have the Dwovians taken the baby?"

Anna screamed, "My baby! Help! Somebody help us!"

One reporter and his cameraman quickly dropped their equipment and tried to get in front of the agents. Q immediately drew his loaded handgun and pointed it in the reporter's face, inches from his nose. The crowd immediately hushed.

"Stand down! This is a matter of national security!"

For one tense second or two everyone held their breath. Then the reporter stepped aside, and the agents quickly resumed moving their detainees down the hallway at a quicker pace. Neil realized that Q's cockiness would be his downfall. Because of the number of agents (five, including Q) and Anna's weakened condition, Neil had never been handcuffed. Q was secretly hoping Neil would make a move.

Anna was still weak and barely able to walk. She and Neil were placed into the vehicle sitting together in the back seat with an agent on either side of them. It was a larger-than-usual SUV, probably custom-made. It was much like a limousine. It was comfortable surroundings, but Anna's heart pounded as she continued to be perplexed as to what was going on. Neil whispered in her ear to explain the situation. Anna began crying and embedded her face in Neil's shoulder. The doors shut and the SUV drove away as reporters stepped into the road to film the SUV speeding away. Cameras flashed and reporters looked at each other in confusion, wondering why the news of the baby was not the highlight and where Anna and Neil were being taken and why. They were clearly as shocked and confused as Anna.

"So, hon, what do you think?" Chepp questioned as he sat on the couch next to Leslie. It was late afternoon and the sun was beginning to set. The snowy scene out of the window and the roaring fire created a calm and cozy setting in the cabin. But it did little to lift the weight of the current conversation. "It seems to me this is the right thing to do," he continued.

Leslie answered with some angst, "It's a major, major decision, Chepp. Maybe the most major decision made by two human beings in the history of the world. I mean it's not like we can turn around and come back lickety-split. We would be leaving our families, friends, careers—our entire lives—with no real guarantee of return."

"Yes, correct. That is what it would mean, technically. But I *do* think we will return. Opie promised. So I don't think that it would mean permanently leaving our families and careers. We go to Dwovy, have the baby to help a race of intelligent beings, and then come home. We can investigate and do scientific research—gathering tremendous information. When we return to Earth, we can resume our careers while also being the first human beings to visit a planet outside our solar system. Think of the opportunity here, Les."

"I know. But the truth is, we have a baby on the way, Chepp. And he or she is counting on us to keep them safe. We really do not know the Dwovians that well. I mean, my mother has always taught me that you have to know somebody for years before you can really trust them. And that's another thing. What about my poor mom? She is excited to become a grandmother, and she is getting older. This trip will take a serious chunk of time out of our lives. She may be gone before we return. Oh, God . . . I don't know what to say. I mean, really, we really don't know anything for sure here and never will. We can't even know for sure how long my mom will live. I know nothing in life is certain, but I'm seriously concerned about never seeing her, or home, again."

"Opie assures me they can bring us back to Earth at a later date. He told me they even have improved their engines to get us there and back faster. This would be a huge endeavor scientifically, Les. Furthermore, our baby will receive support from *two* planets because of his or her significance to both planets. We will be able to bring back potential solutions to the problems on earth with a unique perspective of how they would apply to Earth. The Dwovians do not totally understand our culture even after several thousand years of being here. Have you heard Opie try to use colloquialisms and metaphors? They've had experience, but they don't understand what it is to be human. Their memories are different from ours. Their experiences, their ability to control emotions—these are all different from human beings. They still have a lot to learn, too, and we would be helping them as well."

Chepp spoke with passion. He had clearly made his mind up and was doing his best to convince Leslie. In a way, he felt a bit guilty and hypocritical. It was his fussing about the level of importance Leslie put into her research that had caused them problems in their relationship last year. Now here he was pressuring Leslie to sacrifice her relationships for the sake of scientific research.

"If we are to gain practical knowledge from the Dwovians, it does make sense that it's human beings who will be able to see the full scale of possibilities. If we are able to investigate and bring that knowledge back to Earth, it would be a great blessing to billions of people. In addition, between my scientific degrees and yours, we have a pretty good coverage in expertise. I mean, me with the biology and chemistry and you with the physics and astronomy," answered Leslie. She was beginning to be won over.

"Beyond all that, don't you just feel in your gut this is the right thing to do? I mean honestly. And not only that, we would get to fly in a flying saucer, Les!" Chepp excitedly expressed this last part while standing up, throwing his right arm up, and making spinning motion with his right hand. If that weren't enough, the childish UFO noise he made to go with it made Leslie realize this was something Chepp really, really wanted to do. He looked a bit like a child begging his mom to let him go down the water slide one more time before leaving the public pool.

Leslie answered, "Yeah. I kind of do know this is the right thing to do. At least in my heart." She paused for a moment, then continued. "But think of the weight of the situation that Neil and Anna carried this past six months. It seems like they should be the ones that are offered this opportunity. Or at least they should be allowed to go with us. Ever since Opie told us, I feel sorry that they carried that heavy burden without the final joy of it all."

"Yeah, but it's our baby, Les, that carries the cure. Opie had to use Neil and Anna as the diversion in order for anybody to have this opportunity. He had to play it this way, and now that we are at this moment and you look back, you know it."

"I know, Chepp, but—"

"Listen. Opie even kept the facts from us until today. We haven't done anything wrong. And trust me, Neil and Anna are both just thrilled to be parents. And there is nobody with a more patriotic, sacrificial, and righteous soul than Neil Reese. He would do it all again in a heartbeat. And Anna? She is so devoted to him that she would do it as well," said Chepp, trying to comfort Leslie. "If the situation were reversed, would you be angry at Neil and Anna for doing the right thing for *two* planets?"

"I guess not," she answered. "I suppose I'd get over it. Besides, they've carried the load long enough. They may welcome the simple life again."

"I think they will. And like I said, once we fly out of here and the whole world sees that, then Neil and Anna can share everything freely. And after debriefing, I am certain the government will let Neil, Anna, and Abigail go home. There will be no further need to hold them. Besides, the media will be pressuring the government on every angle after they stole a baby from a hospital. You think the media is going to let that go unchallenged?"

"Probably not. I think everybody on planet earth will demand to know what happened to that baby and her parents," she said.

"Did I tell you the baby's middle name yet? They named her Abigail Leslie Reese," said Chepp with a smile.

Leslie looked up at him and her eyes began to well up.

"Really?" Leslie was choked up.

"Yep. Neil just called a little while ago to tell me."

"Those two . . ." Leslie stood up and hugged Chepp as she shed a tear of happiness.

Chenko sat in his quarters and typed into his jerblonk.

The information you have requested is confirmed. There are four cities on this planet that will need to be targeted for the most efficient and rapid full-scale invasion. The cities are Washington in the continent called North America, London and Moscow in the European continent, and Beijing in the Asian continent. These will be the first priorities in terms of overtaking powerful governments. However, the militaries of these nations are widespread and in the clandestine locations. I have sent that information to you also. Professionally I am optimistic about our plans. Personally, I cannot wait to establish the Dwovian empire on this stable planet, even though it currently is a freezing hellhole. My best to the high command. Hail Dwovy! Chenko.

Swoosh—his wall panel dissolved into an opening with just the slightest sound and motion of air. Grenko walked in behind Chenko as he finished typing. He saw a message with the confidential high government seal on the screen of the jerblonk.

"What are you doing?" asked Grenko.

Chenko quickly flipped shut his jerblonk.

"Nothing. Just messaging my family," he answered calmly.

Grenko knew that wasn't right, but he played along. He wondered why Chenko was lying. Perhaps Opie had sent an official correspondence to Chenko regarding the new plan to quickly leave Earth and for security reasons only Chenko had received the information. Grenko trusted Opie completely and had no reason at this point to be suspicious about Chenko. So at this time, with the urgency of the new plans, he decided it was best to dismiss the lie. So he reacted with normalcy.

"Oh. What's the latest with them?" Grenko he asked.

"Well, my brother is starting the academy, and my father has teamed up with the famous scientist, Lourenco, on a new invention," Chenko answered, perhaps too quickly and too smoothly. He should have rehearsed it better and been more prepared. Chenko felt self-conscious, but apparently it was a good enough response for Grenko.

"That's outstanding, Chenko. Congratulations!" he answered.

"Thanks," Chenko answered back.

"Well, I just wanted to check in to see where we are in preparation for releasing the draminkos. What is the status?"

"Draminko programming is done, sir. All pods of draminkos have been energized in the reactor and are ready to be deployed. Locations for explosive charges have been identified. Charges are ready to be delivered and activated on signal," he explained.

"How many eruptions are we talking about? Nothing that will interfere with our bugging out quick, right?" asked Grenko.

"After consulting with the commander, we have decided to go with only three eruptions. Apparently, the Earth beings are concerned about a shift in their environmental conditions by volcanic eruptions. They often worry about their planet warming. They should be worried more about warming their planet before the next cycle of glaciation. They are still quite primitive in their understanding of their environment," he answered.

"I know. They have no plan at this time for warming their planet, so far as I can find in my research. But as you mention, Chenko, their technology is primitive. They do not yet understand the importance of crystals yet alone the glaciation and thawing cycles. They are still learning about their planet, and we have slowed their progress," he said, reminding Chenko of his own interference in the Earth's development

"Well, at any rate. With three eruptions, and the number of programmed draminkos, the sleeping effect and associated lifespan shortening will be reversed to a 67 percent level in the next two hundred Earth years. The 95 percent level of remediation will be reached within five hundred Earth years. The commander felt this was a reasonable compromise," said Chenko.

"Well done, Chenko. And your calculations have been confirmed?"

"Yes, Grenko. Confirmed."

"Then be ready to proceed when the commander gives the call. That's all for now. Continue in your duties if you are done with your correspondence to your family. We must remain ahead of schedule and at the ready," he said.

Just then, a crystal began to glow on both Chenko's and Grenko's bracelets.

"Sunset is here. Third nourishment will be ready soon." With that, Grenko turned and, *swoosh*, exited the room. Chenko had his privacy once again.

CHAPTER

28

Opie had now joined Chepp and Leslie in the cabin.

"And you are certain—100 percent certain—that it is our baby who has the genetic cure?" asked Leslie, looking out of the cabin window.

"Yes. I have confirmed it three times," answered Opie. "I am certain."

"But Neil and Anna do not know this yet, right?" asked Leslie as she turned and looked back toward Opie who was standing next to Chepp who was seated on the sofa.

"We cannot tell them until after we have left the planet, for security reasons," he answered.

"But with the rate we will be traveling, how soon before they will get the message?" asked Chepp.

"Initially we will be traveling at near light speed, Dr. Duplay. With the new engine programming code sent to us from Dwovy, we will be able to make a jump up to six times the speed of light according to our scientists. But the signal we send back to Earth must be traditional radio waves. So it will still travel back to your planet at the speed of light," he answered.

"Uh, yeah. I get that. We do understand relativity around here. Remember Albert Einstein? I'm just asking how far from Earth will we be before we can send the message back?" smartly asked Chepp.

"We can send the signal shortly after leaving Earth. I would say that the message will be received at this cabin within fifteen minutes of our ejection from the atmosphere," Opie answered.

"Okay, but you said Neil, Anna, and Abigail are currently being held by the government. How do we get the message to them? They are unlikely to return here to the cabin. That would compromise this location," asked Chepp.

"Yeah," agreed Leslie.

"Excellent point. I think sending a message to Dr. Warstein may be the best option. Her identity is still unknown by the media and your government. We can send a message directly to her phone. I will quantum encrypt it so that only her phone can decipher it," said Opie.

"Right. Then she will make a careful effort to get word to Neil and Anna," added Chepp.

"I will request they keep the baby deception secret until we return," said Opie. "Humans are suspicious enough of us because of our past deceptions. I prefer the truth about the baby be confessed upon our return to Earth. We will bring many gifts and offerings from my planet to yours when we return, and the draminkos will have had time to begin reversing the damage we created. This should help oil the squeaky wheel and get the camel through the eye of the needle," said Opie.

"Huh? I think you mean it will help butter the people up before sharing the bad news?" explained Chepp.

"Okay. As long as something is getting lubricated and people will be happy, that is what I am hoping," said Opie.

Leslie laughed to herself and shook her head left and right.

"You need to keep working on your understanding of human culture, Opie. What you just said could be considered pornographic in some sectors of American culture," she said.

"How so?" questioned Opie.

"Uhh, let's just get back to the plan, Commander," said Chepp. "We will have plenty of time to discuss things like this over the next few months. We just need to know where to be when and what we need to do before leaving," said Chepp.

"Hang on, Chepp. Since he is still learning about human culture, I really do need to ask a couple of more questions first. Opie, you do have the ability to provide us with fresh, clean Earth water and healthy Earth food and a place to go to the bathroom, right? You do have all those things figured out, right?" asked Dr. McCabe.

"We can provide you with the necessary, sustaining elements and traditional comforts. I have Manko restocking the ship with Earth food right now. It is we Dwovians who will be eating the unusual Earth diet on the way back to Dwovy. Our Dwovian food supply is all but gone. And water is not an issue. We have the ability to create plenty of iron-rich water on our spaceship using special crystals and energy from our reactor. Our plan is to stock plenty of your filtering water pitcher devices to remove the iron from our water supply for you."

"Terrific," said Leslie. "That's a big relief to me."

"You can rest assured that we have thought of everything as far as sustaining you and your family from here, to Dwovy, and back again, Doctor," said Commander Opie. "You are our guests and almost holy beings from our point of view. You are of utmost importance to Dwovy."

"You hear that? We're like royalty, honey!" Chepp said with a big cheesy grin as he looked at Leslie. Then he looked over to Opie. "What matters do we need to take care of from our side of things? For example, are we supposed to pack anything? And when do we let the planet know that we have left? I mean, our families and coworkers are eventually going to realize we are missing."

"It is best if we do not tell them anything until we are gone. In the message for Neil and Anna, I can request that Neil contact your families and others as he sees fit to let them know you have gone with us. We can announce our estimated return date in approximately ten Earth years also. This may relieve some of their anxiety," said Opie.

"Yeah. That sounds about as good as anything I can think to do," said Leslie. "As long as our families find out first."

"I agree," said Chepp. "But I do want to go over this flight plan one more time, Commander. You say we will initially fly toward Dwovy at near light speed and then eventually jump to a speed much greater than light. How confident are you in this new Dwovian technology? I mean, are you sure it's going to work? And how dangerous is this?" asked Chepp.

"I can assure you that Dwovian science and technology is not performed as it is on Earth. Oftentimes you humans release computer programming that contains bugs and risk using unproven technologies before their time. You are an impatient species. Dwovians do not release new technology until it is tested thoroughly and deemed perfect. If our High Council has announced this new technology, then it is ready. Trust me," answered Opie in his metallic voice.

"You mean like your foolproof plan to cause human's to sleep, which resulted in drastically shortening our lifespan and causing an increase in autism among Earth children?" asked Chepp, being a bit of smart aleck.

"Keep in mind, Chepp, that we did not have human beings to actually test the draminkos on before proceeding. It is actually quite impressive how close Dwovian scientists came to their established goal from a world away. They only had small amounts of human DNA to work with in developing their plan," answered Opie in defense of his kin.

"Fair enough," said Chepp. "You got me there."

"If it helps calm you, we have been aware of the existence of hyper–light speed for some time. Apparently our scientists have finally worked it out to perfection. Our spacecraft was designed and built with the intention of traveling at hyper–light speeds once the proper engine programming could be determined. However, it was not ready five thousand years ago, so the trip here took sixty-six Earth years of time because we were traveling at light speed. Going back, the trip should take approximately nine Earth years. By the time we return you to Earth, I suspect we will be able to make the trip in about one Earth year or less."

"Chepp, whether it is light speed or hyper–light speed, we are still going to have to trust these fellas driving the flying saucer," said Leslie. "It's a moot point. So can I change the topic for a minute and get back to Chepp's question? If we come, what do we need to pack?"

"Certainly, Dr. McCabe. Excellent question. Chepp you may wish to bring your razor for shaving unless you intend to grow a beard. Dwovians do not grow hair, and we have no need for such hygienic tools. And both of you will want to bring a toothbrush

WHEN I OPENED MY EYES

and about ten years of toothpaste, unless you are willing to try the Dwovian method of rinsing with sprekle. It's a timed rinse that cleans your teeth and kills dangerous germs in your gum line. However, it does not leave your breath smelling clean as we have found this actually has some practical application in caring for our health," explained Opie.

"Uh, Leslie, add about three hundred tubes of toothpaste and a hundred toothbrushes to the shopping list," said Chepp in a humorous tone like nobody else could.

Leslie laughed.

"Yeah, I think a decade of morning breath will not be good for our relationship," she agreed.

"I apologize in advance for any foul-smelling breath of the crew. We will be eating an Earth diet, and there is no telling what the long-term smells will be. At least you don't have to smell the breath of my previous commander, Hero. It was wretched. He did not always follow the rinse schedule over the last hundred years, and it took its toll on his gums and breath. I think he became too absorbed in the mission and was becoming senile in some ways," shared Opie.

"Let's buy some spearmint gum for the Dwovians, too, hon," said Chepp.

"Now, about toilet tissue and baby wipes . . . ," said Opie.

Both Chepp and Leslie focused their eyes on Opie with great attention.

"We clean each other in a feline fashion, using our tongues. Can you reach your rectums with your tongues?" asked Opie.

"Auwaullghhh!" both Chepp and Leslie said as they made contorted faces.

"You have *got* to be kidding!" said Leslie in shock.

"I think this is where I say, 'Gotcha,'" said Opie. "And you think I don't get Earth humor."

Leslie and Chepp looked at each other, and then at Opie, and then they began to laugh. Opie laughed too.

"There's a fine line between funny and gross, Opie. But you are getting the hang of it—kind of, I guess," said Chepp.

"So you do use toilet tissue, right?" asked Leslie.

"Yes, the equivalent. Our bodily waste is burned in the reactor core, so we do not build up and waste on the spacecraft. And instead of having a large supply of disposable fibroid to wipe with, we use rags that we place in a bin. They are thoroughly cleaned, completely sterilized, and recycled in our spacecraft," answered Opie. "That reduces our load as well. It would take quite a lot of room to carry sixty years' worth of toilet tissue for the crew."

"Hey, honey. I just thought of something. We really will be going where no man has gone before, huh?" quipped Chepp.

Leslie laughed heartily.

"I don't get it," said Opie.

Chepp and Leslie laughed even harder.

⟳

In a small room about the size of a typical jail cell, Neil sat on one side of a stately wooden table. On the other side sat the man with the identity best known among his colleagues as Q. There were no windows in the room and a one-way mirror at the other end. The room was modern and comfortable looking, but it contained no pictures or plants. Besides the table, there were five chairs in the room. Four were on the side of the table with Q, and the other Neil sat in on the opposite side. The room was overly warm, and Neil was thirsty. He had been offered nothing to drink since being abducted from the hospital twelve hours earlier. It was clear to Neil this was an interrogation room.

"Mr. Reese. Tell me about your relationship with the Dwovians," said Q.

"If I tell you, then what do I get?" asked Neil.

"Once you tell us what we need to know, you, your wife, and your daughter may go home," answered Q.

"How do I know you'll keep your word?" asked Neil.

"You don't. But I think you will believe me when I tell you that you, your wife, and child will never be reunited until we get the information we want. I think you know based on what has happened so far that I certainly mean that."

"I can't wait to sue your ass for this, Q," said Neil with a steely-eyed glare.

"Tell me about your relationship with the Dwovians," demanded Q once again.

"What do you want to know? They showed up in my house one night and took my wife. I was able to capture one of them during that interaction," he said.

"How did you capture him?" asked Q.

"They came with syringes full of some kind of drug. I surprised them and stole one of the syringes out of their hands and injected one of them with it. He lost consciousness and I tied him up," answered Neil.

"Why did you not immediately contact the police or government authorities about this?" asked Q. "Surely you knew this creature could pose a danger to the Earth."

"I did think of that but decided against it. As someone who has served in the military, I know how our government thinks. They are much more interested in the big picture than the details of one human life. Getting my wife back was my first priority," answered Neil.

"How did you get your wife back?" asked Q.

"We worked out an agreement with the Dwovian we captured. We call him Opie—he looks just like little Opie from the old *Andy Griffith Show*."

"An agreement? What kind of agreement?"

"He agreed to help us get my wife back if we agreed to keep the government and military out of it as long as we could."

"And that didn't raise a red flag for you? You weren't concerned about why he did not want the government involved?"

"Of course it did. But have you ever had your pregnant wife abducted by aliens? I wanted my wife back. So I worked with him. If it makes you feel any better, I did interrogate him first and established what I believe was the truth about why they are here. I saw no immediate danger for Earth beyond what we have already experienced. So I agreed to his terms."

"You agreed to *his* terms? What did he tell you? What did he tell you that would cause you to trust him?" asked Q.

"He told me everything that you have been hearing through the news releases. They came to find a solution to a disease that is killing off his people. He told me that my wife had conceived the child with the genetic cure for the Plinks illness. That is why they abducted my wife."

"And you just believed him? You had no reason to question the information he was providing you?" questioned Q.

"Of course I questioned it. We used a truth serum, and I still found myself questioning it. But I saw no better option for getting my wife back than using his technology to get to where my wife was. I had to make a decision, and I decided to trust him."

"Did you visit their base of operation? Have you seen their technology?"

"Yes. They have a flying saucer. That is where my wife was being held."

"Where is the spacecraft located? How many spacecraft do they have?"

"To my knowledge, they only have one spacecraft on the planet. It is a small crew of six Dwovians," answered Neil.

"Where is the spacecraft located?"

"I don't know. We used their technology called a router to somehow beam to their spacecraft. I have no idea where it is. It could be in space, for all I know."

"Mr. Reese. Do not lie to me. We have been able to establish the fact that there are no intelligent signals coming to Earth from space. The communication of the Dwovians on Earth has been terrestrial signals. They have a base of operation here on the Earth. Where is it?"

"I'm not lying. I don't know. The router uses some kind of crystal technology and you just flash from one location to another. It's not like I can look out a window while traveling from one location to another through a flash of light."

"Did the spacecraft have windows? Is there anything you saw that could be helpful to us in determining the location of the spacecraft?"

Neil realized that this was the key thing Q really wanted to know. It was clear the government was determined to go after the Dwovians. He needed to do his best to delay their progress.

"Gosh, I don't know. It's hard for me to think about it while I am so thirsty. Can I get a drink? And I really would like to know my wife and baby are okay before I say any more."

Q looked toward the mirror and with a nod said, "Let's get him some ice water in here." Then he opened a laptop which had been sitting closed on the table. The screen lit up. Q turned it toward Neil. It showed video of Anna breastfeeding Abigail in a rocking chair in a comfortable-looking room that resembled a nursery one might see at a church. It had a crib and some toys and a changing station. There appeared be fresh fruits and bottles of water on a table in the room for Anna. Neil was comforted to see the video.

"That's a live feed," said Q.

"There is no way I can know that. But I do feel a little better seeing that. I swear, if you harm my wife or baby in any way, I'm coming right for you, Q," said Neil in the most serious tone he had expressed in this entire interrogation.

Just then, the door behind Q opened and a young man, probably only in his twenties and wearing a suit, delivered a pitcher of ice water and some cups. As he sat them down on the table, he leaned over and whispered into Q's ear. After Q acknowledged that he understood, the man turned and left the room again.

Q poured a glass of water for them each. Neil was so parched that he immediately picked up the glass and drank it all. The cold water going down his throat was so welcomed by his stressed body. The last twenty-four hours had been rough going for him emotionally. He had observed his wife giving birth and become a father for the first time, and that was the calmest part of his last day.

"Again, what did you see on the spacecraft that might help us locate it?" asked Q.

"Well, there weren't any windows. So I don't know what I can tell you that will help."

"Mr. Reese. I'm doing everything I can here for you. But time is of the essence. My associate just informed me that we have had three simultaneous, significant volcanic eruptions occur in the last half hour. One on an island in the pacific that the military uses as a base, another in Belize in South America, and another on a small island west of Europe. We believe the Dwovians are responsible. We must have the location of their base of operation."

"They probably are responsible. They are releasing draminkos to begin reversing the damage to human DNA as they said they would."

"Or they may be releasing draminkos that do more harm to the human race, Mr. Reese. Now, what else did you see while onboard the spacecraft? I need as many details as you can provide."

"Look, Q. Their technology is far beyond ours. They can relocate people with this router thingy of theirs, and they have this ability to make solid object disappear and then reappear, and they have these guns they call bleaks," said Neil. He was beginning to feel a little woozy and he recognized that his speech was getting more relaxed and informal. "What is happening," he wondered for a moment.

"Tell me about these bleaks. You say they are like guns."

"Damn it. You spiked to water, didn't you?" said Neil as he began to realize the odd feelings he was experiencing were drug induced. He looked at Q and began to see a cloudy halo around his face.

"The bleaks. What do they do?"

Neil began to giggle a little as his body relaxed and experienced the euphoria of the drug that was kicking in. It began to feel like Christmas morning, and Q started to take on the appearance of Santa Claus.

"Awww . . . you know, Santa, they shoot that green beam, like the one that hit Chepp in the shoot-out," said Neil with a smile. He was beginning to offer up information, but deep in his inner being, he knew to avoid giving the location of the Dwovian flying saucer. He would fight the urge to tell as long as he could.

"Chepp? You mean, Dr. Duplay. He was with you on the space-craft?" asked Q.

"Oh yeah. My buddy, Chepp. He beat the bleak. Even Opie was surprised at that."

"Where are Dr. Duplay and Dr. McCabe now, Neil? Where are they hiding?"

"Ha! You'll never guess. But I can tell you it's beautiful there. It's a cute little place."

"Where, Neil? Where are they?"

"I'm hungry. Can you bring me a Big Mac, Santa? I want a Big Mac, and I've been a very good boy. Please? Bring me a Big Mac."

Q looked toward the mirror. "Keep digging into his relationships and travel. And get us two Big Mac meals in here. I'm hungry too."

CHAPTER

29

"All right, Les. The commander here needs an answer," said Chepp. "Look at it this way. The government's intention of finding the Dwovian's is *not* just to shake hands and say goodbye. Furthermore, we don't know what level of technology our own government has been able to develop. I'm sure they are working on technology to help them narrow in on the Dwovians even as we speak. Opie can't wait around for us to have the baby here."

"We have completed our mission at this time, Dr. McCabe. Any delay leaving this planet is now a risk to the success of our mission. That is considered a serious crime back on my planet. I am most likely already in trouble with the high command, but Hero's odd behaviors before his death and returning with the cure may butter up the High Council to rule in my favor. I am hopeful."

"You hear that, Les? We need to decide quickly. And by the way, Opie, you used the term 'butter up' there the right way," said Chepp.

"I am highly intelligent, Dr. Duplay, and able to learn quickly. This should not be a surprise," answered Opie, once again showing some insecurity in his supposed intellectual superiority to the human race.

"All right. I'm in. Let's do this, Chepp. If the people of Earth, including our families, think that we're goats, we're goats. If we're heroes, we're heroes. So be it," said Leslie.

"Did you understand that okay, Commander? We accept your offer and will return to Dwovy with you for a short visit. So give us a little time to get packed and then we can jump onboard and scuttle out of here," said Chepp.

"Terrific. How much time will you need?" asked Opie.

"Can you give us about six Earth hours to prepare? We do need to run and get a few things, like the toothpaste," asked Leslie.

"Ten-four. That will work," said Opie. He followed that up with a very quick wave, grin and an audible yell of "Tallyho!" before disappearing in a flash of blue light.

"Well, I'm glad he figured out the context for 'butter up' and 'ten-four', but that kid still needs to work on his goodbyes. I find myself jumping every time he comes and goes," said Leslie.

"Yeah," agreed Chepp.

❧

Neil awoke with the taste of a McDonald's meal still left in his mouth and a light shining in his face. He was lying on his back in a bed. As his eyes began to focus, he saw a modern drop ceiling above him with bright florescent lighting. As he began to sit up he propped himself up on his elbows and began to look around. The room was totally bare other than the bed and a small toilet-sink combination. The door to the room was metal with no handle on the inside. He was clearly still being held prisoner.

As his mind continued to wake up out of the haze, he remembered the interrogation room and some of the questions Q had asked. But much of it was very foggy. He couldn't remember much after drinking the water. He felt like a fool and was angry at himself for making that mistake. "What is wrong with me?" he thought to himself. "How could I let such a simple trick be played on me?" He was determined to never let that happen again. Even if it meant passing out from dehydration he would not trust his food or drink again.

Neil began walking around the room inspecting it. He wondered what he might have shared while under the influence of the drug. There was no way he could know. But he guessed that he didn't share everything they wanted to know or he wouldn't still be locked up. Maybe they really were going to press charges against him. He couldn't rule that out. His heart pounded with fear and anxiety that he might not see Anna or Abigail anytime soon.

"Get a grip, Neil," he said out loud to himself. "Think." He had no idea exactly how much time had passed. But since he could still taste the flavor of a Big Mac in his mouth and he had a recollection of talking about Big Macs, he was guessing about an hour or two at most. He guessed they were interrogating Anna now since she had been on the flying saucer, too. But considering she had just given birth and was nursing a newborn baby, he doubted they would drug her. And she had very little practical knowledge to offer them regarding the Dwovian spaceship. She was drugged much of the time she was there, and to his knowledge, they had all been careful to never mention to Anna where the flying saucer was. That was Neil's idea. He had correctly anticipated, as Opie had, that the location of the spaceship would be of prime importance to the government. So the fewer people who knew, the better.

As Neil continued to move around the room inspecting every square inch of it, he heard a sound through the walls. It was faint, but there was no mistaking it. It was the cry of a baby. I was Abigail. His baby was crying. He ran to the door and began pounding on the metal door.

"Hey! Hey! My baby is crying!" he began yelling. "What is happening? Let me see my baby! Hey! Hey!"

Neil could hear the sound of boots moving in the hallway outside of his cell as he placed his ear on the door. Then he heard the sound of a key entering the lock of his door. Someone was opening the door.

Neil thought about jumping the person, but he did not have time to think of a plan for what he would do after that. It was too late, the door was opening. Neil was surprised to see Q himself.

"Dr. Reese, you and your family are being released and will be allowed to return home. However, we will be placing GPS ankle bracelets on you and your wife," he said.

"Say what? You're letting us go? What gives, Q?" asked Neil. "And what's with the Dr. Reese? You've been calling me Mr. Reese since you met me."

His questions were ignored by Q as if meaningless and unimportant. He continued speaking.

"Your location will be tracked at all times. You remain a subject of interest. Agents will be guarding your home, but you won't notice them. They will blend in. We will be questioning you as needed as things progress. We request you do not speak to others about your experience on the Dwovian flying saucer or about your encounter at this facility. We thank you and your family for your tremendous cooperation."

Neil was stunned and speechless. Of course, he was grateful and excited to hear that his family was being reunited. But he was greatly confused as to why.

"What do you mean by tremendous cooperation? What did we do?" asked Neil. "Seems like we just got started. We were talking and the next thing I know I woke up in here."

"That is not unusual considering the drug we gave you. It can cause a complete loss of memory much like general anesthesia if you have ever had surgery," he answered. "But trust me, you told us everything we wanted to know. All of our questions have been answered at this time."

Neil stepped outside the door and he saw Anna holding Abigail about twenty feet away down the hallway.

"Anna!" he called and began jogging toward her and his newborn daughter. He wrapped his arms around them and gave Anna a kiss.

"We get to go home, Neil. Isn't that wonderful? We finally get to go home with our baby," she said.

"I know. But why? Why are they suddenly letting us go?" he asked.

"I guess they got all the information from you they needed. What does it matter now? It's an answer to prayer as far as I'm concerned," she said. "I'm sure it's all going to work out, Neil."

He leaned his mouth close to her ear.

"They gave me a drug while they interrogated me. I have no idea what I told them. Did they do anything like that to you?" asked Neil.

"No. I just was placed in a room with Abigail. It was like a little nursery," Anna explained.

Neil got a sick feeling in the pit of his stomach. It began to dawn on him that he must have given up the location of the Dwovian flying saucer while under the influence of the drug. Anna still did not understand what was happening here. Neil began to turn pale.

He needed to let Opie and the Dwovians know right away. But he was being carefully watched now—every move. "Maybe that is the game Q is playing," he thought. "Maybe I told him nothing and he is trying to trace my every move and communication." Neil felt even sicker in his stomach. How would he know what to do? He was damned if he did and damned if he didn't. For an obsessive personality and strategic thinker like Neil, this was the last situation he wanted to be in. He would have to make his best guess. He was a human Magic 8-Ball who would decide the fate of his Dwovian friends. Their very lives may hang in the balance.

Chepp awoke with his right arm over Leslie's pregnant belly. He had been sleeping on his stomach, and Leslie on her side facing him. Leslie was just waking up as well. Their eyes met and they smiled.

"I actually slept okay for my first night in a flying saucer," said Leslie. "How about you?"

"Not too bad. I woke up a few times. I had an odd dream about my previous experiences in this metal vessel, but overall, I can't complain," said Chepp. "Having our own mattress is certainly nice."

"Yeah. I'm glad Opie allowed us to bring it. I can't believe he was expecting us to sleep on those short levitating stretchers. You can tell that guy has never had to sleep a night in his life. Yet alone sleep a whole night pregnant."

"Does the temperature feel okay in here for you, babe? Opie adjusted it for us. Seems about right to me."

"Yeah, feels good to me, too," she answered.

"I talked with him about the air, too. He increased the oxygen in our room to help compensate for the thinness of the air. But it's important for the crew to feel comfortable and healthy, and we will need to be out and about on the spacecraft during this trip. So he told me that he would gradually cut the extra oxygen back over the next couple of weeks in our room until we are adjusted. He said we will eventually adapt nicely.

"Really? How would he know that?"

"Apparently they kept an elderly man who was a widower on here for about eight months until he died. It was about one thousand years ago."

"What? Why?"

"He was a short man native to this area who lived in the mountains. Apparently he was not much taller than the Dwovians, he had a grayish complexion, and he had no ears."

"No way!" said Leslie as she and Chepp crawled up off the mattress that lay on the floor. They pulled up the covers and made the bed as Chepp continued.

"So they were curious and wanted to study him closer. After bringing him aboard, they found out he was all alone in the mountains since his wife had passed, and they determined he had advanced dementia. Rather than euthanize him or release him to die miserably in the mountains, Hero allowed Opie to continue studying him until he passed. He said he learned a lot about human physiology and anatomy at that time."

"Wow. Do you think he died from natural causes, or do you think their tinkering with him shortened his life?"

"Who really knows? But it was a thousand years ago, and I don't think I want to ask. We have to live with these people and trust them with our lives for the next decade, so I don't really want to start the trip off accusing them of medical malpractice."

"Yeah. You're probably right about that," she responded. "What's for breakfast?"

Chepp and Leslie wandered out into the main quarters. Opie had programmed the doors to respond to Leslie and Chepp's hands, so they were free to move about the ship. However, they had no access to the other technology onboard.

They found the dining area on the flying saucer and enjoyed a bowl of Raisin Bran with rehydrated, instant powdered milk as they conversed with the Dwovians about their upcoming trip. The powdered milk was not bad. Opie had Manko steal a large box of first-rate powdered milk from a military base commissary. Using their crystal technologies, the Dwovians were confident they could reproduce the chemical structure and maintain a milk supply for Leslie and Chepp.

The bulk of the rest of the food the Dwovians had stocked for the trip was high-protein foods, most of it dehydrated. The food supply was tightly packed into several storage rooms in each wing of the spacecraft. Dwovians did not require as many calories of food per day due to their slow metabolism. But with Chepp and Leslie onboard, they were packed to the gills.

Opie entered the dining area. He was wearing the typical one-piece robe (more of a kimono) that all the Dwovians wore. But he was now wearing a white robe to indicate his leadership role in the mission ahead. He spoke in Dwovian first, rattling, whistling, clicking, and popping away. Then he turned to Chepp and Leslie.

"I just told the crew that if we remain on schedule, we will leave this planet in six Earth hours. Be sure to stow away your gear for the launch out of the planet's gravitational field. So that goes for you two as well," he said.

"What do you mean 'stow away your gear'? How bumpy is this ride?" asked Chepp.

"It's not so much the bumps as the overall acceleration. We will reach about seven of your g's during out launch. So strap down anything that might be damaged or do damage if it moves," he explained.

"Seven g's? Holy cow!" exclaimed Leslie. "Is my baby going to be okay with that?"

"We have special launch seats that distribute the stresses on our bodies safely. You will be fine. We are moving those seats into position now. Because you are taller than us, your legs will need to dangle off the seats, so there may be some effects in the way they feel during and after launch, but our calculations show that you will have ample blood supply to your organs and blood pressures will maintain so that you are unlikely to lose consciousness."

"Cool. Sounds very safe," said Chepp. "Is there some kind of legal disclaimer we need to sign?"

"Huh? Have I missed something?" said Opie in his metallic, computerized-sounding voice.

"Nah. You're good. Go charge your reactor or whatever you have to do. We will go button down the hatches," said Leslie.

"We have no hatches on this vessel. We use the router," said Opie.

"Forget it. Just go do your thing, Commander," said Chepp with a smile.

CHAPTER

30

"Q, you son of a gun! I knew you wouldn't let me down," said director of ETSP, Roger Dagman, as he patted Mr. Quenos on the back on his suit jacket. "Tell me. How'd ya do it?"

"I wrote a program on my computer using advanced mathematical techniques that allowed me to statistically prove where the Dwovians were not. Therefore, the place that remained had the highest likelihood of extraterrestrial presence. After three days of running the program, its converged on an area around Mt. Picaye in Guatemala, sir," answered Q.

"Impressive. I forgot you used to be a distinguished math professor before you came onboard. I guess that stuff wasn't a waste of time, huh."

"No, sir. Not at all."

Mr. Quenos and his superior, Director Dagman, pushed open the door and entered the war room. They both marched in with energy and determination, the steel door locking behind them.

"Listen, folks, this is a code polka dot. I repeat, code polka dot. Red and white. Q is going to lead this raid and I want you to give him full authority. Give him any and all data and updates that you have. Everyone in here, including Q here, has full clearances for all highly classified materials," said Roger Dagman. "Now listen up for what he has to say. Let's get this done."

With a wave of his arm, he turned the room over to Q. There were about a dozen people manning their computer stations and they turned toward Q. The ranking generals and admirals of the armed forces were present, standing around the command table.

"The first thing we need to do is get some birds in the air around Mt. Picaye, in Guatemala," said Q.

"We have a narcotics and counterterrorism base in San Jose, Guatemala. I'll get their half dozen choppers in the air now. We should have intel streaming within twenty minutes," said Field Marshall Bendoza of the army, a distinguished and well-decorated gray-haired man. He nodded to one of the computer nerds in the room who swung his seat around toward his screen and immediately began typing on his keyboard.

"That will work. We also need to bring up the latest satellite photo on sector SAG457. We need to find that spacecraft. The information I have suggests it's made of some kind of metallic, and since none of our previous intel detected it, I'm betting its underground. We need to find the opening to their underground bunker. Let the chopper crews know we are looking for a large opening in a remote area," confidently said Q, clearly enjoying his moments with supreme power.

"Mr. Z, bring up the latest sat pic," directed Marshall Pickman of the Air Force. Another computer savvy young man spun in his chair and began typing.

"On your left, Marshall Pickman," he said almost as quickly as he typed. A high-resolution photo of the sector requested appeared almost immediately on a high-resolution screen.

"Mr. Jones, get word to those chopper pilots," said Field Marshall Bendoza.

"Mr. Spenk, order our closest carrier to move offshore of Guatemala, ninety degrees, fifty minutes west longitude. Check the Panamanian deployments," ordered Admiral Smith of the Navy.

The room was buzzing with energy and coordination but very orderly. Nobody was speaking over the other. Of course, everybody in the room, except Q, was used to this sort of activity. This kind of raid happened about once per week for these high ranking commanders of the military, for one reason or another. This was only Q's fourth time through an event like this in the war room; his boss,

Director Roger Dagman, had only experienced a couple dozen of these where he made the call.

"Zoom in on Picaye," commanded Q.

The display of the photo zoomed in to a scale of two by two miles.

"Now spiral pan and zoom out slowly," he added.

The satellite photo, which had amazing clarity and detail, began slowly moving. All eyes were focused on the display.

"Simultaneously search for any circular or elliptical anomalies with high sensitivity," said Q.

"Elliptical?" asked Marshall Pickman of the Air Force.

"Yes, sir," answered Q. "I believe their vessel to be round in shape. Logic would dictate they used the spacecraft itself or devices on the spacecraft to somehow bore out the hole in which they hide. Depending on the angle of viewing, it may look like an ellipse."

"That's logic and mathematics at work, Fred," said Q's boss, Roger Dagman. "And no, you can't borrow him."

The photo continued to move with various gray lines and crosshairs moving around the display as the computer searched any and all anomalies in the pixelated photo.

"Birds in the air, General," shouted Mr. Jaison, the assistant to Field Marshall Bendoza.

"Ten-four," he replied.

"There!" shouted Q. "Right there, stop! No. Go back, Z! Right there!" Mr. Quenos walked to the monitor and pointed his finger at a very eccentric gray ellipse drawn on the map.

"Zoom in on that, Mr. Z," said Marshall Pickman.

As the tech zoomed in on the region of interest, the image enlarged and got a little fuzzy. But as Q pointed, it became clear what he saw. It was a highly eccentric elliptical region of missing plant life at the very base of Mt. Picaye.

"No wonder our automatic surveillance didn't find it," said Q. "The opening is tilted so sharply into this hillside that it appears almost as a line in this photo. These military search programs probably figured it was a local walking path since there are no larger construction paths around it. Human beings could not drill a tunnel in a remote location like this without leaving plenty of evidence."

"You're telling me that's a tunnel, maybe hundreds of meters long?" asked Pickman.

"Yes. I believe so. But we will know for sure when we have the choppers confirm," answered Q.

"Twelve minutes out, sir. I'll send the coordinates," announced Mr. Jaison.

"Make it so," answered Field Marshall Bendoza.

⟊

Neil and Anna were now home in their house outside of Pittsburgh. The sun was just coming up, but they had arrived very late at night and pulled the airport rental car into the garage, so none of the neighbors knew they were there yet. Additionally, Q had established temporary fake identities and simple disguises for Neil and Anna, so they were able to fly home with Abigail without media attention.

The house was in reasonable condition, considering it had been unoccupied for the past six months. Shelly had done a marvelous job of house sitting for them, traveling from Penn Tech every other weekend to pick up their mail, do some light cleaning, and give the house a quick inspection. She had hired some neighbor boys to keep the lawn cut until winter had arrived. Now the same boys shoveled their walkway and kept the driveway cleared of snow.

The first month they were gone, Shelly had to regularly fight off the media, but she did an excellent job of playing the part of "family friend" and simple "house sitter." Since the media could find no meaningful connection between the Reeses and Shelly, they assumed that was all there was to it. She must be a casual acquaintance through a mutual friend who was now in graduate school and needed some extra income. They had no idea that Shelly was the main outlet for the worldwide newsflashes about the Dwovian presence.

Neil sat in his lounge chair leaning forward with his head hanging and his hands folded together. He stared at the carpet on the floor as he prayed for God's direction. Anna had just finished feeding and changing Abigail and laid her to sleep in her crib. She had encouraged Neil with a kiss and a hug and sat with him for a few minutes before Neil told her to go lie down and get some sleep. He would be okay, he told her. He just needed some time to think.

The house was quiet as Neil continued to weigh the decision before him. He needed to decide soon what he would do. If he delayed much longer, it may be too late to warn his Dwovian friends. But dare he risk contacting them? He was so stressed by the situation that his fingernails made marks on the backs of his hands as his praying hands squeezed tightly together. "Please, Lord, I need a sign here. I really, really need a sign. It has to be clear what I am to do because I am paralyzed here with indecision." Neil had been in focused prayer for more than a half hour now. The sunlight coming through the window began to hit his face.

"Get up and eat," Neil heard in his heart and mind.

"What?" he thought to himself.

"Get up and eat. Get up and eat."

Neil could not get the soft, insistent thought out of his head.

"I am kind of hungry," he said softly to himself. Then he got up and headed toward the kitchen. He filled the teakettle with water and put it on the burner. He opened the pantry and found a packet of instant oatmeal and dumped it into a bowl and grabbed a spoon from the silverware drawer. He opened the refrigerator only to discover it was pretty much bare. Other than condiments, some pickles, and a few snack packs of pudding that were probably very old, that was about it.

"I guess its oatmeal without milk, huh, Lord?" he said quietly as if in conversation. He grabbed a few paper towels, wet them, and wiped off the table. He sat down at his seat with the dry bowl of oatmeal in front of him. He inhaled deeply, then exhaled.

Ding-da-ding.

"What was that?" he thought. Oh yes, it was his cell phone, which he had in his pocket. He pulled it out to see the news banner across his screen: "MILITARY CLOSING IN ON DWOVIAN HIDEOUT."

"Holy crap! No-no-no!" said Neil in a panic.

He quickly turned on the TV in his kitchen and flipped around for a cable news channel that might have coverage. He had just flipped to the GN3 channel as the news broke. The morning team was showing video of helicopters flying over what looked to be rain forest. He scanned to the bottom of the screen and saw the word 'Guatemala'.

"*No!* No-no-no, Lord! Why?" he lamented out loud. Clearly it was too late to warn his friends.

"We now go live on the phone to Ralph Stryker, who as our audience knows is a senior level reporter for the GN3 network, and dare we say the preeminent reporter on the Dwovians," Neil heard the TV say as he broke out in a sweat and turned up the volume. Ralph went on to explain over the phone that he had nothing to do with the military finding the location of the Dwovians, that their flying saucer location was as much a mystery to him as anyone else on the planet. Suddenly a loud whistle caught Neil's attention as he struggled to listen to the TV. It was the teakettle boiling.

"Neil? Neil?" asked Anna as she walked around the corner into the kitchen. She was in her nightgown and slippers as she came alongside him. She turned off the burner and moved the teakettle to another burner. She noted his pale complexion and the sweat on his forehead and neck.

"What's the matter, Neil? What's going on, honey?" she asked as she looked toward the TV and saw the scrolling banner announcing the discovery of the Dwovian's hideaway.

"This is all my fault, Anna. They're going to end up in big formaldehyde bottles because of me," he said with a tight throat and tears starting to well up in his eyes.

"This isn't your fault, Neil. You tried to help the Dwovians as best as you could. We all did," she said with her typical encouragement as she wrapped her left arm around his sturdy waist.

Just then, there was additional excitement on the news set. The reporters cut off Ralph Stryker.

"Hang on, Ralph. We have breaking news. Something has happened. We have live footage from a news affiliate out of Guatemala City. This is live footage from their news helicopter. You can see an incredible geometrical cloud structure rising up from the base of Mt. Picaye where the American military helicopters were just circling," the cable TV announcer was unusually excited. Neil wrapped his strong right arm around Anna's shoulders and pulled her close as they both intently stared at the screen and listened to see what happened.

"Apparently there has been an explosion . . . a loud explosion. We don't know yet what exploded, but . . . Hang on . . . We're being told it was not an explosion . . . It was a sonic boom, and then nearly simultaneously this incredible cloud formation quickly appeared. It looks like a cloud in the shape of a cylindrical tunnel reaching from the ground up as far as the eye can see. We have footage coming. I believe we have footage of what just happened. Hang on, we have footage of what just happened about a minute ago folks. This just happened. Our affiliates are telling us, if we're translating from Spanish properly, that this just happened about a minute ago. Here's the footage. Let's see . . ."

The footage showed a loud explosion and an almost simultaneous streak of a cloud stretching from the ground up into the sky.

Neil began to breathe in and out quickly with a bit of a chuckle and anxious relief in his breath.

"Please, Lord. Yes," he said. "Please let that be what I think it is."

"What, Neil? What is it?" Anna asked.

"Shhh. Let's listen," he said politely as the color began returning to his face.

The TV commentator continued with several people talking in the background behind him. This was huge news and other reporters at the station, even techs and cameramen were gathering to watch the footage streaming in.

"What is that? Is that military?" the announcer was asking his fellow news companions while trying to give live coverage. "Was that a rocket launched by the military? Play that again. No. I don't know. Someone here is saying that cloud formation is the cloud formation caused by a sonic boom. But it is usually more conical in shape. This one is nearly cylindrical, which would indicate an incredibly high velocity. One of our techs is saying they believe this may be the Dwovian flying saucer launching. Slow the video down. Can we slow the video down? Okay. Let's see what we have in slow motion. This is as slow as we can run it. Amazing! Look! Right there! That frame right there! It is blurry, but that appears to be a disk shape from my vantage point! It certainly does not appear to be a rocket shape. We are going to need to get confirmation, folks, but it sure looks to us here, in the studio, like that was a flying saucer launching from who knows where. Somewhere near the ground, this thing just comes flying out of nowhere! This is incredible. Again, this is breaking news from Guatemala in Central America. We're going to take a quick break and see if we can get a better picture of this and get confirmation from our military contacts. Stay tuned. This is the GN3 network. We're everywhere you need us to be. We'll be right back."

Neil smiled and hugged Anna, picking her up off her feet. He kissed her on the cheek.

"Everything is good, hon! They got away! I know they did! I know in my heart what that was. Godspeed, Opie and crew!" he said as he spun Anna around.

"That's great, Neil. See, I told you everything would be okay," she said.

"You did, didn't you? You were right," he said. "Hey. I'm hungry. You want to celebrate with me by having a bowl of oatmeal with no milk?" he asked with a chuckle.

"Sounds delicious!" Anna said with an overly animated voice.

"Yep! Let's get up and eat. Ha!" Neil smiled from ear to ear.

CHAPTER

31

Suddenly there was a short, repetitive, high-pitched whistle throughout the flying saucer. It sounded a bit like a birdcall. Opie turned and rushed quickly back into the dining area. His short legs moved quickly under his robe brushing it up out of the way. He was no longer wearing his green Crocs but rather wore the typical Dwovian footwear, which was more like a ballerina slipper with a sturdy but flexible sole. Again he spoke first in Dwovian, and the crew immediately got up from the small table and moved out of the dining area with urgency. Each crew member apparently knew what was happening and what they needed to do.

"We have a code 4 alarm on the command console," explained Opie in English for his human passengers. "Flying machines—military helicopters—are heading this way. There are six of them, and they appear to be converging on this location."

"Well, hell. How far out are they?" asked Chepp. "How much time do we have?"

"They will converge on these coordinates in approximately twenty of your Earth minutes."

"We need to get out of here, Commander, right now!" said Chepp in an emotional outburst. "How quickly can we launch?"

Leslie listened intently but moved close to Chepp's side—tight up against him—and wrapped her arms around his torso.

"The reactor must be pushed to full power. That will take about fifteen minutes. Follow me," Opie answered.

Leslie and Chepp left their dirty dishes, like the rest of the crew, and immediately followed Opie out of the door and down the hallway toward the command center. Their hands tightly gripped her left and his right as they walked quickly. The bright orange light and warm, thin air on the flying saucer was doing nothing to calm their nervous systems. Leslie's heart was beating like a bass drum, but she didn't let it show. She was determined to use her mind to overrule her emotions on this trip, and her stoic face suggested she was successful in hiding her anxiousness.

As they entered the opening to the hexagonal command area, Chepp did not duck quite low enough and he banged his head on one of the structural metal bulkheads around the perimeter of the room.

"Son of a bi—!" he stopped his yelling short of completion as he grabbed his forehead with his right hand.

"You okay?" asked Leslie.

"Yeah. It just hurts," answered Chepp while rubbing his head. "Remind me about those things, huh?"

As they looked around, the command center of the ship had taken on a different look. Where there were solid walls previously, there were now large openings revealing a wall with an impressive array of computer displays and instrumentation panels. Apparently, the outside wall surfaces in the command center were merely facades protecting the instrumentation that is needed to fly the spacecraft. The only wall that looked the same was the reactor wall. That was still a solid wall with slots and holes for plugging in crystal devices.

The ceiling of the command center was now a large display screen with a view of outside the spacecraft. It still appeared to be made out of smooth metal like it had been before, but somehow it was now presenting images in stunning resolution. Chepp was fascinated because it looked as though there must be millions of small holes in the metal through which light was now streaming. The image seemed to show a fisheye view of the entire surroundings above and on all sides of the flying saucer. He could see lights on the outside of the flying saucer illuminating the walls of the deep hole they were in, and he could see up the shaft and see a small dot of daylight at the top. It was astounding how deep underground they really were, and the precision with which the tunnel was constructed was stunning. The walls of the tunnel, even though cut through rock, were virtually smooth. The tunnel looked to be perfectly circular in cross-section, and the tunnel shaft was as straight as an arrow over its incredible length.

"Look, honey," said Leslie as she pointed to the ceiling.

"I know. I was just looking at that. Amazing," he said. "I suspect this image may be created by very high-efficiency fiber optics."

Another change in the command center was the presence of seats with straps where there had been none before. One seat was along each wall in the command center, except on the reactor wall. The seats appeared to be physically a part of the floor. The seat support came up from the floor as if made of the same piece of metal as the floor. Chepp bent over to look, but he could see no welded joints, bolts, or any type of break in the metal support holding the seat and the floor. And none of these seats were there last evening when they arrived on the ship. Clearly the Dwovians' knowledge of metallurgy was far beyond the understanding of humankind.

The seats were in slight recline and were short in length and low to the floor, sized for Dwovians. The sitting surface was covered in a smooth, soft material that behaved somewhat like foam, but it did not have the low-density feel of aerated foam. It felt dense but was just as soft as a pillow at the same time. The seats looked a little bit like seats one would see on *The Jetsons*, although, again, they were reclined backward similar to launch seats you would see in a NASA rocket. They appeared to be dark in color, but Chepp couldn't tell for sure what color they really were because of the orange lighting inside the flying saucer.

Chepp counted. There were five seats along the instrumentation walls, apparently one for each crew member attending the instrumentation. There were three additional seats in the middle area of the command center fastened to the floor in a triangular pattern. The seat at the tip of the triangle sat directly in front of the glassy, black command console with all its interactive computer displays. The command console was now tilted over, leaning toward that special seat—what Chepp suspected was the captain's seat. Opie silently confirmed his guess when he began walking quickly toward that particular seat and sat down in it.

"Get strapped in, everybody. We are 9 dash 9 go for launch," announced Opie. He spoke in English, apparently trying to reduce the need to say things twice. "Neil and Leslie, you are here." Opie turned and pointed with his long spindly gray fingers spread out toward the seats at the middle of the command center. He apparently forgot the Earth custom of pointing with just his index finger, but it was clear the seats he meant.

"I'm so nervous, Chepp. I wasn't ready for this yet. I think I may hurl," said Leslie as she took a break from her plan of quiet courage and began to take her seat.

"Sorry to say, but that makes two of us. I hope they blow some cool air on us at some point during this flight," Neil replied as he sat down on his seat.

They turned toward each other with eyes wide open and a surprised look on their faces as they felt the seat. It was far more comfortable than one would have thought by looking at it. It gave an impression that you were sinking into a deep soft supportive cushion, but the cushion itself was only about two inches thick. It was something like an optical illusion, but with the sense of touch being tricked. It was a "feel-usion."

They each lay back on their seat and shifted themselves downward so that their heads were supported. Their legs did indeed dangle off the end of the seats so their heels hit the floor, but it was not uncomfortable. Leslie pulled her restraining straps up over and around her shoulders and waist. She adjusted them to their largest length and was just able to get the fasteners to reach and click. If her pregnancy had been any further along, it would have been a problem. As Chepp pulled the restraining straps around himself, it was clear that they were not going to be long enough to reach. His muscular male human body was larger than anything the Dwovian engineers had planned to strap in. First he looked toward his right to Les with an open mouth of surprise, then he quickly turned his head to the front toward Opie, who was busy strapping in to his seat. Chepp tapped him on the shoulder.

"This gonna be a problem?" asked Chepp. He flapped the strap around with his hand to draw attention to it as Opie turned around.

"Uh-oh. Yes. You must be properly fastened to your seat. If we were to hit any space debris as we launch through your upper atmosphere, or need to make an evasive maneuver, the spacecraft acceleration may cause one of our walls to smash into your body's inertial path," explained Opie.

"You know, as a physicist, I can actually understand and appreciate your description of that," said Chepp. "You got anything longer I can use? I don't really want to end up a pancake." Sweat was beading up on both Chepp's and Leslie's foreheads. It was approximately ninety-two degrees Fahrenheit on the flying saucer currently, so the perspiration was understandable.

"I do not understand the pancake reference, and no, we have no larger straps. We will need to improvise," came the twangy metallic voice in response. "Why do you have beads of water on your face? Where did they come from?"

Manko overheard the commander's questions and was excited to impress him with his newfound knowledge.

"What you observe, Commander, is called perspiration. Humans release salty water from glands in their skin when their bodies become overheated or nervous. The evaporation of the liquid helps to cool their bodies. It is fascinating. However, the liquid must be cleaned off daily or odorous bacteria will grow on the human body, much like the bacteria that grows in dirty Dwovian mouths. Likewise the perspiration is benign. It will not delay our launch."

"Thank you, Manko," replied the cute-faced little commander. "Do you have suggestions for solving Dr. Duplay's strap problem?"

"Negative," came the reply. Opie turned back to Chepp again.

"You need to find a way to extend your current strap. Or you must find another way to fasten yourself to the seat," said Opie. "Without this, I fear you will be injured and not survive this launch. You have less than five minutes now."

Chepp's heart was now beating like a drum as he had a brief mental image on himself hitting the wall and going splat right in front of Leslie's eyes. Chepp did his best to keep control of his emotions and think logically. If the Dwovians had no materials they could think to use, then hopefully he or Leslie had brought something along.

"Got it!" yelled Chepp as he jumped up out of his seat and ran quickly down the hallway toward his quarters.

"Hurry," yelled Opie.

Chepp had not run this fast since trying to steal a base while playing college baseball. He got to his quarters in a flash, then waved his hand in front of the door. But it did not open.

"Hey! The door is not opening!" he yelled loudly down the hallway toward the command center.

"Chenko, temporarily override the launch position of the doorways, please," requested Opie.

Chenko clicked, rattled, and whistled in Dwovian as he pushed a few buttons on his wall of electronics.

Chepp tried again and successfully gained access to his quarters. He grabbed his duffel bag, quickly unzipped and began digging around.

"Ah-ha!" he said with a smile as he grabbed the item he wanted. Then he ran quickly back to the command center and jumped into his seat. Leslie saw what he had in his hands and began to nod her head as she understood what he was thinking. He turned his head toward Leslie.

"Honey, I'm going to need you to temporarily unstrap and quickly help me with this little project," he said.

"Gladly," she replied.

Suddenly there was the unique sound of duct tape being unrolled as Leslie taped the end to the bottom of Chepp's seat and worked the tape around and around Chepp's lap and under his seat again and again. Then she did the same with his torso. Around and around, there was a continuing sound of tape being hastily ripped from the roll. Altogether she had about ten straps of tape around Chepp's chest and lap. There was quite a bit of Dwovian chatter in the background. The clicks, whistles, and rattles were going from person to person around the room.

"I owe you one," said Chepp with his eyes wide open and a grateful look on his face.

"We are nearly ready. We are 2 dash 2 go," said Opie confidently. "Leslie and Chepp, that means we have only two more steps before launching."

"Quick. Get strapped!" said Chepp as Leslie hopped back into her seat and began working on refastening herself. "How much time do we have?"

"Approximately one Earth minute to launch," answered the commander.

"Got it! I'm in!" yelled Leslie.

She reached her hand over to Chepp and he grabbed it and wrapped his strong fingers around it squeezing firmly. He bowed his head and closed his eyes. Leslie understood and she did the same.

Suddenly there was a low frequency humming and vibration, which began in the background. It grew louder and higher in pitch for about ten seconds and then began to grow quieter. But both Chepp and Leslie could sense the amazing power that was building up even as the sound faded away. It was almost as if the flying saucer had woken up like a mighty beast and was getting ready to break the chains that restrained it. The power surge through the ship could literally be felt as if it were a living power within every element of the ship.

"Here we go!" said Opie. Then he rattled, whistled, and popped a command to his crew and without any warning the ship launched to life.

In a fraction of a second, Leslie's and Chepp's heads were being pressed against their headrests with an incredible force. The skin of their faces was stretched backward as if someone behind them was pulling on it with the palms of their hands. Their eyelids were stretched so far that they couldn't keep their eyes open properly. Their eyeballs felt pressurized, like they were swimming one hundred feet underwater. It was a struggle just to keep their mouths shut and they had to strain to keep their tongues pushed forward in their mouths to keep from choking. It felt as if there was a three-hundred-pound sack of sand lying on top of their chests and it was hard to inhale. What they could make out through their eyes was an incredibly quick trip through the long tunnel followed by a bright flash of blue sky and clouds. Within seconds the intense feelings began to reduce and the sky above them began turning dark. Within twenty seconds they began to see stars.

"Lordy!" Chepp was able to force out of his mouth and throat as the G-forces began to wane. His senses were overwhelmed by the whole experience.

"Double yeah!" Leslie managed to say as she apparently had a similar psychological response to the launch. Neither was emotionally ready for the intensity of the power surge and sensory overload. Within forty-five seconds, they could feel the stress on their bodies relieving. Opie and his crew continued to rattle and whistle information back and forth. About three minutes after launch the feeling of weightlessness began to dominate. Opie unstrapped himself and gently floated out of his seat. He grabbed a small indentation on the side of the command console panel that was apparently meant as a handle, and he placed his long fingers on the black, glassy display, which currently had instrumentation lights and monitors lit up all over it like a Christmas display. He slid his fingers downward across the screen on a blue bar display and amazingly a sensation of gravity slowly began to take over the ship in proportion to where his fingers were on the display. The sensation of weightlessness dissipated, and Chepp and Leslie looked around as the crew began to unstrap.

Even though the ceiling display showed the velvety deep black of space with only pinpoints of starlight above, they felt as if the flying saucer were at rest again. Chepp and Leslie noticed the stars changing position, so they knew they were in motion at a very high speed, but they could no longer sense the motion with their bodies.

"We are stabilized. You may unstrap," said Opie, looking at his human friends. As Chepp's and Leslie's heart rates began to fall and the adrenaline surge was processed by their bodies, they began to breath deeper and more slowly.

"So everything went smoothly? We are safely on our way?" asked Chepp to be sure.

"Yes," answered Opie. "Our speed will continue to climb slowly over the next couple of days, and then we will engage the new engine program and begin traveling faster than the speed of light. We are all looking forward to that. It will be a first for this crew."

"Yeah. Us, too," said Leslie as she was finally unlatched and moved over to help untape Chepp.

"Very ingenious solution. I am glad you were able to preserve your life, Chepp," said Opie as he nodded toward the silver duct tape.

"Thanks. I can tell you're all emotional about it," said Chepp in the way only Chepp could. Leslie smiled as she struggled to tear the tape.

"I may need something to cut this off"

"Reach in my left pocket for my pocketknife," suggested Chepp. She did and in little time had Chepp free from his makeshift restraints. As he stood up and stretched to stand upright, the duct tape came rolling slowly across the floor.

"Apparently we are still accelerating," said Chepp as he pointed at it and then bent over to pick it up. Opie and the crew continued with their Dwovian gibberish as they each now stood in front of their instrumentation panels and made the necessary adjustments. From Chepp's point of view, things looked well under control and routine. He wrapped his right arm around Leslie and gave her a reassuring squeeze.

"The crew will meet in the conference room in ten of your Earth minutes. It is not necessary for you to attend. If you have questions, I will explain later. This is routine," said Opie.

"Thank you. What should we do in the meantime?" asked Leslie. "Perhaps we can help clean up anything that dislodged in the dining area? We left that room in a hurry."

"You may go back to your breakfast, or clean up any messes, or roam the ship freely. Perhaps you might consider checking your quarters since you did not have time to properly stow your personals before launch," suggested Opie.

"Ten-four, Commander," said Chepp. Leslie and Chepp turned to leave the command center, and then Chepp turned back quickly.

"Hey, by the way. This ceiling . . . the images . . . is that created by fiber optics?" asked Chepp.

"Yes, essentially. I can answer in more detail in the future, but the image is an actual view outside the spacecraft. The view is essentially the way things would look to your eyes if there were no cap or walls on this spacecraft. It gives us a live 360-degree view and does not rely on any energy source. That way if we lose power temporarily we can still see outside."

"Mega cool!" said Chepp. "I can't wait to learn more about these technologies. Thanks, Commander." He turned and continued with Leslie toward the hallway that led to their quarters and the dining area. Fortunately, he remembered to duck going through.

"It is amazing to be in space. It doesn't feel like what I expected," said Leslie.

"Well, remember, there is some kind of artificial gravity on this thing. So it doesn't feel a lot different from standing on Earth right now. Although, I feel a little lighter on my feet than normal, don't you?"

"Yeah. I thought maybe I was just a little lightheaded yet from the launch, but you are probably right. This must be the natural feel of the gravity on Dwovy," Leslie suggested.

"We will have to ask Opie, but I believe that will be right. It makes sense that their gravity would be less than Earth's, considering the type of star their planet orbits. Their star is cooler than our sun, so their orbit would have to be much closer to their star in order to sustain liquid water. And that would mean they have to be a smaller planet. Otherwise, the tidal forces from their star would rip the planet apart," explained Chepp as they arrived at their quarters.

A wave of Leslie's hand and the door did its magical Dwovian disintegration. Their jaws dropped as they saw the inside of their quarters. Their mattress was leaning up on end against the one wall, Chepp's laptop lay in broken pieces on the floor, and the belongings in Chepp's duffel bag were spread all over the left side of the room.

"You left your bag open, didn't you?" asked Leslie.

"Uh . . . yeah," he answered. "But remember, I was in a hurry."

"Typical. Men . . . You can take them off the planet and they still find ways to make a mess and come up with an excuse," said Leslie with a jab of her elbow into Chepp's side and a sarcastic roll of her eyes. Chepp turned and gave a coy, smiling smirk to her as he grabbed her, pulled her close, and planted their first space kiss on her pretty face. She grabbed him back and wrapped herself tightly around him. She broke this kiss and spoke.

"The crew's going to be meeting in about ten minutes. I've got an idea," she said with sexual innuendo in her voice. With one hand behind her back, she waved and the door rematerialized.

⤫

"I'll be right there, Commander," said Chenko. "I need to send the communication to Shelly like you asked."

"Very well, Chenko. Meet us in the conference room post-haste," commanded Opie as Chenko began to type at his instrumentation wall in the command center.

As soon as Opie had entered the hallway, walking toward the conference room in the science and engineering wing, Chenko changed screens. The crew was unaware of his jerblonk's program upgrade that allowed him to communicate with Dwovy almost instantaneously. However, he would not need that feature for this communication. This communication was going back to Earth via primitive radio waves.

Start. Launch successful. Invasion force due in one Earth year. Draminkos programmed to further increase need for sleep to reduce resistance and casualties. One hundred million American dollars transferred to the bank account as we agreed. Await further instructions at the following coordinates in Buenos Aires, where you will find the serum to reverse the effects of the draminkos. Out. Chenko. Finish.

Chenko hit Send, smiled briefly, and walked toward the conference room and the unsuspecting crew.

About the Author

Kip Trout grew up in western Pennsylvania, near Pittsburgh. He attended the Pennsylvania State University, where he obtained both a BS and MS degree in physics. He lives in Windsor, Pennsylvania, with his wife and three sons. He is currently employed at the York Campus of Penn State, where he has taught physics, mathematics, and astronomy for over twenty-five years. He is the author of numerous scientific publications, covering topics such as laser microphones, ultrasensitive bubble levels, Einstein's relativity, and the Tarzan Swing. While his professional career is in the natural sciences, he enjoys science fiction, inventing in his garage, and the great outdoors. Ironically, he hated science in elementary school.

CPSIA information can be obtained
at www.ICGtesting.com
Printed in the USA
BVOW03s1802040917
493834BV00001B/13/P